The NPC

by Thomas A. Gilly

The NPC, Fourth Edition

To my wife Patti; for her love, patience, and support.

Chapter 1

Raythen sat on a wooden trunk, reclining against a wall, protected from the sun by the gray, creaky porch of the Dead Basilisk Tavern. His floppy, shapeless black hat hid his eyes, a toothpick was motionless between his lips. He looked comfortable in the shadows, visible to the road and yet presenting the ease of someone resting on cushions in the privacy of his own bed. He was rough, dusty, and mostly covered by a tattered black cloak, under which one could see the outline of his folded arms. An unobservant passerby would probably assume he was asleep. An unobservant passerby would also miss the hints of leather armor visible through the holes of his cloak and the tip of a scabbard poking out.

Across a dirt road was the tiny Harkins' farm. Old Man and Old Lady Harkin were in the field turning over dirt with crude hoes, toiling in the sunlight. They were dressed in brown, sack-like peasant garb that made them look like potatoes that had sprouted human limbs. Farther off, two cows in a pen watched their owners from bland white faces as they chewed their cud, and several pigs rolled and grunted in a mud pit. Beyond that—beyond the edge of the last irregularly tilled plot of earth—lay the dark, fathomless forest; where the trees formed a foreboding phalanx and nameless things slept during the day in their shadows. Raythen, silent and motionless, was waiting for something to happen. It didn't take long. It never did.

He heard them approach from his right, stepping onto the splintered planks of the porch. Two people—one with heavy footfalls, the other light. He opened his eyes to slits and covertly watched their feet. The leading person wore green leather boots. The one behind wore silver segmented sabatons and golden greaves. They stopped about two meters away. A male voice said, "We're here to see Briggash."

That's the way, Raythen thought. *With authority.* He said nothing.

"Hey, you awake? We're here to see Briggash."

Raythen summoned his right phand. A translucent blue disembodied hand floated in the middle of his field of vision with the palm open, facing away from him. With a though he made it extend its index finger, move forward, and tap the left leather shoe.

> *Hellfurry*
> *Elf Male*
> *Druid: 34*
> *Guild: We Step In Stuff*
> *Hit points: 2143*
> *Mana: 2890*
> *Gear Score: 1002*

Now the warrior.

> *Lenasin*
> *Human Female*
> *Paladin: 36*

Guild: Perfection
Hit points: 2473
Mana: 1943
Gear Score: 2115

Probably not dating, not in the same guild. Bet they just met, because you don't lead with your weaker player unless you're some druid dude trying to impress a lady.

Raythen considered himself to be somewhat of a romantic at heart, even if the character he played in *Gryphon's Claw* was supposed to be a ruthless scoundrel. He would usually go easy on a guy trying to score, but if you're going to impress a lady you should at least try to play smart.

Really, I wouldn't be doing her any favors by rewarding his foolhardiness. Well, let's see how the druid plays this out—if he shows any promise I might let him pass.

Raythen let out an extended yawn that stretched his mouth and jaw into dramatic contortions. His toothpick miraculously stayed in place on the edge of his bottom lip. He tilted his head back and let them see his long, tan, stubbled face. "You say something?"

Typical elf druid, leather armor etched with a design of leaves and trees and stuff. Long straight blond hair—pointy ears sticking out. He held a staff casually in his right hand; it was horizontal to the ground with some colorful feathers dangling down from its knobby end. The paladin was wearing a gray metal breast plate with a slight feminine outline and a silver helm that had golden wings flaring up on each side of her head. The helm also had a vertical nose guard. Raythen thought a nose guard looked flattering on women, it brought out their eyes. Her mouth was in a tight smirk that seemed to mean something that he couldn't read.

3

"You're going to take us to meet Briggash," the druid said, taking an impatient step forward. "We have important information for him, blah blah blah. So come on, just bring us to him."

Well that's it then, Raythen thought. This was, after all, a role-playing server, and the druid was not playing his role convincingly. You had to have respect for the game. *Sorry druid dude, this is not going to impress the lady.*

Raythen started another yawn. He rolled his shoulders in an apparent preparation to stretch his arms. With a quick, fluid motion he instead rolled onto the floor toward them as his cloak flew open, sword in one hand, dagger in the other, ending in a crouch at the feet of the druid. The druid's staff was brought into a defensive line in front of him as his left hand went to take hold of it. Before he could do so, Raythen sprung up and struck his face with the pommel of his short sword, his dagger thrusting low at the bindings of the leather armor. A solid stab, but not critical, the inner leather folds allowed only half of the blade to penetrate into the druid's side. From his peripheral vision Raythen saw the feet of the paladin shift to the druid's right to get a swing in. Keeping close to the druid's body he spun to the druid's left, ducking below his rising arm and stabbing his dagger down into a skinny hamstring. This was a solid hit, eliciting a curse from the druid as he fell backwards. To his surprise, Raythen saw that he was spinning directly toward the paladin, who was taking a step back in order to swing her long sword down onto his skull. Fortunately for him, the druid was now falling into the path of that swing. Raythen helped him along by rolling into the back of the druid's legs, causing him to topple toward the pally. Springing back to his feet, he saw that the pally had managed to check her swing and dodge to the side of the falling druid.

4

There are two different strategies you can take when dealing with multiple opponents. Go after the weaklings first; dispatching them quickly so they are out of the way when you confront the strong ones. Or, go after the strong ones first; hoping you can avoid getting killed by the weak ones who can get a shot in while you are preoccupied. Raythen usually preferred going after the strongest first, but in this circumstance he had already wounded the weakest—he might as well finish it and be done with him. The druid was obviously not a serious player—Raythen wanted to see what the pally was capable of on her own.

She held the sword with two hands and stepped forward, leading with her left foot and thrusting the sword straight at him. He parried with his short sword and threw his dagger at the druid who was staggering to his feet. The spin was off and it bounced harmlessly against his chest. The pally stepped forward again and made another thrust. Parried. The druid began to cast a healing spell, his staff glowing green. This was actually starting to get dangerous—this duo was now playing smart. Raythen had to get fancy. Stepping back he threw his short sword at the floor at the feet of the druid. It stuck into the wood with a loud thunk. The pally, seeing him defenseless, brought her sword up to take a swing. In a move practiced many times (Raythen did, after all, spend almost forty hours a week on that porch) he leaped past the pally, grabbing a vertical post of the porch with both hands, extending his arms and swinging his body around so that he spun at the druid. He glimpsed the precious look of surprise on his face as his knees crashed into his body. The druid sprawled down and Raythen landed on his feet, grabbing his short sword and pivoting smoothly, slicing his blade down onto the back of the druid's neck. It was a clean cut but the druid still had hit points—the blade stopped at the vertebrae. Raythen pulled the sword out and took another swing. Blood spurted liberally from

5

the neck-stump as the blond head rolled to the pally's feet. She faced Raythen, her sword pointing forward. Grinning, she said, "That was pretty."

With that familiar phrase, Raythen recognized the woman. He grinned back at her.

Chapter 2

Spokesdog steps out of the darkness, surrounded by a starry void. His Armani suit is an understated solid gray, his silk tie an iridescent green, his brown Tanino Crisci wingtip shoes glinting from a recent shine—matching the gloss of the meticulously brushed fur on his head—a head which happens to be that of a golden retriever. His floppy ears perk up slightly as he comes to a halt. His hands are held up in front of him, perfectly manicured human hands, hanging still, ready for a dramatic gesture—a gesture that requires a visual. After a moment that builds the appropriate anticipation, behind him the Sun and the planets burst into view. His hands open and swing toward the celestial objects, and with a voice that is both soft and deeply resonant, he speaks.

"The Solar System—centered with its majestic Sun—is a grand, spinning, relentless machine—a machine of spheres and fire. The harnessing of this soulless colossus has been the salvation of the human race. Freed from its delicate terrestrial bubble, humanity is provided with an abundance of energy and materials to build a wider, grander civilization. Away from the cloying gravity well of Terra, one just needs to push," he pushes an imaginary object, "and mountains are moved. Away from night and clouds, the Sun radiates more energy into space every second than was stored in all the fossil fuels that Terra had ever produced since its creation.

This obscenity of riches allows humanity to grow and build without limits; without the fear of destroying its tired, delicate Earth.

"Two technologies have made this prosperity possible. First, there are the space elevators." Terra looms behind him as thin columns rise out from its atmosphere. "Ebon towers extending from green and blue high up into a colorless void. No longer dependent upon expensive and dangerous chemical rockets, a real economy of scale is created in space. Factories are brought into orbit. Ships carrying workers and machines are flung from the tips of the elevators out to the other planets—the planets that are the spinning, heavy gears in this grand machinery we call the Solar System.

"The second technology is cryosleep. Sending pressurized bubbles, little eco-spheres of Earth, out into space is expensive and dangerous; and, quite frankly, stupid. Freezing humans and sending them with the rest of the cargo is what makes the conquest of the Solar System economically viable. No need to store food, air, or water for the trip. No need to worry about the psychology of boredom. At their destinations there is plenty for the people to do, there is much to build.

"Once humans had successfully launched their frozen selves into space; the Solar System, with its uneven distribution of resources, provided that necessary factor for a dynamic economic system—the trade circuit. Pylons of silicon, magnesium, iron, calcium, aluminum, and frozen oxygen; each the size of a bus, are sent continuously from mass drivers on Luna to distant destinations. Mercury, practically made of iron, sends giant bars of the ore out to the other planets, dragged away from the Sun by beautiful, delicate solar sails. Mars, with its own space elevators, sends out pylons of sodium, potassium, and chlorine. From the asteroid belt, vast quantities of carbon, the ubiquitous building blocks of 22nd century industry, are mined and distributed. Over the storm-filled skies of Saturn, giant gossamer ships scoop hydrogen out of the atmosphere like whales swallowing krill. Frozen hydrogen icebergs are sent back to the inner worlds. Every day an ocean's worth of water is chipped out of comets and shot to dry, thirsty customers.

"A significant portion of these resources are sent to the factory of the Solar System—a place with an abundance of cheap energy but few natural resources—Venus." The white shrouded sphere of Venus appears behind him and slowly approaches. "The surface of Venus is a hell of sulfuric acid rain and heat that can melt lead. But fifty kilometers above the surface, ironically, is the most livable environment for humans outside of Terra. The air pressure is the same as Terra at sea level. The temperature is a comfortable twenty-four degrees Celsius. The atmosphere is still poison, but it is heavier than the nitrogen and oxygen mix that humans breathe." Venus takes up the entire background behind Spokesdog, and the viewer is plunged along with him deep into the clouds. Soon a small black dot appears in the distance, contrasting against the gold-tinged clouds. As the object comes closer it takes on an oblong shape, moving quickly through the thick air.

Spokesdog points to it and says, "A stratos, a city the shape of a giant blimp, five kilometers long, is flying through the three-hundred kilometer per hour winds of the Venusian sky. Four monumental tail fins, each a hundred meters long, stabilize the flight of the city. The top half is transparent and lets in the golden yellow light of the Venusian sky. The stratos is tethered by eight kilometers of cable to an aerosail, a coned funnel with wings that pulls the city along by the tremendous force of the wind, and steers it on its way.

"This Venusian stratos, along with others like it, powered by the Sun shining down from above and shining up from the reflecting clouds below,

9

produce the majority of the manufactured goods in the Solar System. Molecular assemblers, machines that create items one layer of molecules at a time, produce anything the heart desires—from leather shoes to aircraft engines—with a quality as near to perfection as is possible—a level of quality that is now demanded by all customers in the Solar System. The energy needs of these assemblers can only be met at an industrial scale on Venus. And Terra, freed from the burden of production, has healed its environment and is now a paradise. Thanks to Venus."

Spokedog faces the viewer directly and clasps his hands together. "So you see, Venus is not only where merchandise is made, it is where dreams are made. It is where you go if you want to make money; it is where you go if your nature doesn't incline toward a *Terrestrial* paradise—because hey," he gives a knowing wink, "paradise can get boring. Venus is where you go if you want to become somebody. It is where the action is. It is where you can reach your full potential. And, contrary to popular belief, you don't have to be an engineer or a scientist to go. Full travel expenses are being paid to qualified support, security, and entertainment personnel. So if you ever dreamed of living on another world, this is your chance. It might even be more than just your chance; it might be your destiny."

He licks his chops briefly, clasps his hands behind his back, and switches to a more formal announcer's voice, "This edutainment has been brought to you the Venusian Employment Council. And don't forget, lunch is on me. Woof."

Chapter 3

She managed to stay on her feet for about forty-five seconds. She was a few levels lower than he was and not as practiced in sword fighting, so forty-five seconds was respectable. She was on her back, her helmet off, her blond pony-tail out, and her sword lying meters away. His sword was pointing down at her throat.

"Hi Sweet GG. Whose avatar is that?" Raythen asked.

"A friend of mine," she replied casually. "When she told me she had an account on *Gryphon's Claw* I decided I wanted to see what you did at your day job."

"What about the druid?"

"Just a pug. I knew I couldn't take you alone. I thought I might be able to get in a lucky shot while you were distracted by him."

"Nice." He sheathed his sword and extended a hand. "I guess you want to go see Briggash now."

She took his hand and he helped her to her feet. "Aren't I supposed to beat you first?"

"The rules are you're supposed to convince me," he said, "and I have some leeway as an NPC. The character I play would appreciate your sneakiness in sacrificing the druid. Come on."

After she retrieved her sword and helm he led her into the tavern. The wood interior didn't look much better than the wood on the porch, being

11

weathered by spilled drinks, piss, and spit rather than rain, snow, and sun. Raythen was grateful that smell was not included in the virtual world. Faint light shone in from filth-caked windows. To the left was the bar, standing on it was a dwarf wearing a stained apron, using a length of his red beard to clean out a mug in his hand. The round wooden tables in the room had been hacked and gouged more than kitchen cutting boards. In one of the few unbroken chairs an orc wearing chainmail slept with his face in a puddle of his own drool on a table. The drool made the gouges look like tiny little river valleys.

The dwarf said, "Raythen, who's 'dat you got 'dere?"

"Hi Olaf, I'm taking her down to see Briggash."

"What? His dinner t'aint for two hours!" He let out a raspy laugh at his own joke, showing a gap-toothed grin.

"Just let him know we're coming."

"Sure thing Raythen." Olaf walked to the end of the bar where a rope hung from the ceiling on a brass ring, extending to a small hole in the floor. He gave it two quick tugs before going back to his cleaning.

Raythen led Sweet GG back to a small storage room. There wasn't much space to move among the barrels and crates. Tipping a barrel onto its edge, Raythen rolled it aside, exposing a hatch in the floor with a rusted iron ring in the middle. Lifting the hatch by the ring he revealed a ladder that descended into darkness.

"Ladies first," he said, motioning downward.

She carefully lowered herself down the hole. Raythen followed, closing the door above them and plunging them into a darkness that was only relieved by a yellow flicker far below. It grew as they descended what could now faintly be seen as a stone-lined shaft.

"What I wouldn't give for exo armor in this world," she said. "Jumping is way more fun than climbing."

She finally clanked her sabatons on the stone floor and made room for Raythen. There was one narrow passageway through the wall opposite the ladder. Their light source, a torch, was protruding from a hole in the wall. Raythen nodded to it. "You take that." She did. "After you," he said, and she started walking.

"So what do I have to do? I don't want to screw this up for the real Lenasin. I kind of promised that I could finish the Briggash quest line for her."

He snorted a laugh. She frowned at the derogatory sound. He said, "At the end of this passage is a door. You knock on the door three times, pause, and then two more times. The door will open and some mook will bring you to Briggash. Then you tell Briggash you have the gem."

"The gem?"

"Yeah, the gem. The Stolach Ruby." He paused. "You do have the Stolach Ruby, don't you? The thing you get from that thief in Hardor."

She couldn't have forgotten the ruby, could she?

She stopped and turned toward him, the torchlight glinting off her helmet and making her face orange.

"You mean this one?" She reached behind his ear. When she pulled her hand back a red gemstone the size of a walnut was held between her thumb and forefinger.

"Nice manual dexterity for being in an unfamiliar avatar," he said, and then squinted at her suspiciously. "You are Sweet GG, aren't you?"

She winked at him. "Probably."

"Because Edargo tried to pull a fast one on me like that once—which, really, was just plain wrong."

13

Still holding the torch in her fist, she crossed her arms so it went behind her back. "He tried to pretend he was me?" The movement of her body, the squaring of shoulders, slight sideways thrust of hip, convinced him that this was indeed Sweet GG. In some worlds you could have bots move your avatars for you, but not in *Gryphon's Claw*. This game was about real skill, a direct connection between a person's sensory-motor cortex and the avatar. That's why Raythen enjoyed it so much.

"No, this was a couple years ago. He was pretending to be some other girl. And . . . um, I think you're burning your hair."

"Oh frak!" She pulled the torch away from her and held it at arm's length. She turned around so he could see her singed ponytail. "Does it look bad?"

"Eh, well." He patted out the still burning ends. "Naw, it's fine."

"How long till it fixes itself? I told Lenasin I wouldn't do anything stupid."

"Don't worry about it. It'll be fine."

"Good!" She smiled brightly at him. "So, you're going to help me kill Briggash, aren't you?"

"I can't touch the boss mob, just the adds. There are three of them. I can guarantee taking two of them out. Maybe all three, depending on who's playing them."

"Kk, so I kill the boss mob. Cake."

"Ask him for the map. When he refuses, don't wait for him to make the first move. Attack. Then I'll draw aggro from the adds."

"Kk."

They reached the door—it was made from thick wooden planks and iron bands. A ghoul-faced iron knocker hung at eye level. Sweet GG knocked the secret knock. After a few seconds the door swung inward part way, bright firelight streaming out. A bulky, man-shaped silhouette asked, "What business do you have?"

Sweet GG said, "I'm here to see Briggash."

The face of the mook, becoming visible as it jutted through the doorway, leered at her with its crags and scars. "Briggash doesn't take his whores until midnight."

"I have the Stolach Ruby."

"Do you now? Let's have a see."

She showed him the gem, holding it out of arm's reach.

"He might be interested in that," he said. "And if he's not, you're welcome to stay till midnight." Another leer.

Raythen phanded him. Mook One was being played tonight by Marcus Firth. Easy enough in a straight up fight, but shifty. Marcus stayed behind the door as he opened it all the way, keeping behind them as they entered. They were in a square, stone-walled chamber. A fire roared in a massive fireplace that took up most of the wall to their right. Directly ahead, sitting on a rough-cut stone throne, was Briggash. He was an immensely fat ogre, about three meters tall. Bald with many chins, his designer was obviously inspired by Jabba the Hut. A way-too-small breastplate was strapped to his belly. An axe the size of Sweet GG was leaning against the throne. On a table in front of him were carefully stacked gold, silver, and copper coins, some reaching heights of over a meter. Raythen noted the positions of the other two guards; one seated at the far end of the table, playing with some coins, the other leaning in the corner across the room to their left with his sword out. Phanding, he noted they were being played by Keli and Shin. Keli, the one leaning, wasn't too bad. She was aching to get out of the mook pool. He'd have to be careful with her.

Briggash appraised Sweet GG, grinning and showing his pointy fangs. "What tribute do you bring me?" he said in a loud, guttural voice appropriate to an ogre.

"I don't bring tribute, I'm here for a trade," Sweet GG said.

Briggash laughed, spraying spittle. "No one comes to trade. They give."

Sweet GG held up the ruby. "I have the Stolach Ruby. I heard you were interested in it."

Briggash's eyes widened at the jewel.

"I will trade you the ruby for the map of the Torlan Temple," Sweet GG said quickly.

Briggash sprayed his laughter again.

Sweet GG hurled the ruby at his face, pulled out her sword, and leaped onto the table—toppling coin stacks, sending them glittering and tinkling to the floor.

Raythen saw a small tactical problem. Sweet GG was between him and one of the adds. That add would go after her flank and she would have no chance. Otherwise his logical first choice was Marcus. Frowning, he made a quick decision and leaped up on the table, spinning around so he and Sweet GG were back to back. Shin sprang from his chair and swung his sword at Sweet GG's legs. Raythen blocked it with his sword and kicked him in the face, sending him falling backwards.

Briggash was up on his feet now too, reaching for his axe. Sweet GG swung her sword at his head; he blocked it with his thick, bare arm. The sword cut a meaty gouge into it. Keli and Marcus rushed the table. *This is way too defensive*, Raythen thought. He leaped high into the air, flipped, spun, and landed behind Marcus. As Marcus turned to face him Raythen plunged his dagger down the base of his neck between the clavicle and scapula. Sticking solid, he used the dagger grip as a handle to move Marcus's unbalanced body in front of Keli who swung her sword hard into Marcus's side. He turned in time to see Shin thrusting his sword at him. He pivoted to his side to lessen his profile, Shin's sword grazing his chest. Raythen wrapped his arm around Shin's sword arm and lifted up his own legs, putting all his weight on Shin's arm. As Raythen fell back, Shin fell forward, Raythen's heels planted under Shin's rib cage. Shin was upside down, flying backwards into Marcus and Keli. Quickly back on his feet, Raythen deflected Keli's swing. She had overextended and he was able to pivot to the side, jabbing at her with his dagger. Shin was lying on Marcus's belly—the two were getting in each other's way as they tried to get up, looking like a failed game of Twister. This gave Raythen a couple of seconds. He swept at Keli's ankles with his leg, but she saw it coming and made a little hop. In doing so she spread her arms for balance. Raythen used the opening to thrust his sword into her throat.

He got to the others before they could untangle themselves. A sword through Marcus's exposed belly, and a blow to the back of Shin's head.

Raythen turned to see how Sweet GG was doing. She wasn't. She was dangling upside down, Briggash holding a sabatoned foot with a club-like fist. Her helmet was off, showing a bruised face and tangled hair.

"Never come here again!" Briggash yelled, swinging his axe at her head.

"No!" Raythen cried, tensing his body to spring at Briggash, barely stopping himself, remembering his role. Sweet GG's head thunked into the fireplace.

Briggash looked over at Raythen quizzically, glanced at the heap of his dead mooks, and then looked back at Raythen. "She a girlfriend of yours or something?" He bobbed the headless body up and down.

17

"Yeah, actually she is."

Briggash frowned. "Sorry bro." He dropped her body, which clattered loudly on the stone floor. "Didn't you tell her she was too low to solo this?"

Raythen shrugged, regaining his composure. "It's not even her character. She's just visiting."

"Oh, cool." The ogre sat back down, wiping the blood off his axe against his thigh.

Chapter 4

Raythen opened his eyes. He lifted his head, sat up straight, and stretched his neck, first left then right. He was naked, covered only by the groin-arch which was now in the process of retracting itself into the leather recliner he had been lying on for over thirty-six hours. Through the course of that time the recliner had monitored and responded to his various biological needs—robotic appendages and suction hoses hygienically removing waste, cleaning what needed to be cleaned with warm sprays of scented water, drying him with soft tissues.

He stared blankly through the open door of his recliner room at the daylight streaming in from the window in the living room, reflecting off the shiny faux wood panels. The only pieces of furniture in his recliner room were the eponymous recliner and an OmniServe table to its right—a black box that would pop up whatever food or beverage he summoned. He swiveled to the left and rested his feet on the cool floor. The walls were windowless and white. He arched his back, rolling the muscles under his light brown skin, and stretched his arms. A hundred years ago he would have been the greatest athlete in the world—fastest sprinter, most powerful swimmer, tireless marathon runner—but today he was just a little above average. Medical science was given the responsibility of keeping people healthy who spend ninety percent of their waking life in a recliner. It did a very good job. Physical augmentation gave people complete fitness with no work on their part at all. Raythen didn't need to exercise but he did anyway—he enjoyed it.

He stepped into the living room, scratching his tangled brown hair as he came into the sunlight. His apartment was small, sparsely appointed, and neat. There was no bed or bedroom, the couch in front of him could be commanded to become a bed, but he usually went for days without using it, preferring to sleep on his recliner.

Time for a jog, he thought.

He went into the closet and put on some shorts and sneakers. His apartment was on the tenth floor. Out into the hallway, into the elevator. The lobby—clean, beige, with a couple of green couches—was empty of people. The AI doorman, shimmering light-blue, the color of all augmented reality entities projected into the mind's view of the world, tipped his hat and said, "Going for jog today Raythen? Excellent weather for it. You might even get a glimpse of the sky beyond the clouds."

"Really? That would be something."

The doorman nodded and the glass door slid open.

Outside, Raythen stretched his legs at the base of the stairs. Looking up, there was no discernible sky, just a blanket of golden sulfur dioxide clouds that radiated sunlight with nearly equal intensity from all directions. The cloud's apparent motion was toward the stern of the stratos. A Venusian day is two-hundred and forty-three Terran days, but the stratos, pulled by the aerosail, circled the planet once every four Terran days. Approximately twenty-four hours of sunlight followed by twenty-four hours of night. Not that anyone really cared about the solar day on Venus. Everyone's clocks were synchronized with Coordinated Pulsar Time.

The stratos that was Raythen's home was called Lu Shing City. It had a population of a little over nine thousand people. The ground was higher at the edges than in the middle, sloping down to a central lake surrounded by parks. From his current vantage point, about halfway up the slope between the lake and the stern, Raythen couldn't see the lake or the parks. His view was blocked by the sculpted glass and silver skyscrapers owned by the rich and powerful. Driven by aesthetics and envy, they would tear down their buildings and put up new, fashionable ones every year or so.

The street outside his building was quiet and pleasant. It was wide enough for two cars, although there was rarely any traffic. All food, water, clothes, and whatever supplies people purchased was sent through the underground tunnel network. The road was lined with ferns, palmettos, and mahogany trees that had been genetically adjusted to the alien sun and cycles. Small tropical song birds and red ground squirrels kept themselves busy, rustling about. Raythen started his jog. He was the only human in sight.

Raythen summoned his phand. He clicked the menu button on his HUD and scrolled through some new music his brain implant had selected for him. The imp, placed in his brain when he was fourteen, had a good notion of what music he liked to listen to. He picked a wooku wooku band called Baobell. After the opening riffs he thought, *Not bad.* He moved his chat window from the right corner closer to the center of his vision and made it semi-transparent so he could read while he watched the road.

<BeeTwo: post> "Rask has all the manners and sophistication of a baboon."

<Doomsday: post> "If colonel, infantry, BoB."

<BeeTwo: post> "And the colorful baboon butt."

<Doomsday: post> "Twenty-Two Panzer Fours, thirteen Panzer Fives approaching Vervi."

<Edargo: post @Doomsday> "Shouldn't you be in a game channel or something?"

<Dark Fuji: post #DFContest> "I have a proposition for you all."

<Edargo: post #DFContest> "I've been waiting years for you to say that DF."

<Rask: post #DFContest> "A proposition from Dark Fuji is like a kool-aid from a necrophiliac."

<BeeTwo: post> "Rasked!"

<BeeTwo: post> "Baboon."

<Dark Fuji: post #DFContest> "Time travel ménage a trois."

<Thorben: post #DFContest> "Curious."

<Doomsday: post #DFContest> "The problem with living in a world where everyone over twenty has the body and libido of a twenty-year-old is this entire obsession with sex."

<Dark Fuji: post #DFContest> "Travel through time. Find two people contemporaneous to each other who you think I would like to have join me in a ménage a trois. Format: (Year) Name1: Name2. You can have more than one entry, but any following entry must have one member from the previous try."

<Doomsday> post #DFContest> "(1943) George C. Patton: Erwin Rommel."

<Rask: post> "Few know this, but when BeeTwo was eighteen years old he was the love slave of Commodore Whent. The Commodore had a seven-centimeter diameter cock (currently preserved for view in the Ceres Enclave), which soon made BeeTwo's sphincter useless for its original purpose. One day some Peace Corp volunteers found BeeTwo orally servicing members of the DugDug Mine Corps since he had been cast out of Whent's harem. They were horrified by the condition of BeeTwo's anus

and attempted to repair the damage with some impromptu surgery. Since the volunteers were experts in botany, things did not go as planned. When it was over BeeTwo had two anal openings. Happily, the lower one was only about a centimeter in diameter and provided extremely tight pleasure, which the Peace Corp volunteers and observing DugDug workers soon enjoyed. The moral of the story: aim for the lower hole."

<Edargo: post @BeeTwo> "Rasked!"

<BeeTwo: post #DFContest> (2191) Shelley Kym: Kim Shelly"

<Dark Fuji: post #DFContest> "Doomsday is in the lead."

<Rask: post #DFContest> "What's the prize?"

<Edargo: post #DFContest> "BeeTwo's lower hole."

<Doomsday: post> "lf colonel, infantry, BoB."

<BeeTwo: post @Doomsday> "No one cares about your bulge battle."

<Dark Fuji: post #DFContest> "The winner gets a 2-hour cinematic feature of their life. Original soundtrack and 3-minute trailer."

<Rask: post #DFContest> "(390) Hypatia of Alexandria: Alaric I"

<BeeTwo: post #DFContest> "(1 million BCE) Og: Crog"

<Thorben: post #DFContest> "(1936) Hedy Lamarr: Rita Heyworth."

<Dark Fuji: post #DFContest> "Doomsday is still in the lead."

<Rask: post #DFContest> "(390) Alaric I: Stilicho"

<Dark Fuji: post #DFContest> "Hmmm. Rask and Doomsday are tied."

<Rask: post #DFContest> "(390) Alaric I: Vatsyayana"

<Edargo: post #DFContest> "That Alaric really got around."

<Rask: post #DFContest> "Yeah, he liked to Rome."

<Dark Fuji: post #DFContest> "Yeueeww. Bad pun."

<Edargo: post #DFContest> "Bad-ump-bump."

The joke went over Raythen's head. He clicked on the name of Alaric I.

Alaric I (Gothic: Alareiks; 370 - 410) was the King of the Visigoths from 395–410. Alaric is most famous for his sack of Rome in 410, which marked a decisive event in the decline of the Roman Empire.

Yeah, that was a bad pun alright.

<Thorben: post #DFContest> "(1946) Rita Heyworth: Orson Welles"

<Edargo: post #DFContest> "(1960) Woody Allen: Truman Capote"

<Dark Fuji: post #DFContest> "We have a winner!"

<Thorben: post #DFContest> "Which?"

<Dark Fuji: post #DFContest> "Edargo. Good combo of comedy and drama. Rask, you almost had it, but placing Vatsyayana at 390 CE is sketchy."

<Edargo: post #DFContest> "Zowow!"

Dammit. Raythen thought. *Edargo is going to be insufferable after this.*

He was jogging uphill, toward the protective bubble of the stratos. He noticed that someone was jogging next to him to his right. The jogger shimmered blue and was slightly transparent. He was a tall, lanky man with his hair high and tight and a t-shirt with the letters "VDF" on the front. Raythen minimized his chat window and said, "Hi Sarge, how's it going?"

"It's going. I see you're still keeping fit the old-fashioned way."

"You kind of drilled the habit into me."

"Good to see I taught you something."

"You couldn't drag any of the enlisted out?" Raythen asked.

"They're all on leave. Got the track to myself."

When Raythen was in the Venus Defense Force, Sarge would wake everyone up early and tell them they had to jog with him because he hated to jog alone. At the time Raythen thought it was just a pretense, but now he guessed that it must really be true for him to search him out to be his virtual jogging partner.

"I saw you in *Exo Arena* the other day," Sarge said.

"Oh yeah?"

"You showed those civies what a real trooper could do."

"Thanks," Raythen said, feeling genuine pride. Sarge was never much for praise.

"It's not like the real thing though, is it?" Sarge asked. "The feeling of being in a real powered exoskeleton?"

It was true. There was nothing in the worlds to compare with being in an exoskeleton battle suit. The speed, the strength—you were a different kind of creature in an exo suit—an angel, a demon, a master of your environment.

"You still have your sockets?" Sarge asked, glancing quickly at the small of Raythen's back.

The sockets—two holes, each about two centimeters in diameter and twelve centimeters apart, penetrated deep into his hip bone. His hip bone was reinforced with a lattice of carbon nanotube polymer. You don't so much wear an exo suit as be suspended inside it by two carbon polymer rods. When he had left the military they offered to remove the holes, but he decided to keep them. There were some civilian jobs driving vehicles that required hip-suspension, but he hadn't ended up with any of those jobs. He ended up with a virtual career. When he wasn't working in *Gryphon's Claw* he was usually free-lancing in *Exo Arena*, controlling a virtual exo suit.

"They're still there," Raythen said.

"Good."

Sarge increased the pace. Raythen kept up.

"What's up Sarge? You low on your quota?"

"No, not that. I just figured you for a career trooper. You have a level head. Best thing to have in the force. Not like most of the yahoos under me."

Sarge was being generous with his praise today.

Raythen shook his head, "It's not like it matters. It's not like we're at war or anything, or likely to be in one."

"It's not only about war. There was that incident on Falstaff."

Falstaff was a stratos that had collided with a light cruiser. The cruiser had penetrated the protective bubble and crashed onto the habitable surface. The VDF exo troopers were sent in for an emergency rescue mission. It was the only time they had been deployed on a real mission during Raythen's four years of service.

"We saved a lot of lives that day," Sarge said.

"Yeah. That was . . . something."

The road curved to the right, parallel to the transparent canopy of the stratos. "Hold on a second," Raythen said. He slowed down to a walk, continuing straight, going into the ferns. A squirrel screeched its displeasure and ran away. Raythen approached the edge. The canopy was clear enough not to be there. He looked up. All golden clouds. He looked down. All golden clouds. No sign of sky and no sign of ground. He rested his forehead on the warm, hard surface. A couple of times in his life he had seen the surface of Venus with his own eyes. Very quickly dark patches had appeared and vanished. They were recorded in his imp, along with everything else he had ever seen and heard since he was fourteen. He liked the fact that he had seen the surface. Almost proud, and yet embarrassed that he could find pleasure in such a stupid thing, like he was some old tourist.

"What the hell you doing?" Sarge asked.

He swiveled his head to look up, with the side of his face pressing against the canopy. No sign of sky. The doorman had been wrong.

"Just looking for the sky," Raythen said.

"Just finding an excuse to slack off and change the subject."

"No, I'll think about what you said."

"Yeah, sure. Now let's do forty k. And no rests!"

Chapter 5

Raythen ran across the black-rock landscape, between boulders the size of houses and the occasional twisted, purple tree. In the upper right field of his vision the small map on his HUD showed the positions of the other five people on his team, each represented by a small red dot. They were travelling in twos; he and his wingman Edargo were in the southwest corner. About half-way north were WuNeNe and Kingston. Up in the northwest corner were Feyfire and Triptisch. All were moving east. He was running at eighty kilometers per hour, each step amplified by the plastimuscle of the exo armor that wrapped around his body. Covering the plastimuscle was a hard, sleek exoskeleton that curved to his body as organically as something created by nature. Edargo was keeping pace, fifteen meters behind and left.

Raythen highlighted his chat box and thought words into it.

<Raythen: tell @Edargo> "Woody Allen and Truman Capote?"

<Edargo: tell @Raythen> "Brilliant, eh?"

<Raythen: tell @Edargo> "So how did you come up with those two? I thought Dark Fuji was exclusively lesbian these days."

<Edargo: tell @Raythen> "You haven't been following her life very closely, have you? This is where having an unhealthy, and perhaps a little creepy obsession with other people's affairs pays off. She's currently shacking up with these two old guys. I'm talking over a century old. They

were famous artists or movie directors or something—you know, the kind of people who idolize Woody Allen and Truman Capote. Recently she's had this fixation with classic cinema."

<Feyfire: post &RedTeam> "Bogy, one o'clock."

A blue dot appeared on Raythen's map east of Feyfire. Blue Team had moved in fast from the other side, Red Team was only about a third way across the map. The blue dot vanished as Feyfire lost visual. No lock.

<Raythen: post &RedTeam> "Request pincher."

Raythen was breaking etiquette by making a strategic request, since he was just an NPC, but he had played against Sweet GG's team enough times to make a good guess of what was going down.

<WuNeNe: post &RedTeam> "Negative."

Red and Blue were tied, two games each. Raythen hadn't lost a five-game match to Sweet GG in over a month; and his stats were closing in on Slipknot's, the best *Exo Arena* player on Venus. If he lost this one he would never be able to catch up to her—unless she had an uncharacteristic losing streak. Unfortunately, Raythen was not in charge, he couldn't call the shots. He hoped WuNeNe was paying attention; he was willing to bet Blue Team was massing in the north, zerging through a gap in the mountains rather than going for the flag that was in the middle of the map. But he had to keep tracking east, obeying orders, like he was paid to do.

<Feyfire: post &RedTeam> "Bogies, two o'clock!"

Raythen saw three blue dots this time, in a V formation, the open mouth of the V facing Feyfire and Triptisch.

<WuNeNe: post &RedTeam> "Feyfire, keep them occupied while I go for the flag."

Feyfire and Triptisch were engaged now, their dots mixing it up with the blues.

<Edargo: tell @Raythen> "I want this win bad. I could sure use the bonus."

<Raythen: tell @Edargo> "We're going to have to pull north soon. They're trying to wipe us."

Triptisch's red dot vanished, as well as the blue dot closest to him. The first fatalities of this game.

<Feyfire: post &RedTeam> "Can't hold out, I'll try to lead them away."

Her red dot moved fast back the way they came.

<Feyfire: post &RedTeam> "Fuck . . . fuck!"

Her dot vanished.

Raythen was running toward a range of hills about a fifty meters high trailing north to south. If Edargo ran along the base of it on flat ground going at full speed while he gave him cover along the top, they might be able to reach the flag before it was all over up north.

<Raythen: post &RedTeam> "We're going for the flag."

He turned left, Edargo followed.

<WuNeNe: post &RedTeam> "No! I'm going for the flag. Go on those hills and head north to cover us. After we get it you stay at our rear and block."

<Raythen: post &RedTeam> "Copy."

<Raythen: tell @Edargo> "You hug at the base of the hills and sprint to the flag. I'll go to the top and do like he says until he's dead."

<Edargo: tell @Raythen> "Sure, let me get in trouble for disobeying orders."

The blue dots were gone from the map; the remaining blues were no longer in anyone's visual range. It was now five to four—still not bad. WuNeNe and Kingston were moving toward the center at full speed.

Raythen leaped twenty meters to the top of a boulder at the base of the hill and sprang off it to another further up the side. He continued leaping until he was on the ridge, and then ran north. Edargo was already ahead of him making for the flag. He scanned the landscape north and east for any sign of Blue Team.

<Kingston: post &RedTeam> "Bogies, four o'clock."

Two blue dots were closing in on him and WuNeNe. Kingston moved to engage while WuNeNe continued toward the center.

Raythen wondered if those two blues were part of the original group from the north. He calculated the probable time it would have taken them to reach WuNeNe—no, those must be the safeties.

Kingston's dot vanished. Five to three.

The two safeties were not chasing down WuNeNe. They were maintaining their position. They didn't need to follow, Raythen guessed, because the other three were coming down on an intercept course toward WuNeNe. This would actually be the best thing that could happen at the moment for Raythen, because it meant the blues weren't near the flag. The flag was their last chance. If only WuNeNe could take at least one down with him.

<WuNeNe: post &RedTeam> "Raythen, get here quick! Cover me while I go for the—"

WuNeNe's dot disappeared.

<Edargo: tell @Raythen> "Just you and me amigo."

<Raythen: tell @Edargo> "We'll reach the flag a few seconds before them. Grab it and run south-west. After two clicks make a bee-line for home. I'll cover."

<Edargo: tell @Raythen> "Any plan where I'm the hero is fine with me."

Raythen reached around to his back with his right hand and grabbed his rail gun. The KR-79 Special had a meter-long barrel; a clean, smooth cylinder, ten centimeters in diameter. The bore, however, was only five millimeters, out of which it shot tiny pellets of steel and uranium alloy at nine times the speed of sound.

The flag, currently black, was planted at the bottom of an enormous rock-lined sinkhole the size of a football stadium. As the sinkhole came into view, Edargo, now about a half kilometer ahead, leaped down into it. The ridgeline of the hills Raythen was running on ended at the southern side of the sinkhole. He scanned the far edge, magnifying the view, looking for any signs of Blue Team. With his phand he traced a line on the map from WuNeNe's last position to the flag. Fifty-three seconds of travel time. WuNeNe had died forty-one seconds ago. Raythen made a new plan.

<Raythen: tell @Edargo> "Get the flag and head south, to our side of the hills."

<Edargo: tell @Raythen> "Not base?"

<Raythen: tell @Edargo> "No, you might hit the safeties."

<Edargo: tell @Raythen> "Kk."

Raythen leaped down the hill to the east side of the sink-hole and then ran along its perimeter north-east. Edargo grabbed the flag and it turned red, showing the team that had control. As he headed toward the south side of the hole Raythen saw movement at the far edge. His HUD locked onto it. Then all three blues fired at Edargo, the whizzing sounds of their rail guns revealing their positions. Raythen got three locks. They were leaping down the sinkhole as they fired.

Raythen aimed at the closest and fired. A leaping target is an easy target. When you leave the ground your trajectory is all up to gravity and wind resistance, easy things to calculate. Raythen knew he had about a second and a half before his targets could get a bead on him. He fired for that time and then moved away from the rim, out of their line of sight. He backtracked a few meters and moved to the rim again, establishing a lock and firing. He gave himself a second, but this time it turned out to be about a tenth of a second too long. A stream of pellets grazed the left side of his abdomen. The impact spun him ninety degrees as his reactive armor made tiny explosive pops to prevent penetration. He rolled out of sight and ran north a few meters before approaching the edge again. There were only two blues now; they were both focusing on Edargo who was racing up the side of the sinkhole. Raythen fired. This time the one he was locked on didn't bother to fire back at him. They both wanted Edargo who had been firing back at them as he leaped and climbed, trying his best to move in a zigzag pattern. But with two concentrating their fire—

<Edargo: tell @Raythen> "Shit shit shit!"

Edargo was down.

One blue left. He was making short, quick, unpredictable leaps, firing up at Raythen. Raythen continued to move toward the edge, fire a burst, and then move away. But he didn't have time to dance; the safeties would be closing in, he had to end this now. He approached the edge, got a lock, and kept firing, running along the edge toward the south. He hoped the blue was damaged enough not to return fire—he was sure the blue would die first, but he couldn't afford any damage to himself before the last two arrived.

The gamble paid off. The blue fell down motionless. The safeties would be here any second. What to do? Assess. Two to one. He had two obvious choices: either grab the flag and run, or hide and try to ambush them. If he grabbed the flag and they arrived before he got out of the

33

sinkhole he was dead meat. On the other hand, they would probably split up before approaching the flag, making an ambush problematic.

He came up with a third alternative. There was a rock down near that flag that might just do the trick. It might be a stupid idea, it might get him laughed out of the post-game show, but the other alternatives didn't look all that promising.

He jumped down into the sinkhole.

The flag waved its red banner from a solid metal pole that had planted itself upright next to Edargo's wrecked exoskeleton, black flakes scattered about from the reactive armor, a leg lying by itself a few meters down the embankment.

They're going to be here any second, Raythen thought. Let's see if this works.

Chapter 6

Sweet GG ran up the hill, trying to keep her eyes on the red flag on the embankment below.

<Torvald: tell @Sweet GG> "You think it's Raythen?"

He was running down the western slope toward the flag.

<Sweet GG: tell @Torvald> "I'd bet you a dollar."

She reached the crest of the hill and started going down the east side, scanning first the western horizon then back to Torvald. He was at the bottom of the sinkhole moving toward the slope where the flag stood.

<Torvald: tell @Sweet GG> "He must have gone to our base to cut us off."

<Sweet GG: tell @Torvald> "I don't think so."

She was at the bottom of the hill and now running along the eastern edge of the hole.

<Sweet GG: tell @Torvald> "He'd do better here in the rocks."

Torvald was moving up the slope toward the flag.

<Sweet GG: tell @Torvald> "You better circle around the flag; make sure he's not hiding behind a rock."

<Torvald: tell @Sweet GG> "Copy."

Without slowing down he started to circle the flag at a radius of about twenty meters.

Sweet GG reached halfway to the northern edge and turned back, continuing to scan around her.

<Torvald: tell @Sweet GG> "All clear."

<Sweet GG: tell @Torvald> "Copy. Go for it."

Torvald ran straight for the flag. As he approached it he noticed a large boulder, about the size of a hippo, surreally rising up from the ground next to him. He hopped to the side in a sudden start as he realized Raythen was underneath it, holding it up like Atlas holding the world. Torvald swung his gun around to fire, but the boulder was already flying toward him. There was no time to dodge—the boulder crashed on top of him and he was sent to the ground—his head and chest pinned. He tried to leverage his arms to push the boulder off, but as he did so he felt his legs get shot to pieces.

"Damn!" Sweet GG exclaimed, leaping down the embankment, getting a lock on Raythen. He had grabbed the flag and was running away. She still had the advantage, she should still win.

The flag flew in the air away from Raythen. He had thrown it. For the barest instant she followed the flag with her crosshairs rather than Raythen. In that time he had spun and dodged away, aiming and firing. She fired back, attempting lateral moves on the rocky slope. Pellets impacted her torso. She saw her shots hit his left shoulder, which he was leading with to lessen his profile. His left arm flew off in a shower of black. After a small hop she expected to land on her right foot but instead felt nothing, tumbling down into the boulders. Her view spun—boulders, sky, boulders, sky. Black dust obscured her view and pellets tore through her exoskeleton armor body.

Chapter 7

Raythen hated the post-game show. He and his team mates were out
of their virtual armor, sitting at a long table wearing form fitting red
uniforms. Facing them from across the table were the members of Team
GG. Raythen and Edargo's teammates were from Terra, visiting Venus on
a business trip and passing the time in *Exo Arena*. All of the Terrans except
for Feyfire were East Asian. East Asian was the "in" race style on Terra.
Edargo was an early adopter on Venus. Feyfire was Elvish, currently the
most popular alt-race style. Raythen didn't know what the current alt-alt
race style was. If he did it probably wouldn't be the alt-alt style anymore.
He himself had tired of keeping up with race style when he was in his
teens, so he did what many with his indifference did; he had undergone a
procedure that gave him what is commonly called the "Rio" look—a mix
that made his race indeterminate, with his avatar being a fairly close match
to his physical appearance. Sweet GG sat directly across from WuNeNe.
Since Raythen had known them, the members of Team GG had never
changed their races. Sweet GG was East Asian—Korean or Japanese—
with long straight white hair that fell over her shoulders like snow on a
mountain slope. Her face was an oval of innocence. Towering to her left
was Torvald—he was European with tight black curls on his head and a
face like a concrete block. He was purposefully ignoring Kingston in front
of him. Across from Feyfire was Lilith, a willowy African who was almost

as tall as Torvald. Across from Triptisch was Vittany, a conventionally handsome blond man who was never much for words. Across from Raythen was Cass, who could have passed for Vittany's sister, and across from Edargo was Killion, a bald and stocky Mayan.

To the far left, at the head of the table, sat the game commentator. Today it was Tashi Mahalingam, the second-best *Exo Arena* announcer on the planet, an indicator of the wealth of these particular Terrans. Most post-game shows Raythen participated in were commentated by AI bots, since most weren't paid for.

"An outstanding match culminating in a nail-biting tie-breaker!" Mahalingam exclaimed, straightening his tie. "After a strong start by Team GG, Team WuNeNe managed to climb out of the pit, literally and figuratively, and stage a spectacular come-back!"

Mahalingam held up a large red beverage cup with a straw in it and said, "This match recap is brought to you by Galaxy Gulp—drink Galaxy Gulp—because you are fucking thirsty!" He threw the cup out into the virtual audience. "And by Jeef Underwear." He leaped on his desk, revealing that he wasn't wearing pants, just tight green Jeefs. He grabbed his crotch and said, "Hey! Look at my package!"

He dropped back into his seat, straightened his tie, and said, "Let's take a look at this fight in game two where Team GG really showed its stuff and we can see why it is one of the strongest teams on Venus!"

The screen above Mahalingam displayed a surreal ancient ruin with gargantuan statues of imaginary alien beasts. Twisting spires reached toward a red and orange sky. The camera panned around the city and then zoomed in close to three Red Team members running down a cratered boulevard. In the playback the names of the players hovered over them—

WuNeNe, Kingston, and Feyfire. They were running for the flag, which was ahead in the center of a spacious square.

"Using speed and a large force, Team WuNeNe made a direct run for the flag, but Team GG was waiting for them!"

Now the view was angled behind three blue exos running, firing, and dodging. The firefight was presented with dramatic slow-motion leaps with limbs being blown off as Mahalingam highlighted the strengths and weaknesses in their strategies and moves.

<Raythen: tell @Sweet GG> "You really woke them up that game."

<Sweet GG: tell @Raythen> "Arrogant snobs. They needed to be cut down to size. Check out the ratings. We've got some watching from Terra."

Raythen looked at the stats above the replay screen. 2,934 viewers from Venus. 9,342,576 viewers on Terra.

<Raythen: tell @Sweet GG> "Damn! I know he has good stats but didn't realize he had such a following."

<Sweet GG: tell @Raythen> "He's the CEO of Blufarga, Inc. I think those are his employees hoping he gets fragged, like this move here."

On the screen Sweet GG leaped out from behind a statue and fired point blank into the back of WuNeNe. As the dust settled she grabbed the flag and ran for the blue base.

<Raythen: tell @Sweet GG> "Bump."

<Sweet GG: tell @Raythen> "hehe"

Mahalingam turned to the audience and said, "That Sweet GG, she makes it look so easy! Her style! Her grace! She's giving me—" Mahalingam leaped back up onto his desk, suddenly wearing a belly dancer costume. "—EXOPHILIA!" The walls and ceiling exploded, and a line of belly dancers behind him stretched left and right to the horizons.

Raqs Sharqi music blared as Mahalingam and the dancers rhythmically shouted " EXOPHILIA" to the beat. A ten-meter-tall exo trooper strode out of nowhere toward Mahalingam. Unlike the usual exo trooper, his faceplate wasn't blank, it had a jagged metal-toothed mouth. It loomed over Mahalingam, let out a Godzilla-like cry, and then grabbed him and popped him into his mouth. The belly dancers scattered in terror. The giant trooper turned to the players, lifted his fists and howled. After a moment of posturing it squatted over the chair and shit out something that congealed back into Mahalingam, who straightened his tie again and continued his commentary as the giant trooper strode off.

"It looked like it was all over for Team WuNeNe, but then came this move in game four that turned things around!"

Of course, they weren't going to show Raythen's move that won game five and the match. Mahalingam knew who was paying the bills. They showed a fairly decent move by WuNeNe.

<Edargo: tell @Raythen @Sweet GG> "You guys sending love notes to each other?"

<Sweet GG: tell @Raythen, @Edargo> "Fuck off."

<Edargo: tell @Raythen, @Sweet GG> "If you guys aren't sexting or anything I would like your opinions. You think I should change to this look in meat-space?"

He turned first to Raythen and then to Sweet GG, tilting his head and putting on an exaggerated grin.

<Sweet GG: tell @Raythen, @Edargo> "I like the impishness, though it looks too young. Teenaged."

<Edargo: tell @Raythen, @Sweet GG> "Did I mention it was designed by Gringo Jones?"

<Sweet GG: tell @Raythen, @Edargo> "About a dozen times."

<Edargo: tell @Raythen @Sweet GG> "Raythen, you really need to go East Asian. It's to the point where I'm embarrassed to be seen around you."

Raythen noticed that Torvald was staring at him. Proverbially boring holes into him with his eyes. Torvald was probably just chatting with someone else and not paying attention to where his virtual eyes were pointed. Still, he was getting creeped.

<Raythen: tell @Sweet GG> "Is Torvald okay? Is he mad at me for pwning him?"

<Sweet GG: tell @Raythen> "No no! Not at all. He was very impressed by the move. He said it was very creative. And I agree—it was very pretty."

Torvald suddenly turned away from him toward Mahalingam.

<Torvald: tell @Raythen> "Nice move with the boulder today. It caught me by surprise. You really, um, rocked my world."

<Raythen: tell @Torvald> "lol"

Raythen felt awkward. The only member of Team GG he really got along with was Sweet GG herself. The others always seemed cold and distant. They were all engineers at United Shendry Corporation, very involved with their work, apparently. Kind of nerdy. Raythen had this underlying suspicion that Torvald had a thing for Sweet GG. They worked together in meat-space, which, to Raythen's consternation, made him jealous. Just a little bit jealous, nothing pathological that needed therapy or meds. Raythen realized he had a desire, maybe something more . . . a yearning? To meet Sweet GG *in the flesh*. He hadn't had meat-space sex since his teens. This was nothing unusual on Venus where most people you were involved with lived on different stratoses, hundreds or thousands of kilometers away.

41

<Sweet GG: tell @Raythen> "You busy after the post-game? I have an hour before I have to go to work."

A jolt of excitement went through him.

<Raythen: tell @Sweet GG> "I've got nothing going on."

<Sweet GG: tell @Raythen> "Perfect!"

Chapter 8

Raythen and Sweet GG were lying on a goose-down mattress, naked and exposed. The mattress was on an Egyptian barge that floated on the Nile. A white awning billowed in the breeze above them, protecting them from the noonday sun. The barge moved without oar-man or pole-man, guiding itself with its own intelligence. Papyrus reeds and date palms waved in the breeze on both shores. Crocodiles, doing their best log impersonations, watched with mild interest. Sweet GG was lying on her back, her arms stretched over her head. Raythen was lying on his side, facing her, propped on one elbow as his free hand stroked her thigh.

Virtual tactile sensation was only about a quarter of what meat-space sensation was. He pressed his fingers on her smooth white skin, wondering how it would feel to stroke her real thigh, and if he could endure that much physical stimulation.

"We really shouldn't have done that," Sweet GG said, and sighed.

"What? Why?"

She looked at him with a forced frown. "I should be punishing you for beating me so badly today. No sex for you!"

"Too late for that." He poked the side of her breast and she grabbed his finger, pulling it to her mouth to take a bite. When he tried to pull back she grabbed his wrist with her other hand.

"Hey hey!" he said. "Any more of that and I'm throwing you in the river."

"Fine by me, I can use a swim."

"There are crocs in there."

"You'd like to see me eaten by a croc, wouldn't you?"

She said it jokingly, but with an underlying seriousness that might have some meaning, or might be a test, or might mean nothing.

"No!" he exclaimed, and immediately thought he might have overreacted, so that maybe she thought he would like to see her eaten by a croc.

"So if I jump in you'll save me?" She released his hand. "You didn't save me from that ogre."

Oh, that, he thought. "I couldn't save you from the ogre. I *wanted* to, but I don't want to get fired."

"You're not working now. Get your gator fighting gloves on."

"Gator fighting gloves? What the hell are gator fighting gloves?"

But she was looking up now, distantly. More distantly than the awning, anyway. Raythen didn't really know a lot about Sweet GG. He didn't even know what her real name was. He did know that she had a PhD in quantum physics or something like that. And he also knew that she was lousy at pretending she wasn't busy doing something else when she was busy doing something else. His last girlfriend, Marta, had managed to play and win a Grand Master tournament of *Magic: the Gathering* while they were having sex, and he hadn't known it until he saw the standings the next day on her status page.

He watched her, patiently, glancing up at the time on his HUD; 7:51. Her work started at 8:00. After almost a minute passed she looked at him kindly, acknowledging his patience. She smiled apologetically and said

44

"Hey . . . um . . . I'm going to be real busy for the next couple of weeks. I'm going to be AFK."

"AFK?" He didn't quite understand.

"I'm going to be AFK for a couple of weeks."

"AFK for a couple of weeks?" He had never heard of someone being offline for that long.

"Yeah, I have this big demo . . . big contract and all. We can text each other, but I really won't be able to do anything real-time. The team won't be doing *Exo Arena* either." She rubbed his arm gently.

"Yeah, okay," he said, trying to be casual like it was no big deal. He smiled. "Is this contract going to make you a trillionaire?" He scrutinized her. "Two weeks AFK, it better make you a trillionaire."

She lifted herself onto her elbows and kissed him softly on the lips. "Not quite a trillionaire, but it's really important for the company."

He continued to scrutinize her. "What exactly is it you do again? I know it's way above my head but if you can tell me what it is exactly that you do it may help me out here with this patient understanding of you being AFK for two freaking weeks."

"Well . . . as you know . . ." Her lips and her chin stretched with exaggerated moves as she spoke, revealing a great deal of consideration going into what she said. ". . . I do research in artificial consciousness, with cemi fields. So, I make A-Cons, which is really sensitive stuff, legally, because of all the fraking laws and red tape and hoops they make you jump through when you make conscious entities. And that's about all I can say about it because my company is very concerned about competition and they might think that you were sent to seduce me into telling you our precious industry secrets, and that if I say anymore they'll send me to

Titan." She scrunched her eyebrows and stuck out her lower lip, making a sad face.

"Okay, okay," Raythen shook his hands, palms out toward her. "I get that it is super secret stuff. But there's something I've always wondered, just on a basic level. What's so great about A-Cons? What makes them so much more special than AI?"

So much so you have to be AFK for two freaking weeks!

Her face brightened. "Ah! I can help you with that. I have just the thing!" She lay back down on the bed, staring up, her hands on her thighs. "I have some interns I teach part time. I put together this presentation. In fact, I'm thinking about submitting it to Spokesdog so he can make it an edutainment. Would you like to take a look? It would help me out too; you can tell me what you think. It's for beginners so you can tell me how it explains the fundamentals."

"Okay, sure. How long is it?"

"Not long. I'll send it to you and you can look at it whenever."

An attachment icon appeared on his HUD showing that she had sent him the presentation.

"You text me telling me what you think, okay?" She was getting excited and girlish. Raythen thought it was cute. In fact, it was giving him another woody.

"I'll give you a little background real quick," she said. "You see, it's about simultaneity. In the 21st century there were two big scientific mysteries. The first was how self-awareness is made by the brain. The second, the biggy that lots of people were working on, was reconciling Einstein's General Theory of Relativity with quantum mechanics. It turns out that the solution to both of them depended on the concept of simultaneity. According to General Relativity, the idea of two things

46

happening at the same time made no sense. There really was no such thing as a simultaneous event. But in human consciousness, a person experiences multiple pieces of information that are in different points in space in their brain all at the same time. So getting back to your question about what the difference is between AI and A-Con, an AI doesn't experience the information that it is manipulating and reacting to, while an A-Con does. And it can experience multiple pieces of information at the same time. Like the human mind. Like *your* human mind does so fraking well which makes you such an unholy terror on the battlefield. Time-consciousness is really, really, really difficult to architect. Scientists have tried to build A-Cons from scratch but they generally come out insane, which is why most are based on human templates. When you're in *Exo Arena* you're keeping track of the recent past and extrapolating what you think will happen in the future and planning your reactions, but the amazing thing is—and this is something humans do very easily—that the awareness of the past and present and future exists in a single complicated state in your brain at a single point in time. Because the information of the past and anticipation of the future exist in the present, this is experienced by us as a seamless flow. On top of all that there is the problem of motivation. While a conscious entity is experiencing the world it needs to have some sort of overarching motivation in order to get it to act toward specific goals. Just think about all the *little* actions that need to be done in order to get anything *big* done at all. You need to be motivated to perform each little action in order to reach a larger goal. So when you're architecting an A-Con, you have to design a system of motivation that has it perform the actions you desire, and it has to be flexible enough to handle real world situations. This is not easy. Even though science has figured out the fundamentals of how the universe works we still have trouble predicting and designing complex systems like A-Cons. There are still some serious mysteries with complex systems, like, for instance, how much phi can a cemi field hold? That's a biggy."

From the blank look on his face she could tell she was losing him.

"I'm sorry, I'm running on. I have to get to work. I really get excited about this geeky stuff, I know. Look at me; still talking when there's science to do! I'll let you go." She sat up, looked down at his half erect cock, adding, "And no more time for that!" She gave it a gentle swat, and then bent toward him giving him a deep kiss on the lips before swinging herself off of the bed and hopping down to the edge of the barge.

Her white hair billowed like the awning above, her slight but muscular back hunched, seemingly against a cold that he couldn't feel. She turned in profile so he could see her soft, intelligent, perpetually innocent face. "I'm going to make a dramatic exit now," she said, and swan dived into the dark Nile.

Chapter 9

Raythen once again sat on the wooden trunk on the front porch of the Dead Basilisk Tavern. A player approached him from the right. She was dressed in buckskin—probably a ranger. She stopped about a meter away. A few moments passed before she spoke.

"You Raythen?" she asked contemptuously. At least this one was role playing.

From under his hat he watched her open midriff. She had her hands on her hips. He didn't say a word.

"Are you Raythen?"

Still, he said nothing. Her hand reached behind her back. It returned slowly with a long, curved, overly-decorated dagger. He waited until it was pointed at him.

"You tell me—" was all she got out before he jumped up in front of her. With a flash of his short sword her dagger was knocked away onto the road. He gazed down into her shocked, rounded eyes. She was a head shorter than he was—half-elf—her slightly pointed ears sticking out from her red hair. These young kids (he guessed she was probably less than sixteen) really got into the role playing. Reciprocating was the least he could do to.

"Did you want something?" he said mockingly. "Something from me?" His short sword was now pointed at her throat.

49

"I . . . uh . . . I want to meet Briggash." She was staring at his blade.

"I don't think you should meet Briggash. I think you should go back to Hillflower Glade or whatever sweet grassy land that spawned you, and stick to hunting the occasional lost kobold that wanders into your path. Briggash is not nearly as kind as I am, and if you had the gall to pull a dagger on him, your hand would be lying out in the road . . . followed by your head. And maybe a few other parts he might fancy to lop off."

She nodded quickly. "I just thought I would . . ."

"You just thought you would be going home now."

She nodded again. "Can I get my dagger?"

Raythen didn't answer. He sheathed his sword and sat down again, not looking at her. A moment later both she and the dagger were gone.

"You should have given her a poke," Olaf said from the doorway. "She was only level twelve for Christ's sake! What the hell was she thinking?"

"Just feeling her oats," Raythen replied. "Getting bored with killing the little critters. I can appreciate that."

"I would've given her a poke. She looked like she could use a good poke."

Raythen was grumpy. Sweet GG was AFK. And he didn't feel all that comfortable about Olaf making sexual innuendos about some kid who was probably under-aged.

"You'd give anything a poke. You'd give Mrs. Harkin a poke." Raythen looked up at the Harkins in the field and called out, "Hey! Mr. Harkin! You mind if Olaf gives your wife a poke? Or how 'bout your cow? Olaf's in a poking mood!"

Mr. Harkin looked up at them from his hoeing, grinned, and waved.

"Shut up!" Olaf squealed. "There might be some PCs in earshot!"

Raythen scowled. "Okay, okay, keep your shorts on." He looked down at Olaf. "All your pants are shorts, aren't they?"

"Remember, I'm the comic relief!" Olaf said indignantly. "You're the dangerous rogue!"

"Yeah, whatever."

Olaf came around to face him. "What's up with you? You cranky about something? You just had the biggest *Exo Arena* win this week on Venus . . . probably in the whole System. You should be happy. I bet you made a few bucks on that."

"Urmmm," Raythen said and then craned his head, listening to something. "Two PCs coming. You better get inside and start practicing your comedy."

Olaf quickly disappeared.

A few moments later they came into view from around a bend in the road. A warrior and a wizard, mighty in form and aspect. The warrior's golden armor fit perfectly to the contours of his rolling muscles and glowed like the living skin of a sun god. His helmet was of the ancient Greek style, the type Leonidas wore, with a long red plume draping down his back. His shield, also gold, displayed the image of a red dragon in flight in a mosaic in rubies. He held his sword drawn in his right hand. The sword did not look like it could be sheathed in any scabbard. Over a meter long and rapier thin, it glowed white hot, as if eternally fed by the unearthly furnace that spawned it.

The warrior's mystic companion was equally impressive. On his forehead was a white, smoky crystal held by a gold headband. Long, black hair flowed and seemed to join into his shimmering black robe. None of the wizard's limbs were discernible in the robe; he floated over the ground rather than walked. A staff floated by his side—topped with a white

51

dragon's fang wrapped into place by a silver cord. The black, gnarled wood of the staff could have easily come from the First Tree. The wizard's face was pale and beardless, with a long, hooked nose and deep black eyes.

Raythen lifted his head and watched the pair as they approached Harkins' farm. The warrior went up to the wooden fence and tried to lean against it nonchalantly with his elbow. Instead, his elbow missed the fence entirely and he spilled forward, his torso folding over it. As he struggled to regain his balance Mr. Harkins came over to help him up. Instead of accepting his help the warrior pushed him away, swearing. The wizard stared forward, expressionless. The warrior looked around to see if any PCs saw him. There were no other PCs around.

Both the warrior and the wizard were now completely still. Mr. Harkin shrugged and went back to hoeing. The great and clumsy duo was like a pair of painted statues. Several minutes passed by. Raythen suppressed an urge to go up to the warrior and kick him over. He had never seen two more twinked noobs in his life. They barely knew how to move in their avatars and yet they had gear that would take five years of constant play to acquire. They couldn't have been older than fourteen. They probably had just had their implants put in.

The wizard moved first. A hand extended from the blackness of his robe. A jeweled ring encrusted each finger. It pointed in the direction of a cow and did some complicated gestures that demanded great anticipation—and then . . . nothing happened. He repeated the gestures. Still nothing. Several seconds passed. He repeated the gestures more deliberately, this time with a minor variation. The cow exploded. Flesh and blood rained down on the duo and the Harkins.

Raythen slowly got up off his crate. There was a certain unwritten principle that had been violated by these two. You shouldn't be able to buy characters this powerful without having some sort of skill at using them. These kid's parents must be crazy rich. The wizard's staff alone was worth at least a million dollars.

The warrior went through the fence gate and lumbered toward Mr. Harkin, lifting his sword in the air. Mr. Harkin jumped back, screeching and looking appropriately frightened as the slim glowing blade missed him, swinging into the ground and igniting some yellowed weeds with its flame.

"Stay still, fuckhead!" the warrior yelled. Mr. Harkin held his hands up in fear but obliged by standing in place, providing an easy target.

Mrs. Harkin fell to her knees and begged, "Please don't hurt us. We are just poor peasant farmers! Take what you want! Just leave us alone."

The warrior swung his sword down on Mr. Harkin. It went through his right collar bone and dug halfway down his chest. Mr. Harkin went through gruesome spasms and fell backwards. The sword sizzled as blood boiled off its glowing surface. Mrs. Harkin screamed. The warrior and wizard were now laughing.

The wizard said "Cool. Hey, watch this!" He pointed at Mrs. Harkin and made a gesture. It was a low level spell he must have practiced before because it worked the first time. Her screaming was cut off, like something was caught in her throat. She dropped her hoe and stared at the wizard's hand.

"Nice, silence the bitch" the warrior said.

"Yeah, watch this!" The wizard gestured upward and Mrs. Harkin slowly floated into the air.

"Ohhhkay," Raythen said under his breath and stepped off the porch. In his right hand was his short sword, in his left his dagger. Neither the warrior nor the wizard was looking at him. He came up behind the wizard

53

and thrust his short sword into the center of his back. As he had
anticipated, an invisible force field protected him. The force field deflected
the sword, but not completely—it brushed against the wizard's side and
drew blood. Before the wizard could react, Raythen leaped straight up and
plunged the dagger down at the top of his skull. The force field deflected it
as well, but Raythen compensated, guiding the blade like bird pushing
against a gale. The blade found its mark in the meat of the wizard's
shoulder.

"Ow, hey, what the fuck?" the wizard cried. He turned his head
around. "Hey! This low shit did damage! What the fuck!" He tried to spin
around to face Raythen, but only came around half way and stopped.

Raythen made another plunge with his short sword, but this one was
completely deflected by the force field. The wizard grabbed his staff and
raised it. Raythen spun around behind him, out of view, and stabbed again,
giving him another flesh wound.

"Get the fuck away from him!" the warrior yelled. Raythen guessed
that, at best, it would take the warrior three seconds to get within striking
range. He struck again with the short sword. Miss. He struck again.

Sometimes, even against the best defended foes, you make the perfect
shot. The sword plunged deep into the wizard's back. His legs and torso
became unnaturally rigid while his arms flailed wildly. He fell forward to
the ground. Raythen turned his head to see the warrior only two steps
away. He jammed his foot into the wizard's back and pulled out the short
sword, spinning and parrying as the warrior's sword came down at him.
The glowing blade sent sparks flying between them. Raythen fell away and
rolled, trying to get behind him. The warrior stood up straight and spun
around quickly—a little too quickly because he spun away from Raythen,
exposing his back. Raythen was familiar with the armor; he had once

fought against an old guy wearing the same kind. It was made from the silk of Honness spiders that lived on the Plane of Fire. He hadn't been able to scratch the old veteran, and had been beaten quickly. However, this warrior was certainly no old veteran. Raythen came in close and made a jab at his side. The short sword hit straight on but slid off the armor, doing no damage. The glowing sword swung at him. Raythen moved, but not quite as fast as he could have. It was time for theatrics. The sword's tip passed about a centimeter through his shoulder before arching down to the ground. Raythen howled in pain, turned around, and ran over the tilled field. Glancing around, he saw that the warrior was following. Behind the warrior, the wizard was getting to his feet. Not good. Beyond the blood splatter where the cow had been the field fell into a wallow pit where pigs lolled lazily about. Raythen hollered and waved his arms at them. They jumped to their feet and scattered. He then waded into the knee-deep mud of the pit. Turning, he saw the warrior crest the edge, running down at him with his sword held above his head with both hands. Raythen faced him, short sword and dagger drawn. The warrior was coming down at full speed.

Too easy.

He stuck out his leg as he moved out of the warrior's way. The warrior went face down into the muck, steam and bubbles rising from where the sword had entered and disappeared. Raythen jumped on his back, straddling him like a pony. The warrior's arms waved ineffectively at his sides. His legs moved like he was trying to swim.

Time was crucial. The pigs would be back. While great pains had been made in this game to simulate realistic combat, farm animal AI was very simple. But how soon before the pigs came back? Thirty seconds?

One minute? The wizard would arrive any second. It might be best to make a run for it now.

Some porcine faces showed themselves above the rim of the wallow-pit. They strolled calmly back into their muck, oblivious of Raythen and the warrior. One lay down on the warrior's head. Perfect. Raythen stood up on top of the helpless noob, leaping off him to get to the dry edge of the pit. He scrambled to the top.

The wizard was floating ten meters in the air. He was spinning around, trying to see where his friend had disappeared to. He stopped spinning and looked down at Raythen.

"Time to go," Raythen muttered and ran for the tree line. There was a loud, electrical crackle and he was momentarily blinded. His legs stopped working. As he fell forward he balled his body so he rolled instead of sprawled. Stopping at a crouch he tried his legs. They were smoking, but they were working again. He leaped up and ran for the trees. Under the cover of the leaves he knew he could lose the wizard. He heard another crackle and there was another flash of light. At first he thought it was a miss, but then he noticed that his cloak was on fire. He was almost at the trees. He saw his shadow grow in front of him as though the sun was chasing him. That was no lightning bolt—that was a really big fireball. As Raythen leaped into the underbrush of the forest the trees around him burst into flame.

Chapter 10

The voice was honey and sex and song and forest spring.

Especially the forest spring, which is where it came from.

"What the hell happened to you?" it said. The owner of the voice floated lazily on her back in the transparent water. Around her were lily pads and purple lotuses. Dragonflies with rainbow wings flitted. Her sea-blue skin glistened; her green hair flowed into the water like a fan around her head. Her breasts were tiny twin islands bobbing in the water.

Raythen sat on the edge of the spring. His hat and cloak were still smoldering. "Hi Edargo. I had a run-in with a couple of noobs, twinked to the max. I'm probably getting reported right now."

"Yesterday this MetaChristian kid comes over and demands that I remove my kelp bra," Edargo said from his naiad body. "I told him I couldn't take it off; I couldn't override his parental locks. But he insisted a friend of his saw me naked even with parental locks on. I couldn't do anything, you know, it had appeared as soon as he was in the zone. I told him there was nothing I could do. So do you know what he did to me?" Edargo rhetorically waited for a response. Raythen shrugged his shoulders. "He killed me. Then he camped me for about an hour. I mean, how Christian is that?"

"How do you know he was a MetaChristian?"

"Had to be. They're the only ones who use parental locks. Poor kid. Can you imagine going through puberty without being able to fap to some bodacious NPCs? No wonder they're all fucked in the head."

Raythen checked his hit points. He was up to quarter strength. The last fireball that hit him had left him with only nine hit points. It had been close. Dying would have taken all the satisfaction out of pwning the noobs.

"They might be camped out in front of the inn, hoping to get another shot at me." He gave it some consideration. "Nah, they probably reported me."

"Why would they report you," Edargo splashed away a dragonfly that had landed on his big toe.

"I attacked them first."

"Ooooh, ahhhh . . . a bit out of character for Raythen. Yeah, they have cause. You can't enjoy your time being Uber unless the lower level characters cower before you. Yeah, you're screwed."

"I created Raythen. I should be able to add 'moody' and 'unpredictable' to his profile."

They sat in silence for awhile.

"I think I messed things up with Sweet GG," Raythen said suddenly.

"What? What do you mean 'Messed things up?'"

"She told me she can't see me for a few weeks. She says she's 'busy.'"

"Listen," Edargo said, "you can't have anything serious with a woman like that. I mean, she's got a real job making real . . . whatever it is she makes."

"A-Cons."

"Really? Wow. Be honest, I mean, she's just slumming around with you. You're a big shot in this world, I mean you're one of the biggest shots

I know, but a woman like that moves in a whole different universe. She hangs out with guys who own stuff . . . I mean like stocks and stratoses and factories and things. Don't beat yourself up about it. You need to think about something else. Like about getting me a different job here. I mean, it's not so bad being an aquatic sex kitten, but I think I could do much better with Olaf's job. I would be a kick-ass Olaf. It's my destiny to be comic relief. I do awesome improv. Is Olaf funny? Sure, he's got his bit, but his improv is lame. I'm quick on my feet, yet look at where I am, I mean, how many PCs come out here to my swamp? Not many. Just the occasional horny MetaChristian. That's it. Do they appreciate my sparkling wit? I don't think so, and we get paid by the eyeballs."

"I don't know," Raythen said, completely ignoring Edargo's tangent. "Is she blowing me off or is she really busy? What kind of work keeps someone AFK for weeks at a time? She has to be blowing me off, right?"

A deafening thunderclap roared in their midst, accompanied by a blinding bolt of light. When their vision cleared, a robed and hooded figure was standing in front of Raythen. It pointed a pale, gnarled finger at him and said in a voice that both screeched and echoed, "I am High Lord Varun. You have displeased me by daring to attack the noble warrior Longestcock and the most wise mage Pissonu. For that you have earned the dishonor of the cruciatus curse!"

"Ah crap," Raythen said. Red lightning poured out from Varun's finger and danced around Raythen's body. He felt mildly painful pinpricks that indicated that he should be writhing in agony. He obliged, and added some harrowing screams. Longestcock and Pissonu were undoubtedly watching and would need this kind of show to be appeased.

Sure, it was demeaning, but this was too good of a job to risk losing.

After Raythen had writhed around on the ground for a few minutes, the robed figure said, "You are to be banished to the Nether Deep for a full DAY and to know the horrors of the grobious acid worms!"

A swirling black vortex appeared above Raythen. He floated slowly toward it, kicking and screaming. Soon he was spinning in sync with the vortex; his body dissolved into smoke and was sucked inside.

Raythen was standing in an empty doorless and windowless stone lined cell. A broad shouldered East Asian man wearing a fashionable pin-striped suit was standing in front of him.

"Hi Carlos," Raythen said. "Nice avatar, did Gringo Jones do that?"

"Gringo's out. This was done by Netta Lee." He smiled, spun around three-sixty and did a little jig. "I can get you in to see her."

"No thanks."

Carlos's smile stayed on as he said, "You're going to the wandering monster pool."

"I know."

"Don't kill anyone more than a level higher than you. No matter how much the noob twink deserves it. Kk?"

"Sure thing."

Chapter 11

"Balestra!" Raythen leaped forward and jabbed at Edargo who jumped back. They were standing on a thick log that spanned a twenty-meter-wide crevasse. Below them at an improbable distance was a red glowing river of lava. They were wearing exercise shorts and holding rapiers, facing each other in fencing stances. Edargo already had several bloody cuts on his chest and legs.

"Next time I balestra and lunge, you stand your ground and parry. I'm coming straight at you so just keep your wrist pronated."

"Pronate this," Edargo said.

"Balestra!" Raythen leaped forward again. This time Edargo held his ground and parried the thrust.

"Good!" Raythen said. He backed up a step and motioned Edargo forward to get them closer to the middle of the log.

"Ack!"

Raythen attacked again, catching Edargo off guard. He gave him another cut to his chest.

"Hey!"

"You have to be ready at all times. You're the one who wants to get a promotion. If you want to get out of the swamp you have to know how to fence."

"Fencing is lame."

"Fencing teaches the importance of the thrust, which is an under-utilized skill."

"Give me a battle axe against your little sword and we'll see some pronating."

"This lesson is about balance. You don't want to be swinging a battle axe on this log."

Edargo looked down at the lava far, far below. "Yeah, I guess you're right. Okay. Let's do this."

Raythen repeated his same attack. Edargo parried the blow and then made his own thrust, leaning his upper body forward without moving his feet, upsetting his balance. Raythen parried and wacked Edargo's leg with the side of his blade. Edargo tottered a moment before regaining his balance.

"Shit," Edargo said. "I can't believe all the high level NPCs go through all this training."

"Only the good ones."

"Yeah, well, I'm soon going to have a cinematic movie of my life to put on my resume. That's going to help me stand out from the herd! Has Dark Fuji contacted you about getting all the vids you have of me?"

"Not yet."

"Really?" Edargo's brow wrinkled with concern. "I gave her a list of everyone I know who has decent records of me. She'd better get started putting my movie together. My fans are waiting. And remember, if she uses any vids from your eyeballs you'll get a cut in the profits."

"Oooh I can finally retire," Raythen said and feinted, causing Edargo to flinch.

"Alright, let's get serious," Edargo said. "Make your move; I think I got this lame fencing stuff down."

"You make a move if you've got it down."

"No. You make a move."

"No, you."

Raythen heard a chime that indicated he had gotten a text. He checked his text box with his phand and saw that it was from Sweet GG. Edargo, sensing his distraction, made a thrust. Raythen parried while reading the text:

Guess what? Good news! I actually have some time off! The presentation

He parried another thrust.

went better than we could have expected! They're going to give us a little vacation and

Frustrated, Edargo lifted the sword over his head and swung it down with all his strength. Raythen blocked.

I thought celebration was in order so

Another swing, another block.

I can't think of a better time for

Swing, block. Raythen decided he wanted to put all his attention to the text. He made two quick, twisting thrusts at Edargo's face.

"Hey, hey!" Edargo exclaimed. "You didn't! You didn't! Did you pluck them out?"

Two eyeballs were on the end of Raythen's sword like onions on a shish kebab.

"Oh man, that's cold." Edargo stepped back, and then realized that he was trying to move on a log while blind, and shifted his torso spasmodically, trying to get a balance that he hadn't really lost in the first place but now had, in fact, lost. Arms spun around as he arched backwards off the log and began his long journey to the lava below.

Raythen eagerly read the rest of his text.

Chapter 12

Rafe Melon-Smith-Tagart-Sanchez-McRay-Wilton, the Interior Minister of Venus, sat in his stateroom in the Venus Defense Force air cruiser *Pax Cythera*. Wilton felt a little claustrophobic in the cramped stateroom which was one-twentieth the size of his office in the capital stratos of Adonis. For furnishings it had no more than a round table surrounded by six swivel chairs affixed to the floor, a recliner pressed against the wall, and an OmniServe. He was sitting at the table, stroking his red goatee. He had gotten the goatee shortly before going into politics and now his publicity team told him that it was part of his image and he had to keep it, no matter what other fashionable modifications he adopted. When East Asian became the dominant race-style it had taken him two weeks and several million dollars in stylist's fees to design an East Asian face that retained the essence of his original face and still projected the proper authority while simultaneously keeping that damn goatee.

Such was the price and sacrifice of public service.

Sitting across from him was the glowing blue projection of the Prime Minister of Venus, Jagriti Patel. Whenever Wilton lamented about his own fashion sacrifices, all he had to do was look at Patel. When she had first entered politics decades ago she had decided to go for a stately middle-aged look. It had been effective then; it had gotten her far, obviously, but now absolutely no-one went for any look over thirty. Her publicity team insisted that it would be political suicide for her to change her face now. Imagine being stuck with gray hair and crow's feet! He had actually seen children cry out in fear at the sight of her.

The Prime Minister looked genuinely worried. She could have filtered out any emotion from her projection—she was obviously letting him know that she was concerned and that he should be concerned as well. "I wouldn't have authorized any of this if they weren't building a new stratos," she said. "They've been acting like they have complete autonomy for too long. Our hands are forced—but this operation is going to have significant political fallout even if it goes perfectly."

Wilton took his hand away from his goatee and rested it on the table. "The best-case scenario is that they don't have weapons and we simply walk in and take control. The worst-case scenario is they have military grade communication jammers and rail guns and they decide to fight back. If they make that unfortunate decision we will be legally justified in using overwhelming force to take Corpus Christi."

"What is the possibility that they have jammers aboard their stratos?" she asked. "Have you gotten any new intel?"

"Nothing concrete. Their molecular assemblers are supposed to contact us if anyone tries to manufacture anything illegal. It's difficult but not impossible to hack. The signs are subtle—some latency here, some gibberish there—nothing we can prove with certainty, but something sketchy *is* going on. Of course, the most damning evidence is that they won't let any of our inspectors take a look."

"I'm more worried about jammers than anything else," the Prime Minister said. "I would prefer to send in remote control exos and not have to resort to your *alternate solution* for the main assault."

Wilton noted that even on a secure channel she was reluctant to directly mention his *autonomous units*. He had to do a lot of convincing just to get her to authorize them for the extraction operation. But if Corpus Christi had jammers there was no other way to guarantee that there would be no VDF casualties in a live fire assault.

"It all depends on how they respond," Wilton said. "It's our responsibility to enforce the rule of law with as few deaths as possible."

The Prime Minister shook her head sadly. "It boggles my mind that in this day and age they feel the need to arm themselves."

"They're paranoid. It's part of the sickness of religion. Look at their current publicity campaign—they're saying we want to take their children and force a cure of hyper-anthropomorphization disorder on them. Like we would willingly open up that legal can of worms."

"I'm afraid that cleaning up after this operation is going to be a pretty big can of worms in itself," she said.

"Yes," he said solemnly, "but in the long run it will be worth it." He smiled confidently, comfortingly. He enjoyed her worry. He enjoyed how it gave him control of the situation. This assault on Corpus Christi was going to be the bold move that will catapult his career to new heights.

"After this no one will question our authority again."

Chapter 13

Raythen floated in a green Cambrian sea. Below him was a sandy, rock-strewn sea floor with fan-shaped plants, or maybe plant shaped animals (he remembered from somewhere that there were animals in the Cambrian that looked like plants). A variety of odd creatures swam the sea and crawled among the rocks. Most on the sea floor had multiple body-segments with many legs and tentacles. Eye stalks were popular.

"Approximately five-hundred million years ago there lived a fish," Sweet GG's voice said. Raythen spun involuntarily and zoomed forward toward the sea floor until he was face to face with a small fish that swam tentatively between the rocks. It didn't look like any fish that Raythen knew of, it didn't have any fins, just a tail that tapered to a point. Its mouth was a round suckered hole.

"This fish had a problem. It had three basic drives; to eat, to mate, and to hide from predators." Raythen floated about a meter up and was pointed to a nasty, undulating creature with bulbous eyes and two segmented tentacle-like appendages sticking out from the underside of its round head. It was moving back and forth, obviously on the lookout for something to eat. Raythen was sent back down to the fish.

"These drives were wired into its primitive brain the way a novice computer programmer would design it. A novice computer programmer would assign a number to each drive. One number for hunger, one number for sex, and one for fear. If the fish lacked nutrients, the *hunger* number would increase. When it reached a certain limit it would trigger feeding behavior. This behavior would take the fish into the open." The fish in front of Raythen swam out from the rocks over the sandy floor. It made a quick dart toward a tiny, translucent buggy thing and ate it.

"The number representing *fear* would increase from the visual image of a large creature moving toward the fish."

The large, two-tentacled beasty floated ominously close and the fish darted back toward the rocks.

"What we have been referring to as "numbers" are actually the rates of firing by sets of neurons. External stimuli cause certain neurons to fire faster. When the rate of fire reaches a threshold, they trigger the neurons that encode the needed behavior, whether it be feeding or hiding."

Raythen watched the fish alternate between feeding and hiding as the predator moved in closer and then farther away.

"The problem with this design is that there was no mediation between the different behavior modes. It would switch between the two modes, depending upon which threshold was higher. When both hunger and fear where high, the fish would become locked, switching quickly between the two modes." The fish moved back and forth quickly, going out to feed but then turning back toward the rocks, then moving out to feed again. "Such a fish would soon be dinner itself." The predator lunged forward, trapping the fish in its tentacles, bringing it into its mouth.

"What was needed was a *decision maker* in the fish's brain, something that was aware of all sets of stimuli, and then could choose which one to act upon. If we go back to the novice programmer, she might add a new processing center between the neurons that generated the stimuli and the neurons that controlled the behavior. She might code some heuristics that decided, depending upon the nature of the stimuli, to follow one set of behaviors for a certain period of time. And in fact, this is what evolution *started* to do over millions of years of random mutation in the design of the fish brain. But then, something truly remarkable happened."

Raythen was pushed through the water, racing over rocks and plants and apparently through millions of years of time. He was suddenly very small, close to the sand, moving between the rocks that now towered over him. Looking ahead he saw that he was moving toward another little fish. He slowed down as he approached its head. He was the same size as it, going steadily closer toward its left eye. Then he moved into the fish itself, and he realized that he was the fish. He felt his tail. He gave it a wiggle and moved forward. He tilted to the left and wiggled, turning to the left. He then tilted and turned to the right. Sweet GG's program gave him a few moments to get used to the controls. He demonstrated that he could use them by going around in a full circle. When the program was convinced he could swim effectively, the lesson continued.

"The fish that you saw get eaten didn't experience hunger, it didn't experience fear. It simply reacted to stimuli. But think about the different parts of its brain. It had eyes that sent signals to its visual cortex. The visual cortex would generate patterns, and depending what those patterns were—the patterns of food or the patterns of a predator—certain neurons would increase their rate of fire. At their thresholds these neurons would trigger specific behaviors. It is entirely mechanistic.

"But you, as a fish, experience the neurons of the visual cortex."

Ahead and above, Raythen saw the predator swim into view from behind some rocks.

"You experience the neurons that are firing faster. You experience them as fear."

He had to admit, seeing that tentacled monster, now huge compared to him, did make him a little apprehensive.

"You know the behavior that you have to follow to make the fear go away, you have to turn and swim to the rocks."

It seemed like a good idea. He turned his fish around and nestled between the sand and a rock overhang.

"Sometime during the Cambrian, a fish was born that was the first creature on Terra to actually experience its own neural activity. This was possible because the architecture that transmitted information in the primitive brain also created a conscious electromagnetic intelligence field, or cemi field. The neurons are separate entities, each with its own piece of information, but the cemi field encodes all that information into a single entity.

"A detailed understanding of how the cemi field creates consciousness requires an in-depth knowledge of the Theory of Everything, or TOE, and cannot be covered here. What is important to remember is that the cemi field experiences the entirety of multiple neurons *simultaneously*.

"Once the architecture that allowed the fish to experience the information in its brain came into being, evolution set about differentiating the experiences so that some were pleasant and others where unpleasant. Eventually fish were born who experienced fear and hunger. They experienced touch, smell, sound, and sight and created little models of the world in their brains—in truth they *were* the little model worlds in their brains. Each of those fish had its own cemi field. Each fish was its cemi field."

Raythen opened his eyes. Low, steady vibrations rumbled through his recliner into his skin. He was fully clothed, which was unusual for him when he was in virtual reality—clothes felt restricting and binding while

71

he was lying down. It didn't help that he was strapped in at his waist and across his chest. The tiny chamber was round, the walls covered with soft padding—womb-like. He willed the recliner to a sitting position and spotted the clicky above the oval hatch that was to his left. He phanded it and looked at the text box.

Departure—Lu Shing City: 6:45 (On time)
Arrival—Corpus Christi: 12:10 (On time)
Map. . .
Menu. . .
Service. . .
View. . .

He selected *View*—then *Transparent.* The walls vanished and he was flying through the clouded Venusian sky. The cameras from around the plane gave him a three-hundred and sixty degree view, as if he was the plane. He was excited—Christmas-time excited. He hadn't been out of Lu Shing since leaving the military. And meeting with Sweet GG in Corpus Christi! This was serious—too good to be true. He displayed the itinerary she had sent. It was all paid for—the flight, the hotel, everything. She was going to meet him at the Hubein Regency Hotel. A real hotel in the center of the city, the kind of place he could never get in on his own.

There had just been the one text. No other communication. She said she was busy . . . and she didn't know when she would be arriving. It was strange and mysterious and despite the masculine urge to be cool and detached, he had a stupid grin on his face—he just couldn't help it. He'd have to make sure that wasn't there when she finally saw him.

He felt that he was finally living a real life.

He displayed a live-feed of Corpus Christi in front of him, as if he was already coming into the landing that was hours away. He was surprised to see that there were two stratoses—one directly behind the other. The first was being towed by its aerosail, the other was held fast by a tether behind the first. Rotating the image for a better look and zooming in, Raythen saw that beneath the second city's dome there were no buildings, no trees—in fact there was no ground, just the exposed mechanical innards. They were building a new floating city. He clicked the city menu and selected *News*.

News Bullets: Presented by Hovolex
Theophilus to UP: We Won't Stop Building—0 hr 23 min ago.
—Erin Theophilus refuses to cease construction of the new stratos.
—Erin Theophilus is the founder of MetaChristianity and principle owner of the Corpus Christi stratos.
—The new stratos being built by the MetaChristians is to be called New Sinai.
—Erin Theophilus stated that population growth on Corpus Christi has made the construction of New Sinai necessary.
—The legality of the new city, as well as the legality of Corpus Christi itself, is under debate.
—Religious freedom of individuals is guaranteed to all citizens of Venus.
—The belief in an omnipotent, omniscient, anthropomorphized being has been recently defined as a psychological illness in the Diagnostic and Statistical

Manual of Mental Disorders, called hyper-
anthropomorphization disorder.
—There are laws on Venus against inducing mental
disorders in minors.
—There are an estimated 5607 minors in Corpus Christi.
—Although government officials deny it, representatives
from Corpus Christi claim that there are plans to forcibly
remove all minors from Corpus Christi.
—General Uzziah, the leader of the Corpus Christi militia,
is believed to be building illegal military grade weaponry.
—Prime Minister Jagriti Patel has stated that she is
sending the Interior Minister, Rafe Melon-Smith-Tagart-
Sanchez-McRay-Wilton, to Corpus Christi on the cruiser
Pax Cythera to negotiate directly with Erin Theophilus.

Raythen had known, through vague background information, that Corpus Christi was largely a MetaChristian city, but he hadn't realized that it was the focus of so much drama. Why the hell would Sweet GG meet with him there? It was strange, probably brought about by some necessity.

Sweets can't be a MetaChristian, right?

She had never mentioned MetaChristianity to him at all. She was more egghead than religious freak.

Naw, I bet the MetaChristians hired out United Shendry to work on the new stratos they're building. With all the political noise surrounding it, no wonder she has to keep this hush hush. Yeah, that makes sense.

He laid his head back, closed his eyes and relaxed. Yeah, all was good. But it still made him apprehensive that he hadn't had any communication with her since the initial text.

Chapter 14

Raythen had never been in a hotel suite before. Real hard wood floors and oriental rugs, leather couches with carved and polished wood armrests, the richness of the browns of wood and leather saturated the room. French doors opened to a balcony that overlooked the lake, thirty floors below. He looked around, the clickies were not obvious. The paintings on the walls in their thick frames looked like they were actually painted by human beings. His imp, noticing that his eyes were focused on one, posted a factoid next to it:

Women with a Parasol
Claude Monet
1875
Hand painted reproduction
Original at the National Gallery of Art, Washington DC.

Holy crap, they were painted by humans.

Double doors led to the bedroom. He swung them open and walked in. The centrally located king-sized bed seemed to stare back at him with its two piles of pillows for eyes. It also seemed to be smiling. He smiled back.

When the hell is Sweet GG getting here?

His luggage had been brought up prior to his arrival and his small suitcase was lying on the luggage stand at the base of the bed. He opened it up, and then looked at the three-meter tall dresser against the wall. He pulled open a single cavernous drawer and dumped the entire contents of his suitcase into it. He thought that perhaps he should get some more clothes. A nice sports coat and slacks, maybe. Would that be too fancy? How hard should he appear to be trying to impress her?

The bathroom had a whirlpool hot-tub. Raythen wondered if he had ever taken a bath in his life. He couldn't remember. Maybe when he was a baby.

Now standing on the balcony, he surveyed the lake and parks around it. They were filled with people. He started counting and stopped at one hundred, letting his imp finish the count. 454. But what was truly unusual was the number of children. Running, playing, laughing, screaming; he could hear them clearly from his high vantage point. At least half of the people down there were children. Was it some sort of festival? Some religious holiday? He queried his imp and got a negative. Just an ordinary day. Across the lake was a large cobblestone square dominated by a Gothic cathedral. Its flying buttresses and steeples, faithful reproductions of some medieval edifice, looked heavy and earthbound compared to the modern architecture around it.

He went into the bedroom and got into his jogging clothes.

Raythen had to keep his chat windows closed; there were that many people out on the path going around the lake, he had to keep on his toes to avoid crashing into them. Also, he told his imp to catalog all females in view who might possibly be Sweet GG and flag them. He kept the filter to a ten percent deviation from her avatar, although there was really no guarantee that she looked anything like her avatar.

If she had the time to go strolling in the park, wouldn't she have tried to communicate with him first?

To his right on the small strand of beach there were families with children splashing in the water and making sand castles. Most of these kids were MetaChristians, as were the adults. He felt out of place. This was what it was like to be in a different culture, surrounded by people with a different belief system. A male jogger passed close by him—Raythen turned to watch his receding back and clicked on his head with his phand.

Handle: Hobart
Name: Maxim Fortarski
Status: Married
Occupation: Electrical Engineer
Sig: A day without sunshine is like, well, night.
Last Post: Going for a jog—be back for breakfast.
Religion: MetaChristian (orthodox)

They had *religion* in their dox! That category didn't even exist in his dox. So these folks could tell with a click that he wasn't one of them. Of course he could turn off his dox, but that was a really antisocial thing to do, it would probably make them even more suspicious of him. He clicked on a couple other people. "MetaChristian (reformed)". "MetaChristian (fundamentalist)". He hadn't realized there were so many flavors of MetaChristianity.

His imp pinged someone in visual range. Up ahead a path merged with his that led from a grove of trees. A woman jogged out of the trees. The familiarity of her body, her shape, her movements jarred him.

Sweet GG!

She was, however, a brunette with a short bob haircut. Her skin was the color of lightly creamed coffee. He zoomed in on her face. She was Polynesian, the female equivalent of the male Rio look, for women too busy to deal with race style. But that small, tight, athletic body looked identical to GG's. He had his imp do a comprehensive comparison, excluding the face.

She merged onto his path about ten meters ahead. She ran at a brisk pace, pulling away. He sped up to shorten the distance between them. The results from the imp came back, a 96% match. Not identical. Then again, the imp was comparing this actual body to Sweet GG's avatar. Athletes generally had their avatars be identical to their real bodies for maximum performance. He didn't know for sure what Sweet GG's real body looked like, it was an impolite thing to ask—in the virtual world your avatar was you.

He was about five meters away. He clicked on her head.

> *Handle: Astria*
> *Name: Locked*
> *Status: Single*
> *Occupation: Lawyer*
> *Sig: It's better to be hated than loved for what you're not.*
> *Last Post: Clearing my mind of the latest round of madness.*
> *Religion: MetaChristian (reformed)*

Well, that nailed it then. No way was that Sweet GG. He did notice that she was dressed less modestly than most of the other MetaChristians around them. All she was wearing were her sneakers, her shorts that weren't much more than black hot pants, and a sports bra. That four percent difference between her and Sweet GG he could now see was muscle. Her body had an overt athleticism that was apparent in the rolling fluidity of her leg muscles pumping the sway of her hips and the sweat-slicked sinews of her back. As he drew closer he noticed two things—one, she had hip-sockets, and two, there was a clicky on her left butt cheek. Had she been an exo trooper in the VDF? He brought his phand up to the clicky mechanically, but then stopped short. She would know if he clicked it—he was here to see Sweets, he shouldn't be touching other women's clickies.

But then, what kind of clicky would a MetaChristian woman have on her butt?

Curiosity won out. He clicked. A text bubble popped up next to her butt.

If you haven't been touched by Jesus, you ain't touching this.

Well, yeah, Raythen thought, *I guess that is the kind of thing a MetaChristian woman would have on her butt.*

<Astria: tell @Raythen> "It's not too late you know."

Dammit!

He could ignore it, but he was new here, in a strange culture. He didn't want to be insulting. He bet she was going to try to convert him. *She's a trap.* That's it, some sort of clever sexy religious trap.

<Raythen: tell @Astria> "Too late?"

<Astria: tell @Raythen> "To be touched by Jesus."

Trap!

<Raythen: tell @Astria> "Sorry, I'm not here to be touched, I'm here to meet my girlfriend."

<Astria: tell @Raythen> "lol"

That hadn't come out right.

They were now jogging side by side. She looked up at him and said, "You and your girlfriend must have a chaste relationship. You sure you don't want to be a Meta?"

His imp, guessing that he didn't know the meaning of the word 'chaste', displayed in front of him.

Abstaining from sexual intercourse.

He made an embarrassed laugh.

"Because if you're not going to get touched by your girlfriend you might as well make points with God for it, I'm just saying."

He didn't know how to reply, his mind quickly grasped for some topic, and then he remembered the hip-sockets.

"Did you get your sockets in the VDF?"

"Oh no, those are for doc-ocks. I get sent off to the asteroid belt now and then. If you ever do any work in zero g, doc-ocks are essential. The strap-ons chafe."

He just smiled and looked ahead. They jogged side by side for a minute or so. He always felt so trapped in meat-space—in the virtual world you could just disappear. Should he say goodbye and pick up the pace to get ahead of her? *What if she tried to keep pace? That would be weird on her part, right?*

She grabbed his wrist and jerked him to a stop. Startled, he looked at her wide-eyed. She stood still, staring at a grassy clearing to the side of the track about a hundred meters away with a dozen or so people gathered together.

"Come on!" she said, and started running toward them, pulling him along. Her grip was like iron.

"What's . . . what" he stammered.

She looked back, excited, and said "Come on! It's a flash musical! Turn on the pub."

Oh Jeez, he thought. He turned on the public channel and saw the countdown to a flash musical.

> *Category: Broadway Musical*
> *Play: The Spider and the Fly*
> *Song: Which is Which*
> *Vocals: Rodendris*
> *Restrictions: Couples only*
> *Countdown: One minute, fifty-three seconds*

Of course, he had done plenty of flash musicals when he was in high school. Everyone did. It was a great way to meet girls in meat-space, but he was a bit out of practice now.

"Join!" Astria commanded in a change of tone that actually had threat to it. Palpable threat. He joined. Two blue arrows pointing down appeared in the air, one over one of the men and the other over a woman in the crowd. Above them was the text "Jenny and Ian are engaged!" This flash musical was in their honor. There were over forty people in the crowd now, an equal number men and women. Astria dragged him over where the men were lining up. He looked on the ground for his position marker. There it was. The men were facing the women, the women facing back. He was in the second line in, but the lines were staggered so he had an unimpeded view of Astria.

Crap, what will Sweet GG think of this?

Thirty seconds. Ian and Jenny stood in the space between the men and women, facing each other. Everyone got ready, grins all around. Raythen made an unconvincing smile. He looked over the sequence of moves that were expected of him—scrolling the series of icons that represented his choreography. While he was looking them over they suddenly changed—Astria had altered the setting from 'Average' to 'Professional' for the both of them.

What's up with this chick? he thought in despair.

The music started. The beginning was easy enough for the guys. Just macho posturing while the women paced back and forth with synchronized gyrations and hand movements. Jenny was dancing around Ian, lip-synching the song. Raythen scrolled through his preset choreography to the chorus—that's when things were going to get interesting.

When Rodendris sang, *Who has web and who has wings? Is it the man who's pricked by lipstick stings?* the women's group ran into the men's group. As Astria ran by he hooked his right arm around her waist and she crumpled into it. He sent her back the direction she came; she landed on her feet, holding his right hand with her left. She extended, then he brought her in for a spin that merged into a lift—a lift that involved, he noted, him holding her in the air by one hand, that hand on her forbidden butt. When she came down she gave him a knowing wink.

After the chorus the focus was back on Jenny and Ian, everyone else made simple choreographed poses and some cross moves. It was all coming back to him. He actually hadn't been too bad back in the day.

Second chorus, a couple of spins and another lift. He didn't screw up. When the chorus was over all the men and women were lined up in four rows behind Jenny and Ian, who were doing some fairly impressive moves together. They were not noobs at this. Everyone else was just posing and shaking to the music, nothing to distract from the primary couple. It was, after all, their dance.

Astria was good, really good. She was positioned in front of him and she flashed him a grin as she added some flair to her moves that pushed the boundaries of her scripted choreography. She spun and then faced him, stepping toward him with her hand raised, snakelike. She reached out and slowly stroked his chest with her index and middle fingers. Raythen got more nervous than he already was; she was going against her designated role as support dancer.

Is that your web that makes me stay, or some heartbeat command I must obey?

Raythen quickly glanced to the other dancers. He wasn't sure but he thought he was getting some disapproving looks back from them. He looked down at Astria who was way too close. She was somehow able to undulate vigorously and yet consistently stay millimeters away from his skin. She was completely off script now, the closest thing he could describe it to be was a lap dance—while standing. The song was winding down to its last chorus that was going to bring all the couples back together. Astria backed away from him as the other women were going back to their men. As she receded she looked him in the eyes and smirked. On his HUD he saw her change his choreography again—it was really bad etiquette to change your partner's moves on the fly—and he froze when he saw what she was expecting of him. She continued to recede, five meters away now. He phanded to the script to change it back, but it was too late; she was already running at him. Not to him—at him, at full speed.

Timing was crucial. At three meters away she leaped up into the air and landed on her hands, again launching herself high with a front handspring that arched her body so that she fell with her feet angled down toward him. He cupped his hands in front of him; palms up with his fingers intertwined as he judged her aim. It was excellent. He took the weight of her feet, falling into a crouch as her hands gripped his shoulders. He then jumped up, launching her straight back up into the air. He had put all his strength into it—he had to, she had signaled a triple twisting somersault. As she spun in the air above him, seeming to hover like a weightless ethereal object, Raythen was relieved that he hadn't sent her flying in some random direction and crashing down onto the other dancers. Then he remembered that he had to catch her. As she fell she cradled and he caught her under her arms and knees. He realized that her body was hot and slick with sweat and that he hadn't gripped a real human female in years. Real female skin, with all tactile sensation at full, gave him an overload of experience—and she had some seriously hard muscle under that skin that moved in a living way that was completely distracting.

She looked up at him matter-of-factly. "You did okay."

"Hmm." He nodded.

"You can put me down now."

"Yes!" he said, not so much as agreeing as waking up. He placed her down on her feet.

About a hundred or so people had gathered to watch. They cheered enthusiastically.

"I have to finish my jog," she said. "Going for an even fifty k."

It was then that Raythen was aware of the audible mutters of disapproval around them, and burning glares. Jenny, her face transitioning from confused to angry, was pointing at him and Astria with little jabs as she spoke to those around her. It was very bad manners to showboat during someone else's flash musical, especially during a special event like an engagement. But this didn't seem to bother Astria at all. She ignored everyone else completely. Raythen, in contrast, felt slightly panicked. He wasn't used to being around this many humans in meat-space, and he certainly wasn't used to being glared at by most of them.

"Thank you for the dance, sir," Astria said with exaggerated politeness and a slight bow. "One more thing before I go. In your hotel room nightstand is a copy of the MetaChristian Bible. I would be a bad Meta if I didn't suggest you read it. Not the whole thing, of course, just the introduction. Would you do that for me?"

"I should be heading back," Raythen said, wanting desperately to get out of there.

"Okay, it was nice meeting you Raythen. Read the introduction. It's short." She waved as she turned and started back on her jog. Several of the dancers had to move out of her way, annoyed, since she didn't acknowledge their existence.

The flash mob was breaking up. He didn't know if he should apologize to Jenny and Ian or not, maybe send them a text explaining that Astria was a stranger, and probably crazy. He decided it was best to just make a hasty retreat to his hotel room.

Chapter 15

Where is Sweet GG?

Raythen sent her a text saying the room was great and that he was looking forward to her arrival. He then realized that he was exhausted. He hadn't slept in over thirty hours. With physical augmentation the average person only needed about four hours of sleep a night. Sweaty, tired, and anxious, he thought about the hot-tub in the bathroom. That would probably do the trick. He could watch a movie . . . or what was it Astria had said about the MetaChristian Bible? He summoned a time line. Hovering in front of him was a horizontal line with a hash mark for every half hour over the previous twelve hours. Above each hash mark was a small picture of what he had been looking at during that instant. He clicked on the one closest to the end of the flash musical. It was about three minutes after, with him jogging back to the hotel. Underneath was a scroll bar. He scrolled back to when he was holding her and hit play. He watched the replay of the events.

"One more thing before I go. In your hotel room nightstand is a copy of the MetaChristian Bible."

What the hell's a nightstand?

<imp: tell @Raythen> "A bedside table or cabinet."

Oh, that thing. When Raythen had first seen it he thought it was some sort of fancy OmniServ.

He went into the bedroom and examined the nightstand. Sure enough there were no clickies like you'd get from an OmniServ. He opened the drawer and inside was an old-fashioned book. Black leather cover with gold lettering: *The MetaChristian Bible: with commentary by Erin Theophilus.*

It was an ancient looking artifact, although it was really quite new. He had seen books in the movies, of course, but had never actually handled one. He pinched the edge of the rigid front cover and picked it up. It hung open, obviously requiring some manual dexterity in order to read properly. He cradled the back cover with his free hand and the pages flopped open to somewhere in the middle of the book. He looked at the black ink letters on the white paper. Motionless, they just lay there in manner that was something akin to death. He closed the front cover and opened it again, so he could see the first page. It just repeated what was said on the front cover. He tried to turn the cover page, but somehow ended up on page forty-tree. Using the tip of his thumb he flicked at the edges of the pages until he managed to lift the cover page. The next page was blank.

People in old-times must have had tremendous patience. Maybe the blank paper meant something. *Clear your soul before entering*, or something like that. He got to the next page and was rewarded with the word *Introduction* and lots of other little dead words. Okay, he was getting the hang of this book business. Time for that bath.

He reclined in the tub as jets of hot water massaged his body. Damn, it really felt good. The old folks often commented that young people these days neglected tactile sensations. He was starting to agree with them— remembering what it felt like to hold Astria.

Where the hell is Sweet GG?

He picked up the book he had left on the edge of the hot-tub and opened it up. The water on his fingers were absorbed into the paper and left gray splotches. It was easier to turn the pages though. He went to the introduction.

The dilemma of religion at the end of the 21st century was that science had explained everything. It even had an explanation for the soul itself. The overwhelming evidence for evolution could no longer be denied by any reasonable person. Religion was no longer needed to illuminate the seekers of truth on the "hows" of life. That had been taken care of by Priests of Science who could demonstrate their truth with the undeniable facilities of their technology.

Before science, it was to the Priests of Religion that people had turned when life presented its mysteries. "Who were the first people?" "What are the planets, the stars?" "How do I cure my gout?" If the Priests of Religion had special knowledge about moral behavior and the nourishment of the soul, the people reasoned, certainly they had to have answers to these more prosaic questions. And the Priests of Religion felt pressure to oblige the people to maintain their authority. They looked to the old stories to answer the people's questions; it was the best they knew, but they were often wrong.

What does it mean to be a MetaChristian? The most common answer is, "To believe that the Universe is a computer program that God created to make a species of intelligent, feeling creatures that weren't directly designed by him." And that is the essence of the idea that inspired me to form the first MetaChristian church. I put the "Meta" in Christian to emphasize the belief in the Greater Universe, "Heaven", which exists beyond this one. We cannot know the nature of Heaven, but it is a real place, and our Universe, as vast as it seems to us, is but a small construct in Heaven.

Why do I believe this? Why the need to believe that this Universe, that science has explained so thoroughly, was created by an intelligence that lives in a Greater Universe? Isn't it easier to believe that this Universe has the fortunate laws it does that enables consciousness because it is one of an infinite number of universes, all with different laws of physics? Isn't that a more reasonable belief? Doesn't my belief leave the gaping holes of "Where does God come from?" and "Where does Heaven come from?" But we also have the question, "Where did these infinite universes come from?" Belief in the physical universe is still a belief. Belief that what we see with our eyes reflects an actual physical universe and not a simulation is still just a belief.

We all have choices about what to believe. Here and now I am given two choices; on one hand are the infinite physical universes that have their own independent existence, and on the other hand is God, who has created this simulated Universe that we exist in. Of the two, in my mind the belief in God does have an advantage, and that advantage is that it feels right, in my heart. There is, inside me, the feeling of God watching over me, of loving me, of filling me with hope and forgiveness and meaning. This sensation is the evidence that tips the balance toward God. This is why I believe.

Now to the tough question that everyone likes to argue about: Why did I feel the need to cut half the books out of the traditional Bible to make the MetaChristian Bible? As I said earlier, the ancient priests felt a need to answer all questions. But God had not given them all the answers. What answers had he given them? That is the crucial question. And that is truly *the most important aspect of being a MetaChristian—trying to find out what God has told us.*

God created the Universe so that it would create people, so that it would create us. This is much like a computer programmed genetic algorithm. A genetic algorithm creates a variety of entities, and then a winnowing process separates the useful entities from the unuseful ones. This is what God is doing with this Universe. He created this Universe so it would create us, but we were made by a random process, and certainly not all of us will satisfy his requirements of what it means to be a righteous person.

Now, God could have kept the system random. He could have let human societies evolve on their own, and pick out the righteous as they came along. But instead, at some point in history, God decided to help us along in satisfying him. He revealed his will to some worthy people in order to facilitate his testing of us. And some of these revelations have survived to our time in the Bible. But along with God's wisdom, some other writings, writings by humans, contaminated the texts. It is our greatest responsibility in life to discern what these actual revelations of God are from what is human. We have a tremendous set of tools at our disposal to perform lexical analysis, along with the archeological evidence and other ancient texts to help us determine the origins of the various books of the Bible. I have spent over thirty years studying all of the available evidence, and this version of the Bible in your hands is the culmination of my studies. These words are, to the best of my knowledge, the words of God reaching to us, to teach us to be the people that he wants us to be. It is in our hands to be the good and loving people that God wants us to be. This responsibility is a great gift, and a great burden. As undeserving as I am, I hope to live up to His Love.

When Raythen fell asleep he dropped the book into the hot-tub.

Chapter 16

The Venus Market is where it's at. And where this, that, and the other thing is at. And where as much as ten percent of the population of the planet was at, at any given time. In meat-space Raythen was in the hot-tub, which he decided he preferred over the Recliner while networking—he just had to remember not to relieve himself in it. Almost everyone went to the Venus Market at least once a day, so maybe Sweet GG would be there. A quick check of the roster showed she wasn't, at least not on her GG avatar.

Raythen was riding his hovercycle, sleek as a drop of quicksilver, cruising down a wide golden boulevard. You earned Market points depending on how many positive transactions you made on the Market, and with them you could buy vehicles, store fronts, and advertising. Raythen had saved up for over a year to get the hovercycle. Around him people rode skateboards, bicycles, motorcycles, hoverboards, horses, cars, mammoths, magic carpets, giant robots—and a few poor noobs even walked. The boulevard he cruised down was one of the main spokes that radiated from the Market Hub. The buildings looming to either side grew more fantastical and elaborate as he approached the grand central tower of the Hub. Store signs with videos and music and exploding galaxies and choruses of angels and hentai and gladiatorial battles raged for Raythen's attention. He weaved through the menagerie of traffic, even though it wasn't really necessary, there was no collision detection in the Market—

people could pass right through each other, although it was considered rude if it could be avoided.

The circle of the Hub was a kilometer in diameter—the avenue fifty meters wide. The goal of every marketer was to get a store front in the Hub. At Raythen's current rate of savings he could rent one in about three hundred years. For a day.

The central tower, Market Tower, was currently rented to Lieberkopf—it was plastered with multiple giant images of their current spokesperson Adrian Kulana—who spun, winked, leaped, danced, and fell up and down its shimmering glass sides.

As Raythen turned into the rolling cacophony of traffic in the Hub he had to veer to avoid passing through a red dragon that had swooped down to show off. Its rider waved to someone as it ascended into the sky again. Raythen joined the traffic and just went around the circle, watching people, seeing if someone looked like they might be one of Sweet GG's avatars, or the kind of alt she might have. A lot of people had alternate market avatars, keeping business activities separate from other online lives.

Up ahead, a vehicle caught Raythen's attention—a large litter carried on the shoulders of four bald muscular men wearing loincloths. The rider, partially obscured by a gossamer canopy and curtain, was reclining Cleopatra-like on a divan. He clicked on her—it was Dark Fuji. He pulled up beside her. She slowly lolled her head in his direction, gave a quick bat of her butterfly-wing eye-lashes, and said in a husky, whispery voice. "Hello Raythen. I was expecting to talk to you soon."

Keeping pace with Dark Fuji, Raythen was no longer avoiding the other traffic. A Humvee drove through him. He made all colliding traffic partially transparent. "Expecting me?"

"Edargo has been exceedingly persistent about me producing his feature. I was hoping for some inspiration from the vids that he sent, but I have to admit I am at a loss for that spark. That elusive creative spark. You know that frustration when the muse refuses to speak to you and leaves you an empty husk of . . . of . . . grains of sand in a metal tube."

Raythen didn't know that sort of frustration, but he nodded anyway.

"Biv and Tassel wanted me to be challenged. They wanted me to choose some random person to make a feature—a film. The editing, the background music . . . to create a cohesive story out of the flashes and drabs that construct a modern life. A challenge . . . a challenge! So I picked Edargo. He is clever and interesting in his own way, but in reviewing his life I see now that it seems to embody the very deconstruction of cohesion. He knows many people and enjoys insinuating himself into their lives as an observer. He jibes and makes commentaries, but he owns no narratives of his own. So, in reviewing the hours of vids of his life, I now see before me . . . a buddy picture."

She allowed Raythen to dwell on that, batting her eyelashes at him for emphasis.

"I'm the buddy?" Raythen said.

"You are the buddy."

Raythen nodded. "So you want my vids."

"Yes. He told me you were helping him to become a professional NPC. We'll have to take whatever you have relating to that. I was hoping to have enough material already to make a feature, but we have an incomplete story. The problem—and this is a problem—is that you are now aware that you are making a feature and it will bring artifice to the endeavor. He will have a tendency to ham it up. I think you will be fine. You are solid enough. And you have a following of sorts that will bring more viewers. Another danger—and this is a real danger—is that you may become too much the center. I will have to use some skill in editing. He does have more words per minute than you do, by several orders of magnitude. You might look like a bit of a lug."

Raythen looked back at her, at a loss.

"Exactly," she said. "I know that you are not a lug, but this is in comparison to Edargo, and it has to be *his* feature. You will be a very sympathetic lug, if a lug at all."

"I don't think I'm liking this."

"I am being up front about this because I would like to have a contract that leaves me with complete access to all your previous vids taken in Edargo's presence, as well as any real-time video that occurs between now and the completion of this project. Hopefully we can get this project done in a month or so. In reviewing the vids that Edargo has provided to me I have noticed that you have flagged some of your interactions as private and I am unable to watch them. I realize I am asking a lot from you. That is why I will compensate you beyond the standard VuDyne rate. Two million dollars."

Raythen's eyes widened involuntarily at the offer. Two million was a lot—not FU money, but more than he had ever gotten in a single transaction before. However, Edargo was his best friend and confidant, there were some things he has spoken about in his presence that he wouldn't want put into the public sphere, especially things about Sweet GG.

"The last thing I want is to invade your privacy," Dark Fuji said, sensing his reluctance. "The focus of this feature is Edargo, not you. In the end there will only be two hours of vids that will be made public, and the rights of all the remaining material shall be returned to you. Rest assured that I will be discrete with the vids as I go through the editorial process."

The two million was tempting, but he couldn't risk some of his private conversations with Edargo getting back to Sweet GG. He could have his imp go through the history of his interactions with Edargo and refine the privacy filter for any conversations he wouldn't want to get back to her.

"I need to review my vids," Raythen said. "I'm sure I can give you some more material than you already have, but I'm afraid I can't give you unfiltered access."

Dark Fuji gave just the slightest hint of annoyance. "Yes, you do that." She looked ahead for a few moments, seeing things that he couldn't see. Then she turned to him quickly, "What are you doing at Corpus Christi?"

Raythen didn't want to talk about his current situation. He had an impulse to brush her off and drive away, but he didn't want to annoy her more than she already was. She was one of his more well-connected friends.

"I'm here on vacation."

"Really? There is a lot going on there. I hear there are some opportunities selling live-feeds—to news organizations and . . . other interested parties. You could make some extra cash while you are . . . *vacationing*." She looked at him conspiratorially.

"Thanks for the tip," he said automatically.

"You should have played time travel ménage a trois. Who would you have picked?"

"I don't really know much about history."

She sighed dramatically. "No, that's not it. You are just not interested in games that do not involve killing people. I do hope you decide to take a larger role in my feature. Your laconic nature is a wonderful contrast to Edargo."

She looked ahead again, and enough of a pause passed that he judged he could safely leave. "Thanks again for the tip; I'll check into the live-feeds."

"Yes you do that," she said, not looking at him. "And be careful, things may get a bit hairy down there from what I am seeing in the news. But you were in the military yourself, so you know how to be careful."

"Thanks. Later."

He accelerated his hover-cycle and zipped away.

Chapter 17

Spokesdog stands behind a podium on which hangs the seal of the president of the United States. He wears a dark blue suit and red tie, an American flag pin on his lapel. The orange fur on his head is longer than usual and coifed in a distinctly human style, parted far down one side and combed straight back over his ears, the front shaped oddly like a cap visor.

"Fake News!" Spokesdog yells at his audience. "The Fake News media is lying about me! I won the election by a landslide! I got the most electoral votes since Ronald Reagan! I won the popular vote, millions of illegal aliens voted against me! I had more people at my inauguration than any president ever! I accomplished more in the first six months than any president except maybe FDR! These new taxes are going to hurt me, believe me! If anyone says otherwise it's Fake News! I had nothing to do with Russia during the campaign! Believe me! I never called those shit-hole countries shit-hole countries! Don't listen to the Fake News! I have to tell you, they are all liars! It's Fake News folks! Fake News!"

Spokesdog steps out from behind the podium and rubs the top of his head with both hands. When he removes them, his head has returned to its normal golden retriever fur. He looks at you and says, "Remember Fake News? No? Most of you didn't live in those dark times. The president of the United States could stand up in public and say lie after lie, and tens of millions of people would believe him. He and Russian trolls and right-wing propaganda "news" sites would spew forth disinformation—lies—and at the same time they would accuse reputable news sites of reporting Fake News. And millions upon millions of people believed them. This led to decades of chaos. Human civilization stood at a cross-roads—if the nations of the world had worked together at that time to solve its problems— environmental problems, human migration problems, rampant wealth inequalities—decades of pain and suffering could have been avoided. Instead, Fake News was used to divide people, foster hate and mistrust, while the rich became richer, separating themselves into luxurious fortress enclaves. It is not an exaggeration to say that Fake News almost led to the end of human civilization. Without a common reality to bind people together, how can a mutually beneficial economy be built between people? If the president of the United States himself is saying that American democracy is corrupt and can't be trusted, then what values could people put their trust in?"

Spokesdog parts the curtain behind the stage and walks through it, out into a busy city sidewalk. People wearing mid-21st century clothes are walking by him, oblivious to a human with a dog's head standing in their midst.

"The turning point happened here, in this nondescript office building." He motions his hand to the building behind him. "This is where Ragnar Kekkonen founded VuDyne, in the rented space on the third floor. Here is where he and his partner, David Hicks, put together the first distributed version of the VuDyne program that ensured that anything anyone recorded, and by this time everyone was recording everything, could be validated with encrypted, uncrackable, hashed certificates. If you wanted to know if a digital recording was real all you had to do was validate it with VuDyne. The date, location, and content of any recording that was Vued was saved to an encrypted certificate on the distributed block chain. Any tampering of the recording would break the hash code, letting everyone know that it was Photoshopped or dubbed. Since it was distributed, it was not controlled by any one person or organization. Soon, no one took any recording seriously unless it was Vued, and Fake News became impossible. Here, David Hicks came up with the VuDyne logo, *Information is Life*. And the validation of information once again allowed normal life to continue."

Spokedog turns around to the entrance of the building, opens the glass door, and steps inside. Instead of the lobby one would expect, he finds himself in a black void, standing on a glowing green grid that stretches out to the horizon. Little globes of light flash and wiz by behind him.

"There was one wrinkle. Quantum computers. Remember when I said that the hashed certificates were "uncrackable"? Well, they were, until people built quantum computers. Quantum computers made the distributed block chains vulnerable. Anyone could use the power of quantum computing to hack the block chain. It was no longer secure and reliable. Fortunately, Ragnar Kekkonen had anticipated this and built a centralized infrastructure that mirrored the existing block chain. Once the threat of quantum computers became too great, he flipped a switch—literally, he physically flipped a real switch in his office he made himself—and VuDyne was moved to his private servers. He negotiated with governments and corporations so they would perform regular audits, allowing transparency to his operation that ensured the continued integrity of the data. Civilization depended on a central authority to validate the truth of data, and fortunately VuDyne was there with the willingness and means to get it done."

Spokesdog glows brightly for an instant as his body is teleported to a vast white expanse. Around him are little clusters of people, some painting on easels, some taking pictures of beautiful models, some dancing, some scribbling in notebooks, some singing, some sculpting marble statues, and some just watching everyone else. The view slowly pans up and away from Spokesdog as he continues. "There was an added benefit to the centralization of VuDyne. With a trusted central authority to oversee the validation of recording, civilization was granted a means to protect everyone's intellectual property. Now, using official VuDyne software, artists can use the vast digital tools at their disposal to create music, movies, anything their imaginations lead them to, and stamp it with their VuDyne signatures so no one can steal their creations. Thanks to VuDyne we live in an age where the artistic content generated every hour is greater than the combined human content from before the 21st century. We can create, secure in the knowledge that our contribution to this magnificent endeavor is recorded, appreciated, and fairly compensated. It's hard to believe that the creativity and peace of mind that is the defining characteristic of our modern society is brought to you by a single company. VuDyne.

"This infotainment has been brought to you by VuDyne—*At VuDyne, Information is Life*. And remember, lunch is on me. Woof."

Chapter 18

Torvald was sitting in the dark. He was in a box that was barely large enough to fit the bulk of his exo armor. The exoskeleton's knees were pressed against his armored chest, his arms wrapped around his legs.

He had been in the box for over three days.

He didn't mind. In fact, he was as near to giddy as he had ever been. At times he would start giggling spontaneously—silently, of course, in his mind. The mission required that he remain completely silent. He kept himself entertained with his imp. He was required to spend a certain amount of time going over the mission specifics; map walkthroughs, rendezvous points, alternate scenarios; but when he satisfied those requirements he went back to vids of Sweet GG. The vids of what they had once shared together.

Another giggle-spasm erupted in his mind.

Raythen is here. So close. So close to me. Hee hee.

Raythen was up there on the surface, so clueless, waiting and waiting for Sweet GG. So disappointed.

Sweet GG had broken it off with Torvald several months before she had met Raythen. She thought their sex was interfering with their professional relationship. He hadn't liked it but he understood, especially with all the added scrutiny they were receiving. But then when she started fucking that lousy NPC—that had really gnawed at him. What the hell could she see in *him*? He was an idiot. He wasn't special, like she was, like he was.

The rage he felt whenever he saw Raythen had surprised him. He hadn't thought he could experience such depth of emotion—he hadn't even suspected that such overwhelming emotions could exist. It had opened up the worlds to him, it had explained so much about life. He could read Shakespeare and understand the murderous passion of Othello; he could watch Scorsese's *Taxi Driver* and understand obsession.

And now they had let him out. He was off the Farm and he was armed and armored and soon, so soon he would be free to do what he wanted to do, what he needed to do. Sure, he had the mission to complete, an important mission that would demonstrate to the worlds just how important the work they were all doing on the Farm was. After this mission there would be more funding and consulting with people in power and Parvati would be so proud. She would get all the recognition she deserved. And there would be more missions.

Operation Achaean, his official mission with the Venus Defense Force, would be easy enough—it was a simple grab and bag. What only he and his brothers knew was that there was another mission, a mission called Operation Bonehead. And soon that Bonehead up there would know about the mission too.

Chapter 19

Raythen was jogging on the track around the perimeter of Corpus Christi. Palmetto plants lined the track that weaved serpentine, toward and away from the transparent dome. It was nighttime, the simulated starlit sky cast down an eerie white glow. The stars matched what he would have been able to see if there were no clouds over Venus, but magnified in brightness. The Milky Way splashed across the sky above him, equaling the glow of a full moon on Terra.

Raythen's jogging companion was Mr. Hang. Mr. Hang was a disembodied giant glowing blue hand about a meter tall that floated ahead, pointing where he should jog. Mr. Hang wasn't a talker. He was, however, very insistent with his gestures. Mr. Hang stopped and put up a "halt" with the palm facing Raythen. He then pointed into the palmettos, away from the hull. Raythen was detecting a pattern. Mr. Hang wanted to get a good look at every building around the perimeter, near the hull of the stratos. Raythen plunged into the foliage, pushing away the palm fronds that brushed at his face. Mr. Hang went ahead, passing through the trees, until they reached the clearing and the building. Another apartment complex, about ten stories high. There were more buildings on Corpus Christi than on Lu Shing to accommodate the larger population. Mr. Hang had him look up, left, then right. Mr. Hang beckoned him with a curled finger to circle the building. Yeah, he had the routine down. This was going to take hours, but they were paying well. He followed Hang, stopping occasionally and panning three-sixty. They turned the corner to the front in time to see a family of four approaching the entranceway—mother, father, and two young sons, around three and five years old. The mother was holding the three-year-old who was crying. The five-year-old was in a defiant stance, angry about something or other, eyes down, red faced. Raythen walked by them casually, scanning around them. When you were providing a live-feed to someone it was best not to be obvious about it. He tried to stroll like a clueless tourist, which wasn't all that hard for him to do.

He turned the corner around the other side of the building, looked at the wall and the windows, then down to the tree-line, and then jogged back through the palmettos to the path.

<Tray Wind: tell @Raythen> "Who are you working for?"

Raythen flinched. *Who the hell is that?* Mr. Hang motioned him forward. He kept jogging.

<Tray Wind: tell @Raythen> "Sorry to startle you. I've seen a few of you guys lately and thought it was time for an interview."

Raythen phanded her name in his text box.

> *Handle: Tray Wind*
>
> *Name: Tray Wind*
>
> *Status: Single*
>
> *Occupation: Licensed Reporter (Venus Salon)*
>
> *Sig: The optimist thinks this is the best of all possible worlds. The pessimist fears it's true.*
>
> *Last Post: Don't do that unless you want a wet sandwich.*

<Tray Wind: tell @Raythen> "Interested in a quick interview? Your identity will be kept confidential. And you will get the standard interview fees."

<Raythen: tell @Tray Wind> "How much is that?"

A contract scrolled in front of him, with the important parts highlighted; $1.49 per view, expected views—twenty to thirty thousand.

<Raythen: tell @Tray Wind> "Okay, I'm in."

Raythen knew that Mr. Hang might not want him to be giving an interview about his live-feed job, but Mr. Hang could only see the raw feeds of what he was seeing, he couldn't see any of Raythen's HUD or hear his audio, and so was unaware of the conversation he was having.

<Tray Wind: tell @Raythen> "How long have you been on Corpus Christi?"

<Raythen: tell @Tray Wind> "Two days."

<Tray Wind: tell @Raythen> "Were you hired to be a live-feed before coming here?"

<Raythen: tell @Tray Wind> "Nope, I found the job at the Market after I arrived."

<Tray Wind: tell @Raythen> "So you don't consider yourself to be a professional live-feed?"

<Raythen: tell @Tray Wind> "Nope."

<Tray Wind: tell @Raythen> "Have you ever been paid to be a live-feed in the past?"

<Raythen: tell @Tray Wind> "Just the normal informal stuff. You know, for friends."

<Tray Wind: tell @Raythen> "Who hired you to do this job?"

<Raythen: tell @Tray Wind> "I don't know. It was through an anonymous service."

<Tray Wind: tell @Raythen> "So you're just making some easy money then, eh? Are you a MetaChristian?"

<Raythen: tell @Tray Wind> "No."

Mr. Hang signaled halt and pointed into the palmettos. Another building. He plunged in.

<Tray Wind: tell @Raythen> "Do you have any religious affinities?"

<Raythen: tell @Tray Wind> "Of course not."

When he emerged from the trees he saw this wasn't just the average apartment complex. Ahead of him, about twenty meters away, was a chain link fence. Beyond that was a great black slab of a building, dark and windowless. Mr. Hang had him stop, and then motioned for him to walk along the tree line. Raythen recognized the design of the building. He had worked in one like this when he was in the Venus Defense Force. But this building didn't belong to the VDF. On the flag flying on the nearby pole was the image of a crucifix crossed with a sword, with the words *Corpus Christi Militia.*

<Tray Wind: tell @Raythen> "You seem a little defensive about religion."

Raythen walked along the trees, scanning back and forth at the building.

<Raythen: tell @Tray Wind> "I'm just not religious. Never been."

<Tray Wind: tell @Raythen> "How much do you know about the current stand-off between Corpus Christi and the United Planets?"

<Raythen: tell @Tray Wind> "Just what I've seen in the news."

<Tray Wind: tell @Raythen> "If there is a violent confrontation between the UP and the MetaChristians, which side would you be on if you were forced to choose?"

Raythen had a sudden prick of paranoia. Supposedly it was impossible to fake online credentials. You could block people from reading your dox and walk around anonymous, but any credentials that *did* show on your dox were maintained by VuDyne and guaranteed authentic. Tray Wind's dox stated she was a licensed reporter for Venus Salon, a progressive publication that (he checked quickly online to verify) tended to editorialize against superstition and throwback ideologies like MetaChristianity. And here he was, in the middle of a job that was looking more and more like the surveillance of the perimeter of a target of a possible assault. As Sarge would say, *Turn on your fucking situational awareness you mindless goob!*

What if Tray Wind was really a MetaChristian?

There it was, for an instant, he saw it. Up ahead against the trees, it moved. Mr. Hang, who saw everything that he saw, didn't recognize it— Mr. Hang was motioning him to continue ahead. But Raythen was feeling like an exposed squishy animal. He was on a stratos filled with religious fanatics who were worried about what the UP and VDF were planning to do to them. These people believed in an *afterlife,* which meant that *this* life, this *beforelife* was just about as important as the hors d'oeuvres in a ten-course meal. And now they probably looked at him as the enemy.

Mr. Hang was getting impatient, motioning him forward more insistently. Raythen didn't think that was the best idea. Instead, he leaned one hand against the trunk of a tree, lifted up his foot, holding his ankle in his other hand, and stretched his leg, grimacing as he did so. He was just a jogger who had pushed himself a little too far, that's all.

An exoskeleton trooper suit is surprisingly quiet. It looks like it should clank and click and make that servo whir noise when it walks and comes to a stop. It doesn't. Every exo suit is tested in a sound chamber surrounded by sensors that would make a bat drool in envy. The suit goes through its full range of motion in a routine that takes about three hours. If any sound is heard beyond the wooshing of air, it is sent back to the factory. When Raythen heard the polite clearing of the throat, he knew what he was going to see, because he hadn't heard anything before that. Raythen turned his head and pretended to be surprised.

The exo trooper had his helmet off. It wasn't really off; the active camouflage system that covered the outer skin of the suit projected the actual image of the trooper's face in real time. The trooper might not even be in the suit, it could be operated by remote control but still be projecting the face of the operator. On his shoulder was the cross and sword logo of the Corpus Christi Militia.

"Excuse me sir," the trooper said. "What's your business here?" His voice was polite, but his face was unsmiling.

<Tray Wind: tell @Raythen> "Still thinking?"

<Raythen: tell @Tray Wind> AFK

"Just going for a little jog," Raythen said. "My leg was getting cramped so I thought I would take a little short cut back to the hotel."

"If you're injured we can take you to a hospital."

"Oh no! Not injured. Just a little strained." Raythen gingerly put down his foot and shifted some weight to it. "Yeah, just a little strained."

Mr. Hang floated next to the trooper's head and gave Raythen the 'okay' sign.

"Are you sure you don't require medical assistance?"

"Nope, no I'm good."

"Very well, I'll escort you to the main road where you can walk home or summon a vehicle."

"That sounds fine."

"Follow me please."

The trooper walked ahead. Raythen noticed that he didn't have a rail gun, only the VDF troopers were allowed to have them. He glanced behind and could make out the camo blur of his wing man about three meters away. As they walked around the base Raythen scanned his eyes around, to get as much data as he could for Mr. Hang. There wasn't much to see other than the dimensions of the place, all the real activity was inside or underground. It took them about ten minutes of walking to get around to the front. When they reached the road a taxi was parked with its door open. The trooper motioned him into it.

"That's okay," Raythen said. "I can walk back, I'm fine."

"Sir, for your safety, I insist that you take this ride back to your hotel."

Raythen knew that there was no use arguing. He got into the taxi. There was no other word from the trooper as the door closed. The taxi was already programmed to go directly to his hotel. Mr. Hang floated in front of him, waved good-bye, and vanished. He was replaced by the live-feed contract, which indicated that only twenty-two percent of the job had been completed, meaning he would only get twenty-two percent of the payment. That was fine by Raythen. He accepted the completion form. He guessed that Mr. Hang no longer had any use for him now that he had been made.

As the taxi drove back to the hotel he expected to hear from Tray Wind, but there was nothing. He could have tried contacting her, but decided against it. It was time to lay low.

Chapter 20

Raythen sat in the hot-tub with a hand towel on his forehead, pondering the events of an hour ago. This vacation was not proceeding as planned.

Where the hell is Sweet GG?

This was not making sense. He wished he knew her real name. He had looked at the obituaries that covered the past few days . . . the *obituaries!* Of course no one had died . . . if someone had died on Venus it would have been big news. Any injury that put someone in the hospital was big news, if something tragic had happened to Sweet GG he would have heard about it.

So where was she?

Was this her way of blowing him off? Was this her way of easing her guilt, paying for an expensive hotel room? And then not showing up—to inform him by her absence that it was over? Maybe she had abandoned her Sweet GG avatar, leaving her *Exo Arena* life behind her? If that was the case, why not send him to New Tahiti? That was a real vacation stratos, half of it was beach. Why did she send him to some religious enclave that might actually get *invaded* by the VDF? The cruiser Pax Cythera was just a few kilometers away on a parallel course. That had to be where Mr. Hang was from. The VDF was doing recon. Getting a live-feed from the perimeter. And now he was probably being watched by the MetaChristians as a suspected spy. He wouldn't be surprised if they tossed him off the stratos. And what if they did send him away? What if they got rid of him moments before Sweet GG's arrival, and she thought that *he* blew her off? Or that he didn't care enough to lay low and keep from doing something stupid that could get him removed from the stratos?

What if she saw the vid of him and Astria? He couldn't block it because it had occurred in a public place. What if she saw that and decided he was a douche-bag scum?

He plunged his head under the water, his hands gripping the sides of the hot-tub, his teeth clenched, bubbles streaming up through them—he watched the bubbles collect under the surface of the floating washcloth.

A bell rang in his head.

He sat straight up, wet washcloth flopping over his face.

The bell rang again.

The door bell!

A video screen appeared in the darkness of his closed eyes. It was a feed from his hotel room door.

Living in a world with ubiquitous cameras and instantaneous information, Raythen was spared the moments of joyful anticipation he would have felt if he had to run to the door to find out who was there. Instead, he was looking at Edargo's grinning face.

<Raythen: tell @Edargo> "What the hell are you doing here?"

Edargo put his hands over his face, hiding it, and then opened them up like swinging doors. He said "Surprise! Did I catch you two at an awkward moment?"

<Raythen: tell @Edargo> "No."

He got out of the hot-tub, took the washcloth off his head and started drying himself with a towel. Edargo's face was now projected onto the bathroom wall.

"Where is she? I want to say hi."

<Raythen: tell @Edargo> "She's not here."

Raythen put on a bathrobe.

"Good! We can talk face to face."

Raythen walked across the suite and opened the door. Yes, it wasn't a joke, Edargo was really there. And he had his new East Asian face.

He stepped into the room and surveyed it appreciatively, rubbing his hands together. "This place is *nice!* Much nicer than mine. I'm at the dump next door; my place isn't much more than a recliner room. But *your* girl set you up in style!"

"How did you get here? You can't afford a flight."

"No, you are absolutely correct. I, personally, like you, can't afford a flight to this distant, exotic city. But, like you, I have my own personal sugar momma. But, unlike you, I'm not allowed to touch mine."

In a flash it came to Raythen. "Dark Fuji."

"Ding! Dark Fuji."

"The movie, right? This has something to do with your stupid movie."

Edargo looked offended. "This is my life! Anything stupid about this movie is going to be smart-stupid. As in comedic. When I told DF that you were here with Sweet GG—"

"You told her about Sweet GG?"

"Yeah, sure, it's news, and you didn't tell me not to tell anyone. Anyway, she started throwing out names like Martin and Lewis, Cheech and Chong, Crosby and Hope. She's toying with the idea of calling the movie, *The Road to Corpus Christi*." He grinned. "I'm here to help you with any potential problems you might have with your first rendezvous with the love interest, aka Sweet GG. DF said the situation was 'rife with possibilities.' By the way, have you discovered GG's true identity yet?"

"She's not here."

"You told me that. Did she step out somewhere?"

"She's not here." Raythen looked sour. Edargo was starting to catch on that something really wasn't right.

"You *don't* know where she is?"

"I don't *know*.

"I know that you don't know but what I don't know is why you don't know. If I knew what you did know then I would know why you don't know. And if I knew what you didn't know then I would know. You know?" Edargo had managed all that with a straight face and a single breath.

Raythen's right hand became a fist. Veins were popping out in unhealthy looking places in his face and neck. "Are . . . you . . . turning this into some kind of comedy sketch?"

Edargo pointed to the side. "Don't break the forth wall."

Raythen raised his fist. "I'll break—" and then he realized he had just been fed a line. He dropped his hands to his sides and deflated, his veins going back to their accustomed places. He stood there in silence for a moment. He realized that he was actually glad to see Edargo.

If Sweet GG showed up anytime soon he could always kick the ball-buster out. Hard.

Edargo said, "I saw there was a bar downstairs. I've never been to a real bar before. Let's check it out."

Chapter 21

The bar was a large mahogany semicircle staffed by three smartly dressed human bartenders who moved with the skill and precision of robots. Rows of exotic looking beverages lined the shelves behind them. Wine-glasses hung by their stems from overhead racks. Most of the bar stools were taken but they managed to find two together at one of the ends.

Few of the patrons talked to each other—they simply stared straight ahead, some making conversational facial expressions and occasionally laughing.

Edargo leaned toward Raythen and whispered, "This is so cool."

A bartender slid toward them and put down two coasters. "What can I get for you?"

Raythen didn't drink alcohol. He didn't like not being in control of himself. When he *did* go to the bar—always a virtual bar—there would be a menu hovering in front of his face—always the same menu, since the only drinks available were those that could be dispensed by his OmniServe. There was no menu here, this place was old school.

"I'll have water."

"With or without bubbles?"

"Without."

"I'll have your finest Scotch, neat, my good barkeep," Edargo said.

The bartender raised an eyebrow. "The twenty-five-year Macallan goes for four thousand a glass."

Edargo looked past the bartender to the wall. "I'll have that blended stuff over there at the end, neat, my good barkeep."

The bartender, without the slightest hint of a sigh or eye-roll (which would have been completely justified) nodded and went to get the drinks.

"How's Keli doing as Raythen?" Raythen asked to get the conversation started on a grounded topic.

"Terrible. She's getting her ass kicked. Lines are actually forming at the Dead Basilisk since word got out that you were on vacation. Although, she does have some acting skill . . . kind of a flare that she brings to Raythen's character, especially when she's groveling for mercy."

Raythen winced. The image of his creation and namesake groveling in front of a line of players made him a little sick. Edargo was probably exaggerating—he could look on the boards to see what was going on, but decided not to think about it. The drinks arrived. He took a sip of his water.

"So, what's going on with you?" Edargo asked now with genuine concern.

Raythen related to him the events of the past few days. He could tell that Edargo was looking up vids as he spoke. He was probably watching the flash musical with Astria. When he got to the part about being escorted off the military base, however, he had Edargo's full attention.

"What was the name of that reporter who was interviewing you?"

"Tray Wind."

"Really? You mean that cute elf across the bar?"

Raythen looked across the bar and saw an elf with short wavy blue hair looking straight at them. She had the anime styled elf ears—long and thin, sticking out at wide angles. Her eyes were about a third larger than normal human eyes, with bright green irises. He clicked on her and sure enough it was Tray Wind. She winked one of her huge eyes.

"You really are kind of clueless," Edargo said.

<Tray Wind: tell @Raythen> "Ready to finish that interview?"

Edargo said, "You guys are chatting, aren't you?"

<Raythen: tell @Tray Wind> "Maybe later. I'm talking with my friend."

"Open a channel," said Edargo. "I want to listen in."

<Tray Wind: tell @Raythen> "Let's get a booth."

She stood and walked over to their side of the bar, dressed in a smart blue dress-suit and carrying a glass of white wine. When she reached them she nodded her head to a booth against the wall. "Come on guys, join me for a drink."

Edargo was up like a shot and followed her to the booth, sitting across from her. Raythen got up and slowly skootched in next to Edargo.

Tray took a sip of her wine and gave them a dimply grin. "Heya fellas! Did you know that you two are the only non-Metas at this bar who are also not reporters?"

"I knew that!" said Edargo, as if he was answering a teacher's test question. "I myself thought that was a little odd and I, also, feel a little out of place because of it."

She leaned forward and whispered, "Are you guys VDF agents?"

Raythen coughed out a laugh. Edargo looked at him, annoyed, and said, "While we're not agents per se, it's not that we couldn't be, if that's what you wanted."

"What I want is a good story, a good *true* story. My instincts tell me that there's something going on with you two."

"Nothing going on between us," said Edargo. "We're just friends."

"Why are you talking like this?" Raythen said to Edargo. "You're spewing the worst clichés to this woman. Do you really want this kind of dialog in your movie?"

"You guys are making a movie?" Tray asked.

"Don't break the fourth wall." Edargo pointed at the wall.

"Fuck the wall."

"I just met this wall," Edargo said, patting it gently. "I'd have to get to know if first."

Raythen rolled his eyes.

"It's okay to be a cliché," Edargo said, "as long as you're the best cliché. If you're the person people think of when they think of a cliché, then that is immortality. And money."

"Are you telling me that you two came here to make a movie?" Tray asked. "A couple of NPCs? We are in the politically hottest spot on Venus right now, probably in the solar system. You *do* realize that the MetaChristian church hierarchy is meeting in this very hotel tonight to discuss how to react to the VDF cruiser shadowing the city."

"I did hear something about that," Edargo said.

"And while your records in the *Exo Arena* game are impressive, even champs such as yourselves couldn't afford this hotel."

"That's true," Edargo said. "My friend Raythen is here to meet his wealthy girlfriend for the first time in meat-space . . . and I am here to help him with the finer points of, you know, meat-space meeting."

Raythen glared at him.

"You know . . ." Edargo continued, despite his better judgment—when he started articulating a thought he felt obliged to finish it. ". . . because he's not as experienced as I am at meat-space . . . meetings. And we're making a movie about it."

"That's your story?" Tray said incredulously. "You're making a movie about a meat-space date? If she has all this money why aren't you meeting on New Tahiti?"

Edargo turned to Raythen. "Yeah! Why aren't we on New Tahiti? I've never been to New Tahiti. They have a wave pool."

Raythen felt like he was starting to die a little inside. He yearned to be with Sweet GG. He was supposed to be with her, the real her, upstairs in *their* hotel room. Their own private hotel room to spend *days* together. Not to be cross-examined by Edargo and some reporter elf. He felt the urge to do something physical, go jogging again maybe, but he was afraid he would be followed by the local militia. Lift weights—or maybe he should just sleep. He could go to sleep and escape for a few hours and maybe Sweet GG would be there when he woke up.

He was thinking about excusing himself when blue words flashed in front of him on his HUD. Words he had seen only a few times in his life.

NETWORK CONNECTION LOST

"Whoa," Edargo said. "Is this just me?"

"No, it's not," Tray said. She got a hungry little smile that Raythen has seen on people in the battlefield—from the kind of people you had to watch out for. "It's happening. It's starting right now."

"What's happening?" Raythen asked.

"What do you think," Tray said. "You were in the military. The assault is starting."

Of course! Raythen thought. If the VDF was making an assault they would point their jammers at the stratos to take out the wireless communications. The city defenders would turn on their own jammers to prevent the attackers from communicating with each other along frequencies that were in phase with their own jammer signals. All standard wireless communications would be down.

They heard audio from a loudspeaker, "ATTENTION. ATTENTION. EVERYONE IN THE HOTEL MUST PROCEED CALMLY TO THE NEAREST STAIRWELL AND GO DOWN TO THE HOTEL SHELTER. ONCE IN THE SHELTER YOU WILL BE GIVEN FURTHER INSTRUCTIONS. ATTENTION. ATTENTION."

Tray got out of the booth. "Come on guys, stay close to me. If you want to make some money you can be my camera men."

There was that welcome click in Raythen's mind, that click that meant that he had to be focused on everything around him instead of focusing on himself—and to think about solving immediate problems. The first problem was getting to the shelter. Red lighted arrows appeared on the floor, leading with rhythmic flashes to the opposite side of the bar where a door led to the stairwell. Some patrons were standing about, confused, while others where following the arrows.

"All right, let's go," Raythen said.

"How much money," Edargo said, gulping his drink down and staying close to Tray Wind.

Chapter 22

The hotel shelter was rectangular, the size of a large ballroom. People were filing in from the double doors, two sets of doors on each long wall, one set in the middle of each of the shorter walls. Rows of safety chairs lined the floor, but few were occupied. People clumped together and their low, nervous murmurs ebbed and flowed like ocean surf. The shelter was never used for any other purpose than emergencies and was sparse and safe with padded blue walls and a high ceiling that glowed with a warm white light. Two security guards were at each door; they were helmeted and wore half-exo armor—armor strapped on the body with servos at the joints—as opposed to full-exoskeletons with body suspension and plastimuscle. They were armed only with ouch-sticks that hung from their belts.

Tray Wind was focused. She had positioned the three of them in the main wide isle between the two sections of safety chairs.

"Edargo, your job is the close-up. If I'm talking to someone, you follow the conversation. Look at whoever is talking. Raythen, get the wide shots. Watch the groups, the doors; look for anything that might be of interest. You know what Theophilus looks like, right?"

His imp brought up a cached picture from a recent news story. "Right."

"Good. She should be here soon. If things are confused enough around her entourage I might be able to get a few questions in. That's the big money. We'll only have a short window of opportunity."

"How do you know she'll come here? Why not someplace more private?" Raythen asked.

"The subway is off that door in the back. If they are going to get someplace else safely they're coming through here first. There are at least fifty other reporters here. It's going to be a zoo." She gave a savage half-smile.

A voice boomed from a loudspeaker, "ATTENTION! ATTENTION! THIS IS NOT A DRILL. EVERYONE NEEDS TO TAKE A SEAT. PLEASE TAKE A SEAT IN THE SAFETY CHAIRS PROVIDED AND WAIT FOR FURTHER INSTRUCTIONS."

The room was filling up, with decreasing room for the jostling groups of people to move, but only a smattering of them obeyed and took seats. The muttering was getting louder.

"There she is," Raythen said. She was stepping out of the double doors at the closer end of the room. The security guards pulled out their ouch-sticks and held up their free hands, motioning people away. She was a tall African, her head visible above the bodyguard in front of her, her hair pulled back behind a smooth, rounded forehead. Her great dark eyes projected worry as they took in the scene of the crowded room. She seemed oblivious to the half dozen people who were following behind her and talking to each other with agitation. The security guards at the door started forward but then stopped, looking confused. They had probably been told to both watch the door and Theophilus, and she was making that difficult by moving quickly into the room.

All the reporters simultaneously saw their opportunity and jumped at it. Cries of "Theophilus! Theophilus!" drowned out the bodyguard who was yelling at everyone to get back.

"Come on!" Tray said and rushed in, Raythen and Edargo close behind. As they moved toward the growing mob their paths converged with two meaty looking male reporters, and one shouldered hard into Tray Wind, sending her stumbling to the side. Raythen kicked hard behind the man's knee and he crumpled to the ground. His partner gave Raythen a dirty look that Raythen return before continuing toward their common goal. Tray recovered and they joined the mob, about three layers away from Theophilus. Raythen had training with no-net conditions while in the VDF, but Edargo was clearly disoriented. Raythen jabbed his shoulder to get his attention, locked eyes on him, and then gave him some *Exo Arena* hand signals to indicate their next move. The confusion left Edargo's eyes as he understood, and they moved forward together positioning themselves in front of Tray, forcing their way through the jostling crowd, glaring down anyone who didn't like it. Tray Wind kept close to their backs.

Normally, a reporter rush was aided by augmented reality to maintain order, with each reporter's media outlet logo displayed over them and active chat to help them post questions to the interviewee. With the network jammers preventing normal reality augmentation, most of the reporters were at a loss at what to do beyond calling out Theophilus's name. Several were trying to improvise, remembering old movies where reporters would shout out questions, hoping to get picked for an answer. Most of the shouted questions were stuttered and confused until Tray Wind burst through the mob between Raythen and Edargo and said, "Tray Wind from Venus Salon. Ms. Theophilus, do you believe this network scramble is for psychological warfare or is it a prelude to a military assault?"

Theophilus, who had been turning her head side to side as if searching for someone, stopped and looked directly at Tray Wind.

"Excellent question," she said, and everyone quieted to hear her response. The question itself seemed to help Theophilus, allowing her to make a statement to the jittery crowd. Her face went from a questioning concern to that of determined authority. "I'm sure this is just psychological warfare. It would be insane for the VDF to make a physical assault on Corpus Christi. If everyone would just sit down and be patient I'm sure everything will be fine."

None of the reporters took her advice. Instead they all yelled out questions of their own simultaneously, creating a garbled din. Theophilus strained to hear, to pick out a question she could answer, but was clearly having trouble. She was trying to use this opportunity to calm the situation, but the reporters weren't cooperating. Frustrated by the coup pulled off by Tray Wind, the other reporters started moving forward slowly, forcing Theophilus to take a step back. Concern was washing back over her face.

Raythen's job was to take in the larger scene, so he was first to see the woman that stormed through the same door that Theophilus had come through. She was barefoot, wearing a tight black V-neck mini dress and running toward them with the kind of intensity that made Raythen brace himself involuntarily for an imminent attack. He wasn't far off the mark. She bowled herself through the crowd behind Theophilus and tore an ouch-stick from one of the security guard's hands. Positioning herself between Theophilus and the reporters, she swept the stick in front of her. It was then that Raythen recognized her.

"Get the FUCK back!" Astria yelled. "Get the fuck back or this is going up each and every one of your ASSHOLES! Get back NOW!"

The reporters didn't get back, but they did stop moving forward. Glancing at the disarmed security guard, Astria commanded, "Get Theophilus into that corner and get four more guards over here to make a perimeter around her. NOW!"

The security guard motioned to some of the guards at the other doors to come over. Theophilus said something to someone next to her that Raythen couldn't hear. Astria was examining the crowd, looking like she could leap at any one of them in an instant and tear out their throats with her teeth.

Slowly, Theophilus and her entourage moved into the corner that Astria had indicated.

"I don't want anyone outside our group coming within ten meters of her!" Astria ordered the guards that reached them. The reporters slowly started to back up, keeping their eyes on Theophilus, making sure their imps didn't miss anything good.

"Hey Raythen, isn't uberbitch that woman you danced with at the flash musical?" Edargo asked.

"Yeah."

"Cool."

"Did you get her entrance?" Tray asked excitedly. "Did you actually see her grab the ouch-stick?"

"Yeah."

"Outstanding," Tray said. "Great job gentlemen. Outstanding."

"Thanks," Edargo said. "I'm also available for weddings and bar mitzvahs."

Raythen groaned.

"What?" Edargo said. "I'll bet you every great comedic actor has said that line at least once in their career."

"How much do you want to bet?"

"Camera-men, attention," Tray said firmly.

A dozen men in half-exo armor jogged into the room toward Theophilus. On their shoulder patches they wore the cross and sword symbol of the Corpus Christi Militia. They carried MR-23 assault rifles at the ready and fortified the perimeter set up by Astria. They were followed by a bald man with a pronounced, hooked nose and a long, black beard. He was wearing fatigues and smart glasses.

"There's the big boss," Tray said. "Uzziah. Stay with him Raythen."

"On it."

Uzziah walked through the perimeter and went to talk to Theophilus.

"Fuck!" Tray Wind said.

"What?" said Raythen.

"Uzziah and Theophilus are facing the wall; I was hoping to read their lips."

Uzziah had turned Theophilus with a hand on her shoulder toward the wall before starting their discussion. Raythen instinctively phanded over Uzziah and got a negative buzz and another *Network Down* message.

"Who's Uzziah?" Edargo asked Tray.

"He's the leader of the CCM, the Corpus Christi Militia. Those smart glasses are connected to the local point-to-point network in the walls. They use laser-burst communications to keep in contact with each other. They are going to want to move her someplace soon. We have to stay with her as long as possible."

Uzziah's and Theophilus's discussion became more animated as they turned to face each other, providing a view of their profiles. Uzziah covered his mouth with his hand, but Theophilus's was visible. Raythen highlighted her face with his phand and told his imp to read lips.

126

". . . have any casualties . . . insane to risk . . . be bluffing . . ."

Uzziah once again put his hand on her shoulder and motioned her to face the wall.

Tray poked Raythen's arm. "We should get at different angles. You go to the far left. Edargo, move over to the far right. Watch them close."

Raythen nodded and started to move through the crowd. He was about halfway to his destination when the double doors at the wall he was approaching burst open. Two full exos walked in. Raythen immediately saw the VDF scallop shell logo on their shoulders. Their rail guns were holstered on their backs—they carried glob guns in their hands—wide barreled cannons that could shoot spheres of polymer glue the size of baseballs. One of them said with an amplified voice, "VDF! VDF! This is a police action! Everyone down on the ground now! Everyone down on the ground!"

There was an instant of silence and shock followed by the sound of someone letting out a quick scream of surprise. Most people who were standing fell to the floor. Raythen crouched, maintaining a clear view of the two exos as they advanced toward the corner, toward Theophilus and Uzziah. The CCM troops crouched and raised their assault rifles. Theophilus cried, "Don't shoot! Don't shoot! Civilians!"

Pops from the glob guns came fast as the CCM half-exos were thrown back from the impacts of the heavy polymer spheres that stuck to their armor, imparting their full momentum. Uzziah stood and stared, transfixed. Astria grabbed Theophilus's arm and yelled, "We have to get out now!" pulling her back toward the door they had arrived through. One of the VDF exos leaped forward ten meters, over the crowd and almost scraping the high ceiling, landing between them and the exit. There were more screams from the crowd. Astria grabbed Theophilus by the back of the neck and pushed her down forcefully to the ground, sending her flat on her face. She crouched over her as the VDF exo approached them. He ignored Astria and reached for Theophilus. With a wrathful grimace, Astria swung hard at the helmeted head with the ouch-stick. There was no way the operator of the exo could have felt it, yet the helmet flinched from the impact, from what must have been a surprised reflex action. She followed immediately with a wide swing of her leg into its side. Raythen had never seen or imagined seeing an unarmored person, let alone a woman in a black mini-dress, take on an exo trooper in hand-to-hand combat. The exo grabbed her leg and used it to swing her out of the way. She was sent airborne and landed meters away, sprawling into the crowd between safety chairs. Theophilus pushed herself up part way and stared into the blank face of the exo. The exo reached forward . . . and then stopped.

Everything in the room stopped for a second, because both exo troopers had become as motionless as statues, and by their inaction commanded the attention of everyone. Raythen held his breath . . . it seemed that everyone held their breath. Then the exo looked up. Although no face was visible on the helmet, it was pointing directly at Raythen. The exo trooper quickly stood up, and something in the tilt of the helmet indicated recognition.

Sarge?

The exo jumped directly toward Raythen. The people in between them dived out of way. Raythen sprung up, holding his hands in front of him, palms out. "Hey trooper, we'll cooperate fully—"

The exo lunged forward and grabbed Raythen's left hand. There was the sound of bones cracking. The pain came an instant later—Raythen had waited for it in the timeless fugue state that comes when things happen too fast to think. When the wave of pain did hit him his knees buckled; he was prevented from collapsing by the exo holding him up by his hand. He dangled, arm stretched up. Raythen's imp reduced the pain to something tolerable. The exo then ran for the door, violently jerking Raythen's arm—he was being dragged on his knees along the floor.

Chapter 23

There was nothing he could do. The exo was running through a wide hallway.

This shouldn't be happening.

There was no reason for this to be happening. Jumbled flashes of possible explanations swirled in his brain. Mistaken identity? Was he being rescued? Was he in danger?

Meanwhile, his hand was still being crushed as his body swung along with the exo's swinging arm. Raythen noticed that he was holding the exo's wrist with his free hand, taking pressure off his crushed hand. He gave the crushed hand a quick tug, hoping to free it. The exo squeezed harder.

They stopped at a metal door. The exo opened it and stepped inside, bringing Raythen with him. The lights came on as they entered. It was a storage room for housekeepers. Each housekeeper was a plain white cylinder about a half meter wide and two meters tall, balanced on one wheel. Most of the housekeepers were gone, leaving three rows of ten in the back of the room. The exo dragged Raythen to the back near the first row. Raythen balanced himself on his knees.

"Trooper!" Raythen yelled. He took a deep breath and said slowly, "I'm private first-class Dominic Rex. You can release me now."

The exo's helmet vanished, replaced by a holographic image of the head of the controller. Raythen stared back at his face, confused.

"Torvald!"

Torvald was laughing uncontrollably. Tears were streaming down his face. He looked at Raythen and tried to say something but was wracked by another bout of laughter. While his head was shaking back and forth, his exo body remained still.

The door opened. The other VDF exo stepped inside. Torvald cocked his head, listening. Even with jammers on, two exos could establish a point to point laser network as long as they had an unobstructed view of each other.

"No! No! You get back out and secure Theophilus!" Torvald ordered. He listened again, and then said "No! We don't have time! I'll save the vids. Get out there." The other exo went back out and shut the door behind him.

Torvald turned his head back to Raythen. He grinned and said, "You just have no idea how good this feels. No idea."

"Torvald, let go of my hand."

"I don't have much time," Torvald said and chuckled. "I have an important mission to get back to. I have to make this look like an accident." He glanced about before focusing on the closest housekeeper. "How about getting your head crushed by a housekeeper? That sounds like an accident."

Torvald suddenly turned toward the door. "No!" he yelled, dropping Raythen and reaching to grab the rail gun strapped to his back. As he swung it out, the door and much of the wall around it exploded. Raythen scurried into the housekeepers that zipped nimbly out of his way. He crawled to the back wall and lay flat on the floor. Above him housekeepers exploded and he heard quick *thunk thunks* as hypersonic rail gun pellets whizzed through the wall. He covered his head with his arms as debris rained on him. After a moment he heard the familiar staccato of pellets raining onto a prone exo. Then it was over.

Quiet. Exos were walking out there. One stepped on a fragment of housekeeper and cracked it. He heard the few undamaged housekeepers extend their tentacles and start vacuuming up the debris of their fellows. Then, right next to him, so close the voice exploded in his ear, a woman said, "Hey Raythen, you dead?"

Astria.

He pushed himself up from the floor with his good hand and bent his legs. As he put his weight on his left leg he felt a sharp pain through his thigh. He winced.

"Looks like you got hit," Astria said. "You should still be able to walk. As long as those pellets don't hit bone you don't get much serious damage. They just pass right through flesh. Clean wound."

"Yeah, I know," Raythen said, gritting his teeth and trying again to stand. His imp dulled the pain. Astria didn't offer to help him as he made it up to his feet. She looked at him stone-faced and said, "Of course you know. You are VDF after all. Follow me."

There were three militia exo troopers in the room. One was lying on his back near the wreckage of the wall. His mask had been shot up and was seeping red. Another exo was crouched over him. The third was looking at Raythen, KR-79 at the ready. Astria turned and started walking. Raythen looked down at the scattered pieces of Torvald's destroyed exo. It was empty—no body, no blood, nothing. Astria stopped at the gaping hole in the wall where the door had been and glared at Raythen. He followed.

In the hallway there were two more full exos and several half-exos. Astria motioned to a half-exo to come with them. Looking down the hallway toward the shelter Raythen saw a crowd of civilians watching with interest and apprehension. He didn't see Edargo or Tray Wind among them. Astria grabbed his arm and pulled him in the opposite direction.

"There's a first-aid station down here," she said flatly.

It was a small station with just four hospital beds. There was no one else in the room. Raythen approached the bed and was about to lay down when Astria said, "No, over here," motioning to a small table in the corner with two metal chairs. He sat down with his back to the wall and placed his shattered hand on the table. It had swollen to comic proportions; red, black, and blue. The fingers were at unnatural angles.

The half-exo remained standing. Astria went to a locker and rummaged around.

"I really can't be fighting in a battle zone in this little black dress," she said, more to herself than to either of them. "As good as it looks it's really not very practical. Ah! This is it."

She turned around holding a flat sheet of white material wrapped in clear plastic. The label on it said HAZMAT SUIT. She tossed it on the table in front of Raythen and then peeled off her black dress, standing in front of them casually wearing only a black thong. The half-exo face was not visible through his helmet, but his body betrayed embarrassment as he turned quickly away. Astria tore the clear plastic from the HAZMAT suit, the white material becoming semi-goopy in her hands. She dropped it on her head. Like a living thing it spread itself down her neck, over her bare shoulders, breasts, and torso. It went down the full length of her arms to cover her hands. When it reached her ankles she lifted each foot one at a time so it could cover the bottoms. It was a thin veneer of covering that would do no help for modesty, though Raythen guessed modesty was not an issue with this woman. Her face was left uncovered by the suit, but it did form a hood. She pulled the hood off of her head and ruffled her hair a bit, and then sat down across from him. The half-exo, still apparently embarrassed, did not look at her, but was now facing directly toward Raythen.

"These outfits are really made to be worn over clothes," she said absently. "But in situations like this you have to make do." She folded her hands together on the table. "Now—"

The door opened and two half-exos came in carrying a man in red overalls and no face. The man from the downed exo. The half-exos put the body on the far bed. Their visors were up so you could see the anger on their faces. Monitors lit up around the bed.

"He went for the head," one of the militia members said. "Just the head. He was in an RC and he's going for the head of a manned exo. I can't believe he went for the head."

"There's nothing we can do," the other said.

"There's nothing left of the brain. He can't be saved. He went for the head."

"Godless bastards. No respect for life."

They glared briefly at Raythen while the dead man bled into his pillow—then left the room.

"Okay, Private Dominic Rex," Astria said, knocking twice on the table to make sure she had his attention. "*Dominic Rex*, that is one great name. Like the name of an action hero, or maybe a secret agent. Anyway, I have some questions. First question; why did the VDF have to extract you from the shelter? What was so important?"

"What?" Raythen said, confused. He looked at his hand. It seemed very large and important there on the table. "My hand—"

"Fuck your hand," Astria said evenly. "Why did the VDF bypass Theophilus, who is by everyone's estimation the primary target of this operation, and instead extract *you* from the shelter? Do you have some crucial information for them? What is it?"

For Raythen, the air became crystalline, with him trapped in it, a fly in amber surrounded by people who hated him. This was unfair, this shouldn't be happening, but it was. If he could explain, if they understood . . . but even he didn't understand.

"The trooper who tried to kill me is called Torvald." His voice shook. "He wanted to crush my head with a housekeeper. I think he's insane."

This didn't make sense to Raythen, and he knew, as he said the words, that they sounded ridiculous. There was also the other VDF exo, the one who had entered the room briefly. How could two troopers be complicit in attempted murder?

"So you admit you know the trooper?" Astria said. "Good, that's a good start. Just so you know, my brain tends to filter out bullshit, so the only thing I heard you say was the trooper's name. Which is Torvald. Everything else was blah blah blah. Why did Torvald want to get you out of the shelter? I'm guessing it had something to do with the jammers. Did you give the VDF the carrier frequencies for our jammers?"

"No! No. I don't know the carrier frequencies. If I could just give you access to my vids I could show you what happened. I could show you Torvald."

"It's too bad that the jammers are up and you can't show me your vids. Oh wait! If you know both the VDF frequencies and our frequencies you could bypass the jammers and show me the vids. Okay! Show me the vids."

"There's got to be a direct link to the hardwire network here somewhere. Plug me in and I'll prove it to you."

Astria shook her head. "And now you're trying to convince me that a covert VDF agent couldn't possibly have fake vids in his imp. I don't know how that got through my filter. Dominic—or Raythen, I guess you usually go by Raythen—I don't have time for this bullshit. You folks somehow got two exos down to this shelter minutes after the hull was breached. The only way that could have happened is if they were already stashed on board. So right there we know that our security was compromised prior to invasion. We also know the exos were unmanned, which gives us two possibilities as to how they were being controlled. One, the VDF is riding our carrier frequency. Two, the VDF has hacked the hardwire point-to-point network. We don't really give a fuck about our carrier frequency because we can't use it, since the VDF is also jamming. But the point-to-point network—that is our primary advantage as a defender. If that is compromised we need to know. We need to know badly."

"But he crushed my hand!" Raythen said with exasperation.

"Fuck your hand." Astria held up her own left hand. "This is my third hand. Best damn hand I've ever had." She slapped it hard on the table and thought for a moment. "You know, *you're* going to need a new one. Hold on one second, maybe we can get you ready for that."

She got up and went back to the locker. She returned with a small first aid kit. Sitting back down and opening it up she pulled out a scalpel. Her expression became mischievous.

"Ah, very good. Raythen, to make way for your new hand we're going to have to remove that one. The problem with that is I don't know for the life of me how to make a tourniquet. It would take a while for me to hack through the wrist with this little knife and you just might bleed to death."

She reached forward and grabbed Raythen's hand. He felt broken bones moving freely under her tight grasp. She held the blade of the scalpel millimeters over the veins of his wrist.

"I know what you're thinking," she said. "You're thinking about how long it would take for your buddies to get here after you bleed to death. How much damage would happen to your brain before they brought you back?" She looked at him intently. "What if there was no brain? What if there was no way for them to bring you back, like that martyr on the cot there." The blade of the scalpel touched the edge of his skin.

The half-exo grabbed Astria's arm and pulled it up. She turned to him and opened her mouth to say something, but stopped. The half-exo said, "I'm sorry ma'am. I can't be a party to the torture or death of a civilian by another civilian."

After a couple seconds she found her voice and said, "I think you're taking the good cop role a bit too far, corporal."

"No ma'am, you have no authority over me. I was told to assist you, but you've crossed the line. Keep in mind that everything I see here is being transmitted to Command." He looked up at the ceiling; Astria followed the direction of his faceplate to a small black dot. The dot that connected him with emergency point-to-point network. He released her arm.

"Very well corporal. If you insist on playing nice, call your commanding officer and get your orders on how to proceed."

"That won't be necessary," a voice said from the door.

Chapter 24

Uzziah strode into the room, followed by Theophilus and two more half-exos. He went right up to Astria and said, "The corporal is quite right. You have gone too far. I know you're some sort of big shot on Terra, but here—" Astria stood to face him and he looked at her outfit. "What—" he stammered, "what are you wearing?"

She looked down, and Raythen saw her become embarrassed for the first time. She crossed her arms over her breasts, the rubbing of the plasticene material making little squeaky noises. She looked back up at Uzziah and said, "It's better than that black dress, in a fight anyway."

Theophilus went to Raythen and touched him gently on the arm. "You're injured," she said. Raythen latched onto and drank in the kindness on her face. "Stand up," she said, and he obeyed thoughtlessly. "Let's get that taken care of." She brought him to the nearest bed and had him sit down. Astria and Uzziah continued to argue at the edge of his perception. Theophilus stared at the wall behind the bed and then shook her head in frustration. "I can't phand it with the jammers on. Got to use voice commands." She cleared her throat and said, "Computer, using voice commands for diagnosis of patient Dominic Rex."

A flat female voice responded, "The patient has multiple bone fractures to the left hand and a puncture wound to the upper left leg, piercing the vastus medialis." A section of the wall opened up, revealing a hole big enough for Raythen's arm. "The optimal treatment for the hand is amputation and replacement. Amputation cannot be performed without a licensed doctor present, so it is suggested that a cast be applied until a licensed doctor can be reached. Please place your left arm into the hole, up to the elbow." Raythen leaned forward and put his arm in the hole. Air bags inflated around the arm, keeping it still. There was a *shvump* sound and the bags deflated.

"You may remove your arm," the computer said.

Raythen's hand was encased in a shiny white mitten that stopped at his wrist. Rigid as steel. Theophilus looked down at him with a little sympathetic smile of concern. The two half-exos were close at hand behind her.

"You go by Raythen, right?" she said. Her voice had a near mystical ability to sooth. "Why did that exo trooper do this to you?"

His view misted and he sniffed as he leaned back on the bed. He wanted to curl up and cry. To fall into her and cry and beg for mercy and protection. But he couldn't do that. He couldn't break down. Situational awareness. *Scan, plan, react. Scan, plan, react.* He was in danger. *Scan.* He was in a small room with Theophilus, the leader of the religious group that was under siege by the VDF. She was protected by two half-exos. Behind one of the half-exos, on the table, was a scalpel. He thought about the scalpel. *Take her as a hostage? Can I get her under my control before they could react?* Astria and Uzziah were also still in the room. He only had one good hand. Of all the people in the room, Astria worried him the most. She had attacked an exo trooper. She would not respond well if he tried to take Theophilus hostage.

He then realized that he was still under interrogation and that Theophilus was the *real* good cop. *She thinks I have information they need.*

If they believed that he had important information then he had a bargaining chip. *But how to use it? Pretend to be a spy? Promise information for protection?* The other alternative was a truth that they wouldn't believe. *Act.* Don't freeze up. Say what she wants to hear.

"I can help you," he said.

"Good, we need your help."

But there was another little problem. He was a terrible liar, especially in meat-space. So, really, the only thing left was the unbelievable truth.

"I know one of the VDF troopers. The one who grabbed me. His name is Torvald. I know this sounds crazy, but he wants to kill me."

"Why does he want to do that?" There was no incredulity in her face. Only unjudgmental listening.

"I think he's jealous of me and my girlfriend."

She nodded. "Okay. Okay."

Uzziah came over to the bed and said to Theophilus, "We have to go. We have to get you into hiding. It's time for me and my militia to fight them. It's God's will that today is the day we make our stand against the unbelievers."

Theophilus looked at him, stone-faced. "You say it's God's will for today, but I won't tell you God's will for today . . . until tomorrow."

"God's will is God's will. We have to go." As Uzziah reached for her arm she turned back to Raythen and said, "You need to stay here." She left the first aid station with Uzziah and Astria. The two half-exos who stayed behind took up sentinel positions on each side of the door.

Raythen's leg was still untreated. He said, "Computer, what should I do about my leg wound?"

"In the cabinet on the second shelf from the top there is an applicator for durmapolymer. It is clearly marked. Remove your pants and apply the

durmapolymer to the entrance and exit wounds, covering them
completely."

"Right," Raythen said. He went to the cabinet and found the
applicator. He unbuttoned and unzipped his pants, glancing at the guards.
He didn't want to ask for their help, and they probably wouldn't give it
anyway. With his one good hand he tugged his pants until he finally got
them down to his ankles, revealing his red Jeefs, and sat back down. It was
easy enough to apply the durmapolymer to the entrance wound. He had to
twist his leg around to see the exit wound, but the pants at his ankles were
restricting his movements. Using his feet he pushed his shoes off at the
heels and shook away his pants. Putting his bad leg up on the bed he found
the exit wound and treated it.

Chapter 25

The door opened and Edargo and Tray Wind were led inside by a half-exo who said, "Stay here," and left. The two sentries didn't move.

"Hey," Edargo grinned, and then caught sight of the dead militia trooper on the cot. His head whipped around to look at it when he realized what it was. "Holy fuck!" he said, bending over to get a closer look. "Holy fuck! Look at his face! His face is gibbed! Holy fuck!"

One of the sentries moved between Edargo and the dead man, shoving him back. "Show some respect! He was a friend of mine."

"Sorry bro," Edargo said, then turned toward Raythen and silently mouthed, "That's a dead body."

Tray Wind leaned close to Raythen's ear and whispered, "Please tell me you witnessed his death."

"Nope. I went for cover."

"Too bad. That would have been a Pulitzer for sure." She then looked at his hand. "Are you okay?"

"Yeah bro," Edargo said, "That exo must have really messed up your hand. And why are you in your Jeefs?"

"I got a leg wound in the firefight."

Edargo glanced back at the corpse. "What the hell happened with that exo?"

Raythen felt better talking to them; time and space seemed to be moving at their normal speeds again. "You're not going to believe this. Torvald is in the VDF. He's the one who took me."

"No way."

"Yes." Things were too serious to respond with another 'way'.

"No way." Edargo had different views on 'serious'.

"Who's Torvald?" Tray asked.

"He's a friend of Raythen's girlfriend," Edargo said. "They play on the same team in *Exo Arena*. Yeah. So Torvald grabbed you. Wow. Wait! Did Torvald kill that dude on the bed?"

"Yeah."

"No way!"

"Hold on guys," Tray said. "We need to do this right. We can still get that Pulitzer. I need a proper interview format for the package. Raythen, look at me, okay?"

He looked at her.

"Nobody speak unless I ask them a direct question, okay?"

"Okay," Raythen said, "But can I put my pants on first?"

"Oh, of course," Tray said, and gave a nervous giggle. "I suppose you wouldn't want to be interviewed in your Jeefs."

Raythen reached down and tried to pull his pants on with one hand. He then gave up and said, "Edargo?"

"Hey bro, we're close friends, but . . . aah, whatthehell." He bent down and helped Raythen pull up his pants. Raythen stepped into his shoes and put some weight experimentally on his bad leg. There was some weakness but it didn't buckle.

"Are you okay to sit at the table?" Tray asked.

"Sure."

They all sat down, Tray Wind facing the door, Raythen sitting directly across from her. Raythen thought this interview might be a good idea; it might help bring everything he had experienced into some sort of rational perspective. He could certainly use a dispassionate view now.

"This is Tray Wind of Venus Salon interviewing Dominic Rex in a first aid station in the Corpus Christi stratos. Players of *Gryphon's Claw* and *Exo Arena* might know Mr. Rex better as Raythen, since he's a professional NPC in both of those venues. At 20:34 CPT today, Mr. Rex was captured by a VDF exo trooper. Mr. Rex, in your own words, can you describe what happened after you were taken from the hotel shelter?"

"Yes, um, I was dragged out by my hand into the hallway and um, brought to a storage room." Raythen played back the events on his HUD as he spoke. "I don't understand why I was brought there. He crushed my hand."

"Did the trooper speak to you?

"Yes. Yes he did. He was laughing. He said he was going to kill me. Make it look like an accident."

"No way," Edargo said. Tray gave him a stern look, and then turned back to Raythen.

"What did he say exactly?"

"He said, 'You just have no idea how good this feels. No idea.' But before that he spoke to the other trooper."

"The other trooper?"

"Yes." Raythen paused in thought.

Tray waited a moment and asked, "What did he say to the other trooper?"

Raythen focused back on Tray Wind and said, "That really doesn't make sense. There's no way that an RC exo in the VDF could commit a murder and get away with it. Maybe…maybe a manned exo that was jammed from the network. Every RC exo is under direct observation by a superior officer during an operation. Every one. A manned exo in a jammed environment could get away with murder, but it would be recorded by the suit. He would get caught afterward. There's no way to make it look like an accident. But there wasn't only one trooper, there were two. And he was going to save the vids!"

"Slow down a bit please," Tray said. "Are you saying that the VDF trooper was RC?"

"Yes, the suit was empty. I saw that it was hollow after the battle."

"You're getting ahead of yourself, Mr. Rex. What was the first thing that happened after you and the exo trooper entered the storage room?"

Raythen ignored the question and continued to think aloud. "If he had the choice to save the vids then he had the choice to erase the vids. But that's impossible! If the VDF had the jammer carrier signal, everything Torvald was doing would be open to view by his commanding officer. The vids would have to be saved. But let's say they have access to the city hardwire network from a hidden location, only those in the hidden location would have access to the vids. If they were both at the same communication node then both would have access to each other's vids. No need to save the vids. And the other trooper wanted to watch . . . me . . . get . . . killed? Another member of Team GG? At two locations on Corpus Christi? He had an important mission to get back to. They were both off mission. It makes no sense."

"Could we go back to the point when you and the trooper entered the storage room?" Tray asked, more insistently this time.

"Are you sure it was Torvald?" asked Edargo. "Seriously? The guy's a total boffin. You ever have a conversation with him? Always talking numbers and science and shit."

That was true. All of Team GG were boffins. And Sweet GG was the biggest boffin of all.

Sweet GG! What was her role in all of this? He was on Corpus Christi because of her. Had Torvald known he was going to be there? Where was she? They were just a bunch of research scientists and engineers.

The exo had been empty.

They all turned their heads to the door when they heard a muffled explosion followed by the sounds of assault rifles. The two guards put their rifles at the ready and turned to face each other. Then there were the loud pops and cracks from rail guns. One of the guards pointed at them and ordered, "Stay here!" before they both rushed out of the room.

For several seconds the three of them remained motionless. Then Tray Wind shot out of her seat and went to the door. She turned to them and said, "We don't actually have to do what they say!"

Chapter 26

Tray Wind was reaching for the door when it swung inward, hitting her full in the face. She reeled backwards as Astria rushed into the room. Raythen stood and she turned her eyes to lock onto his. In her hand was a blue cylindrical object about the size of a large cucumber. She held it in front of her as she came toward him, shouting, "What the fuck is this thing?"

She grabbed his collar with one hand and dug the object hard into his cheek. "What the fuck is it?"

Edargo stood and moved around behind her. "Hey lady—" he managed to say before one of her feet caught the side of his head, sending him sprawling. Raythen was bending backward over the table away from her. She pulled the object away from his face, getting ready to thrust it hard into his gut.

Scalpel time.

As she swung the object forward he swept his right hand behind him, scooping up the scalpel and spinning to get behind her. She ducked and pivoted as he tried to wrap is left arm around her throat. He felt the strange blue object in Astria's hand hit him hard in the kidney. He jumped back and there was an instant when they adjusted into their stances. He put the scalpel into a reverse hammer grip. He thought she would probably start with a kick, but instead she bounced forward in a crouched boxing stance.

Raythen powered into her, aiming his right knee for her face. She managed to deflect his knee and get some body blows into him. He slashed the scalpel across her forehead—she grabbed his wrist but he got the result he wanted—blood was flowing into her eyes, blinding her. She moved with greater ferocity, bringing her own knee into his groin. After the flash of pain she kicked him square in the chest, sending him flying backwards into one of the beds. He propped up against it with his elbow and shakily worked his feet underneath him. She paused to wipe the blood away from her eyes. Edargo was lurching unsteadily behind her, reaching with both hands to grapple her. She glanced back and sent an elbow into his nose. He went back down. While she was momentarily distracted by Edargo, Raythen moved forward and swung the cast on his left hand into the side of her head. She reeled. He tried to follow up with another swing but she ducked and came in underneath it. He met her face with his right fist. As her head bounced back he hit the side again with his cast. She stumbled into the table, turning her body away from Raythen to brace herself against it. Raythen went in behind her, wrapping his left arm around her neck, using his weight to fold her body over the table. He moved the scalpel to the forward hammer grip and pointed it at her eye.

"Stop or you're dead," he panted.

"If I had a nickel . . ." she said.

"What?"

"Nevermind."

There was an awkward moment while they breathed, their lungs heaving, blood from her forehead dripping onto the table. Finally, he said, "What is that thing you were hitting me with?"

"That's what I came here to find out."

"Did you find it in the VDF exo?"

"Of course."

Raythen had a theory.

"I think I know how the VDF is controlling their exos."

"Really?" Astria said. "I'm not surprised."

"Yeah. I'm going to let you go now. And if you don't attack me, I will tell you."

"Bad idea bro," Edargo said nasally from the corner, holding his bloody nose.

"Do we have a deal?" Raythen asked.

"Deal," she replied.

Raythen stood and backed away. She straightened up, grabbing the first aid kit and removing some gauze. She turned toward him, wiping blood from her face.

"My theory, and it's only a theory—I don't know for sure because I'm not a spy or anything—is that the cylinder *is* Torvald, or at least a copy of him."

"AI?" Astria asked.

"No, A-Con."

"I don't think so," Tray said. She was standing by the door, swaying uncertainly. "Using unsupervised A-Cons in a battlefield situation would get the UP in huge trouble. They would be breaking dozens of laws."

"Actually," Astria said, "it's not that clear cut. AIs yes. Any AI in the battlefield needs a person who is at least observing it with a hand on the kill switch. But the legal status of A-Cons is a nebulous area of the law right now. A lot of people are arguing for giving any sufficiently advanced A-Con all the legal privileges of personhood."

"It's the only way I can make sense of what happened," Raythen said. "Sweet GG and Torvald make A-Cons for a living. She was working on a top-secret project. This is probably it. They created A-Cons, probably based on their own neural patterns. What you have in your hand is a copy of Torvald, sent here to capture Theophilus. But then he saw me and went off mission."

"Yeah, that's the part I'm having trouble with," Astria said. "Let's assume the UP and VDF decided to use A-Cons to capture Theophilus, stashing some exos here in Corpus Christi with the plan to snatch her up right at the beginning of hostilities. That doesn't sound like a bad plan. She goes to the shelter, they know where she is. The A-Con exos go in and grab her with the idea of rushing her out to some pre-arranged meeting point to get her onto the cruiser. It all sounds reasonable. But, instead of doing what they were trained to do, what they were *created* to do as you say, they instead go on a murderous side-trip against what, a romantic rival? That, I have trouble with."

"It's the only thing that makes sense," Raythen said.

"To you," Astria said, "the guy who threatened to kill me a minute ago."

"There's one way we can really find out," Edargo said. "We can ask Torvald."

They all looked at the blue cylinder in Astria's hand.

Chapter 27

They walked through the main aisle between the safety chairs in the hotel emergency shelter, which was now empty of people. Raythen and Astria led, with Tray and Edargo right behind. Several of the chairs in the shelter had been destroyed and there were impact holes in the walls, as well as blood splatter.

"Two more VDF exos came in while you were under guard," Astria said. "Two more of your supposed pre-planted A-Cons. VDF redundancy in action. But this time we were ready for them. Theophilus has been moved to another location. They're going to have to work hard to get to her now."

"Where is she?" Tray asked.

"Ha!" Astria laughed. "Not a chance. I'm still not convinced that Raythen's not a VDF agent."

"Why him, why not me?" Edargo asked nasally through his swollen nose.

"Because he beat me in hand-to-hand. Sure, he had a weapon and you distracted me, but even with those advantages it's still impressive."

"And what makes you so tough?" Tray asked.

"Because my God is a kickass God who demands results from his subjects. My God looks down on you soft amoral seculars in disgust while eating the Flying Spaghetti Monster with a nice glass of Chianti." She looked back at Tray. "You, I've read your stuff. While you're secular as hell, you're not pro-UP by any stretch. But Ray here, he has mad skills. Even though the reverse hammer grip was a poor choice to fight with a scalpel."

Raythen spun his head toward her, away from the battle damage he had been looking at. "What? It worked, didn't it? What would you have used?"

"Forward saber."

Raythen snorted. "I would have disarmed you."

"Alright," she said. "After this is over, we meet at dawn—with dueling scalpels."

He stopped walking. Everyone else stopped as well. "If you still think I'm an UP agent, why are you talking so chummy right now?"

"Because," she said, "as long as you're with me, you're not going after Theophilus. And we're investigating the cylinder. If this Torvald of yours is really in here, the militia will need to know that these exos they're fighting aren't hooked into any network. We can continue using the hardwire net and maintain our defensive advantage. So let's hurry up and get to the subway. And stay a little ahead, I don't want to get a surprise bonk on the head with that cast of yours."

"This way?" he asked, pointing to the doors they were facing.

"Yeah, right through there."

They entered the subway terminal. A glass wall separated them from the railway. As they approached the glass a single cylindrical rail car zipped through the tunnel and stopped in front of them. A section of the glass wall lifted and the car door slid open. They stepped inside and sat down on the comfy couches—Raythen and Edargo sitting across from Astria and Tray.

"This is like a weird double date," Edargo said. "I'll take the cute elf, you can have the uberbitch."

Everyone ignored him. Astria said, "Car, take us to the nearest AI lab."

"The nearest AI lab is at the Fortuluse Research facility on the twelfth floor," the car answered. "It is fourteen minutes walking distance from the nearest subway terminal. Since both the wireless and wired networks are down, would you like me to give you verbal directions?"

"The wired network is down?" Astria said, surprised.

"Yes," the car replied.

"Fuck. Car, get going to Fortuluse. And yes, give me the verbal directions. Fuck."

After the car finished giving them directions Astria said, "I can't believe Uzziah shut down the hardwire net already. The idiot. If you're right about Torvald being an A-Con then he just gave away our only shot at winning this. And even if we do confirm this A-Con theory, the only way we can contact him is sneaker-net. Fuck."

After a moment, Tray said to Astria, "Do you mind if I ask what your real name is?"

"Yes, I do mind. I'm going to remain anonymous while in the presence of potential enemies."

"Okay, well, just so you know I've been trying to figure it out. I'm guessing you must have had a body-mod either right before or right after you got here, because you don't match the physical descriptions of anyone on the public roster who's travelled here in the past couple months."

"And what makes you think I arrived within the past couple months?"

"I talked to one of the guards who took us to the first aid station. He said you were some hot-shot lawyer sent from Terra specifically to deal with the legal issues from the new psychiatric classification of hyper-anthropomorphization disorder. He said that since you arrived you've been a big headache for Uzziah, trying to dictate a strategy for dealing with the UP. Are you Theophilus's official legal counsel?"

Raythen felt a shift in momentum as the car became an elevator and began descending to the twelfth floor. He gingerly touched some of the swollen lumps that Astria had granted to his face. She might be a hot-shot lawyer, but she was also a kick-ass fighter.

"I plead the fifth for now," Astria said. "But I promise that after this is over I will give you a full interview."

The rail car stopped and they got off at the twelfth-floor station. They were in the midst of the industrial underground of the city—metallic, sterile, and purely functional. It was completely abandoned; all hands had gone to the nearest shelters. They walked through the wide corridors lit by red emergency lights. There were no signs, the walls and doors were blank, but their imps remembered the verbal directions given by the car.

Chapter 28

The first few rooms of the AI lab looked like nothing more than lounges; containing couches, chairs, and small tables. They spent several minutes searching down different hallways before they found the room they wanted. It contained workbenches with racks of tools for intricate electronics work and cables coming out of the table-tops linked to various small devices. On the walls were large video screens. Astria went to the nearest workbench and tapped it—a touch screen interface with keyboard appeared.

"Good, it's live," she said. She put the cylinder down on the workbench and typed in some commands, and after a moment the video screen on the wall displayed the Fortuluse logo. She sat down and got to work. Tray Wind stood behind her to get a close view at what she was doing. Raythen and Edargo grabbed some chairs—rolling them out and sitting down.

"She looks like she knows what she's doing," Edargo said.

"Yeah," Raythen replied. "She knows what she's doing."

"But what are we going to do?"

"We're going to stay close to her and do what she says."

"I think we have to get the fuck off this stratos," Edargo said emphatically. "This whole place is insane. I mean really insane."

"My primary goal is to keep away from any VDF troopers," Raythen said, watching Astria. "Any one we meet might be a copy of Torvald, and I can't take the chance of him seeing me. I don't want to give him another chance to try to kill me."

"Yeah, but didn't psycho-religious-freak-bitch try to kill you too? I mean, this is an asylum and I'm beginning to think *I'm* the sanest person here—which really scares the hell out of me. We need out."

"What scares *me* is that Sweet GG is a part of this. This whole invasion is the project she was working on. I'm sure of that now, and she sent me here. Why would she send me here?"

Astria pulled a cable up from the work bench and plugged it into the cylinder. "Alright," she said, "this here is a diagnostic station for AI modules. Fortunately the same interface is used for A-Con modules. This Torvald of yours should have a fully functional sensory-motor homunculus. If everything works out right he should appear in a virtual prison cell I set up for him." The video screen in front of her displayed a room with metal walls, the viewing angle positioned at one of the ceiling corners. It was empty. "Okay, let's give it a few seconds . . ."

Torvald materialized in the center of the room. He was wearing blue VDF coveralls. Astria turned to Raythen. "Does he look familiar?"

"That's him," Raythen said. Torvald looked at the walls, first to his left, then to the right. Apprehension was clearly etched on his face for a moment before becoming blank as he stood at attention, putting his hands straight down his sides.

Tray bounced from barely contained excitement. "We should question him," she said. "I should do it; I've been trained to do interviews. I'll get him to tell us what he knows."

"He's not going to tell you anything," Astria said. "He's aware that he's part of an operation that is legally questionable at best. Anything he says could reflect badly on the UP. But he isn't my primary concern at the moment." Her eyes burned into Raythen's. He returned her gaze. Several uncomfortable moments passed.

"I know you guys can't be texting each other so you're freaking me out," Edargo said. "Just say something."

Although Astria's eyes were still on Raythen, she responded to Edargo. "Behind you is a headset. I want Raythen to go in and talk to Torvald. I want to see how the two of them interact."

Edargo rose mechanically and picked up a stretchy knit skull-cap off a workbench. He held it up quizzically and said "I haven't seen one of these since I was a teenager." Astria nodded toward Raythen. Edargo held it toward him and said, "Your call bro."

"Let Edargo put the head-set on you," Astria ordered Raythen. "I already scanned you in for the avatar. Have a chat with your old buddy."

"What do you want me to ask him?" Raythen asked suspiciously.

"Whatever comes to mind."

Raythen wasn't all that keen on being trapped, even if just virtually, with the person (entity? creature?) who had so recently tried to kill him. Still, he desperately wanted answers.

"Alright," Raythen said.

Edargo fit the head-set tightly over his skull. Raythen then leaned back and closed his eyes. The chair automatically reclined and held him as he felt the familiar sensation of his body being torn away from itself and becoming incorporeal for a moment before coalescing in a virtual world.

He was standing in front of Torvald, face to face and within arm's reach. Torvald's eyes went wide for a moment and he stepped back, clearly surprised to see him. Yet there was something more to the expression of surprise that made Raythen look down at himself—his avatar was naked except for a bright red thong. He turned his face up at the corner where he guessed the viewing angle was and gave Astria a dirty look. He then turned back to Torvald who was now standing as still as a statue.

"You work for the VDF," Raythen said firmly. No response. "You tried to kill me. Why?" Still nothing. "I figured out that you're an A-Con based on the real Torvald. You were sent here to covertly apprehend Erin Theophilus, but you went after me instead. You wanted to kill me. Tell me why." Still nothing. "Tell me why!" he shouted.

With an emotionless monotone Torvald said, "I am the AI interface for unit UE-276. This unit is the property of Venus Defense Force. If you return this unit to the nearest representative of the Venus Defense Force you will be financially compensated."

"Oh no," Raythen said. "No you don't. I know you're in there. You were surprised before. I saw it in your face. You're in there!"

"I am programmed for emotional responses to facilitate human interactions. If you return this unit to the nearest representative of the Venus Defense Force you will be financially compensated."

<Astria: tell @Raythen> "I think he can feel pain. Try hitting him."

<Raythen: tell @Astria> "What makes you think he can feel pain?"

<Astria: tell @Raythen> "Assuming this is an A-Con and assuming it's copied from a human, the main module would be replicated from neural patterns. His imp would be in a separate module. This avatar in front of you is directly linked to the sensory motor homunculus of the main module. I've blocked off the other modules so I don't think he has access to his imp."

<Raythen: tell @Astria> "If you have access to his imp you can replay when he attacked me."

<Astria: tell @Raythen> "There are several other modules. I'm a lawyer, not an A-Con engineer. I found this one easily enough because it's the primary. The point is, you can hurt this guy, and if you're telling the truth I think you'd want to."

<Raythen: tell @Astria> "I'm not amused by the thong."

<Astria: tell @Raythen> "Purely strategic. I wanted to see if I could elicit an emotional response."

Raythen did want to hurt Torvald, the real Torvald, the one responsible for this. But all he had was this thing, this shadow of Torvald. And yet this shadow shared the same desire to kill him as the real Torvald. He had the same emotions, the same understanding. And there he was, pretending to be nothing more than an AI. Raythen remembered the laugh he had made when he was about to kill him. Torvald could feel sadistic glee.

Raythen pulled back his fist and swung into Torvald's face as hard as he could. He felt the satisfying, fleshy thwack as his fist crashed into Torvald's nose. Torvald reeled back and then immediately straightened into his previous position. Raythen punched him again. There was a crack as Torvald's nose broke. He came back into position a little slower this time. His eyes were blinking as blood poured out of his nose.

"Why do you want to kill me?" Raythen yelled and hit him again. "Why? Is this about Sweet GG? Why did she tell me to come here?" He punched him again. "Where is she? Where is she?"

Torvald head was swaying from the impacts. Slowly a smile came on his lips underneath the blood. "You're an idiot," he rasped. "You have no idea about Sweet GG. You don't know her at all. You're just some stupid fucking NPC. The only thing about you that deserves any attention at all is that you're a little faster than most people, a little cleverer at fighting. You're a talented trained monkey who can barely comprehend what she and I share together."

"You and her," Raythen laughed. "You're not even the real Torvald. You're a copy. Maybe the real Torvald has something with her, but not you. You're expendable. You're the one who's nothing."

"The real Torvald? What does that mean? We're all the real Torvald!" He lunged at Raythen who side-stepped and elbowed hard into his ribs. As Torvald stumbled Raythen kicked him in the back, sending him to the floor onto his face. Torvald might be a decent exo trooper but his hand-to-hand combat needed work. Raythen planted a foot between his shoulders and grabbed his left wrist, pulling his arm straight up. He got a grip around Torvald's little finger.

"Where is Sweet GG and what does she have to do with this?" Raythen asked and broke the little finger. Torvald howled. Raythen grabbed the ring finger. "Where is Sweet GG and what does she have to do with this?" He broke the ring finger.

"You're a monkey!" Torvald screamed. "A fucking bonehead meat-bag monkey! This pain isn't real! Do you think this pain is real?"

"Pain is real if you feel it." He broke the middle finger.

Raythen felt himself get pulled away.

Chapter 29

Raythen sat up straight and pulled off the headset. He flexed his right hand, still feeling the sting from the impacts with Torvald's face. "Did you get what you wanted," he said to Astria, his lips taught.

"I don't know," Astria said. "You two could have been play-acting to perpetuate your ruse."

"Are you kidding?" said Tray Wind. "You think that was an act? To what end? That is an A-Con found in a VDF exo that was on a tactical mission using live ammunition. Do you know what that's going to do to the UP's publicity? Even if they win this battle and get Theophilus, we now have proof that they used lethal force with no biologically-human intervention."

"What really bothers me is that he called Raythen a meat-bag," Edargo said. "I mean, is that what the A-Cons are calling us these days? Isn't that one of the signs of the Impending Robot Apocalypse?"

"I would love to open this thing up," Astria said. "Make sure there's a cemi field in there. But, evidence-wise, it would be best to do that live on the net with a bunch of experts watching. Anyway, considering what I've seen so far I'm going to assume that this thing really is an A-Con."

"If it is an A-Con," said Tray, "then what happened just now could be considered torture."

"Boo hoo," Astria said sarcastically. "The thing is an abomination."

Tray continued, "It has a cemi field just like you and me. It feels, it experiences, just like a human being. You might not feel empathy for it yourself but don't you think that the God you believe in would love an A-Con as much as a human?"

"The God I believe in only loves those who obey him."

"I thought God loved everyone equally."

"It's meaningless to be loved by someone who loves everyone equally. My God isn't about meaningless love."

"You always talk about *your* God, like it's different from everyone else's."

"Of course he is. Listen, I'm Reformed, probably more reformed than most Reforms. I have my own view of God, the details of which are none of your business. You might not be a fan of the UP, but I know from your writings you have no great sympathy for MetaChristians either."

"I believe in freedom," Tray said. "And I'll support the freedom of the Metas to believe whatever craziness they want to believe in, as long as they respect my freedom to be secular. I'm sure that if some of the Metas had their way they would outlaw secularism. Look at Uzziah, his interpretation of MetaChristianity is Biblical literalism. He believes that because the universe is a computer program then God can violate all the rules of physics that are violated in the Bible, including the internal contradictions. You think if he wasn't watched over by the UP he would respect *my* freedom?"

"We have no time for this," Astria said. "We have to get to Uzziah fast. He might be a Biblical literalist but he'll understand the tactical implications of what we know. But before we go I have one demand for all of you."

"What demand?" Edargo asked.

"Raythen, put the headset back on. This diagnostic program works for imps too. I'm going to put a network block on all of you."

"What!" Tray said. "Why? What for?"

"I don't know the situation out there," Astria said. "If the network was to come back on, even for a few seconds, any one of you could send what you know to the VDF. I need to make sure that doesn't happen."

"See?" Tray said. "Here we are talking about freedom and you want to take mine away! For no reason! You know I won't send any information to the VDF."

"You're the one talking about freedom, I'm talking about survival. You wouldn't send your information to the VDF but you would send it to your editors as fast as you could, to get the scoop. And your editors would publish it immediately. The VDF are monitoring all media right now." Astria stood and squared off with Tray Wind. "No exception for you, elf."

"It's not happening," Tray said, not backing down. "You don't have the authority. Hell, you don't have any authority over me."

Raythen watched Astria's feet. It was a subtle shift, but he noted how she angled one foot ninety degrees to the other. Her knees had a near imperceptible bend. Body leaning slightly forward. Tray Wind was standing straight with her knees locked, arms folded, defiant. He and Edargo were still sitting down. He figured Astria would go for Tray's nose or trachea, something to take her down fast. He was closer to her than Edargo so that would probably force her to go after him before Edargo. Still, he had an inkling that she would want to do something to take Edargo out of the equation first. Maybe by throwing something. *Yeah, her left hand there behind the back of her chair. It's hefty looking, but she's strong enough. Yeah, that's probably how it would go down. Then it would be just me and her.*

164

"Authority?" Astria said. "Look around you elf. I have all the authority I need."

Raythen believed her. He was curious about whether or not his assessment was accurate. It would almost be worth it to find out. Unfortunately he had some deranged A-Cons trying to kill him, and this woman knew how to fight. It was much better to have her on his side. "Edargo, help me put the head-set back on. Alright Astria, let's do this. Lock my imp."

Without taking her eyes away from Tray Wind, Astria reached behind her to the touch interface on the workbench and tapped out a combination.

"Bro, you sure you want to do this?" Edargo asked as he pulled down the headset on Raythen's head.

A popup window appeared in front of Raythen with the text, DIAGNOSTIC MODE REQUESTED, PASSWORD VERIFICATION REQUIRED. Raythen phanded his password. Technical readouts scrolled quickly in the popup, followed by red letters saying NETWORK ACCESS LOCK ENGAGED.

"I password protected the lockout," Astria said. "I'll give you that password when this is over."

"What if you can't?" Tray asked.

"Yeah, what if you get killed or something?" Edargo said.

"A professional level diag will be able to override it," Astria said.

"And how long will that take?" Tray asked. "It could be over a day before I get my network back. The story would be dead in that time."

Astria ignored her and said, "While I'm in your head Raythen, you might as well play back the alleged death-threat Torvald gave you in the broom closet. If you show it to me I might even trust you."

165

"That's right!" Raythen grinned. He scrolled down the timeline and played back the vid, which was displayed to all on the big screen. He felt the satisfaction of vindication. When it was done Astria nodded.

"Yeah, that's our homicidal robot. Now give the head-set to Edargo."

Raythen tossed the head-set over to Edargo who caught it, but still looked uncertain. Raythen nodded at him and he put it on. Astria typed onto the panel again.

"I'm not doing it," Tray said. "You have my word that I won't transmit any of the story while the conflict is ongoing. I'll stay in airplane mode."

"Bullshit," Astria said, and finished with Edargo. "I know what you're thinking. You're wondering how many of these A-Con modules have been recovered by the CCM, and how many reporters have access to them. I bet you've already done your lead-in to the story in your imp; you're probably working on the commented report as we speak. If the network came back right now I bet you would have the package ready to go. So put the head-set over your silly blue elf hair and open up the diag. Now!"

"It's not happening," said Tray, defiant. "You can try to beat the crap out of me, but I'm not going to let you into my imp. No way. And you don't have time for this. Are you going to waste time fighting with me while you have crucial tactical information to get to Uzziah?"

They stared at each other for a few moments. Raythen could see the tension on Astria's face, her hand clenched into a fist. For an instant he thought she was going to strike, but then her body loosened.

"Fine," she said. "But you're staying with us and the second the network comes up I'm going to crack your skull." She motioned everyone up with a sweep of her arm. "Let's get going, back to the subway."

Raythen stood and asked her, "Just out of curiosity—" he glanced at Tray, and then looked back at Astria, "—nose or trachea?"

Astria smirked. "Eyes."

"Really?" Raythen said.

Astria held up her fist and then stuck out her index finger and pinky. "Fuck yeah."

"What are you talking about?" Tray asked, looking at them both.

"Nothing," Raythen said quickly, heading for the door.

Chapter 30

Spokesdog stands on the Serengeti plains wearing khaki shorts, khaki shirt, and a pith helmet. One foot rests on a desiccated tree log, his elbow resting nonchalantly on his knee.

"One hundred thousand years ago, this area was a major seasonal migration point for our early homo sapiens ancestors. It is theorized by many anthropologists that right around here, one of the most significant developments in human culture occurred, a development that brought forth the ability that enabled humanity to dominate the planet." He takes his foot off the log, standing up straight and looking around. "You see, at that time most humans traveled in small family bands of a dozen or so individuals. The members of those bands were closely related by blood or marriage and had strong emotional bonds to each other. These close bonds were what enabled people to work together in groups, keeping them from being selfish pricks. When the males in a band reached adolescence, they would leave their family and join an all-male group, called a troop. These troops would travel the country-side, surviving on their own, and when they encountered a family band containing an adolescent female who was of age, they would compete among themselves for the favor of the young lady. Whoever won the favor would join her family band. This system of human behavior worked for thousands of years, up until the coming of a young man—let's call him Utnap—who refused to live by tradition. Come with me back one hundred thousand years—" Spokesdog waves an arm behind him as the shore of a lake appears, and the ground becomes lush with grass, "—to the largest seasonal gathering of the human race in that period, where Utnap has an important talk with his mother Ki."

Dozens of small, portable leather huts dotted the shore of the lake. Tall dark people dressed in leather loincloths and red body paint were mingling by fires outside of the huts. The voices of several hundred people talking and singing and the sounds of pipes and drums were the makings of a festive atmosphere. The view moves away from Spokesdog and focuses in on a young man sitting outside of a hut. Across the fire from him is a matriarchal woman bangled in painted sea-shell jewelry. She says, "I don't understand what you are saying Utnap. It is time for you to join the other young men. I will miss you, deeply, because I love you, but you must find a wife and a family so you can have children of your own."

"Mother, I want to go join the other boys. I want to hunt and play with them and to find a wife. But I can't."

"Is it because you don't like girls, like your older brother Dimuzid?" The view switches for a moment to Dimuzid, elaborately dressed in ostrich feathers, sitting very closely with another young man while they string a necklace of shells together.

"I do enjoy having Dimuzid and his partner Shulgi stay with our family," Ki says. "It is a convenience having more young men around, but I would also like to have grandchildren in the other family bands as well, so we can meet together at the Gathering and you and your wife and children can tell me stories of your year together."

"Mother, I like girls just fine. It's something else. Something else that's very strange to talk about."

Ki looks at him with concern. "What is it? What could possibly keep you from joining with the young men?"

With reluctance, Utnap says, "The other day I was trailing an antelope I had wounded with a spear." The view becomes wavy as it changes to a flashback of Utnap jogging through brush looking at the ground. His voice is heard over the flashback, "As I came out of some trees I saw a lion standing before me, not five strides away. I could not move because I was so afraid. But the lion didn't move either. He just looked at me for a moment, and then spoke my name!"

"The lion spoke to you?" Ki says, surprised.

Spokesdog, walking up to the lion, says, "At the time, there was no tradition of talking animals—no Aesop's fables, no Mother Goose. However, there was also nothing in these people's worldview that expressly *forbid* animals from talking, so while the idea of a talking lion was new, it was not discounted out of hand."

"The lion spoke to you," Utnap's mother repeats. "He knew your name?"

"Yes, he said it quite clearly."

"How did he know your name?"

"I don't know, but he knew other things that he should not have known. He said—"

The lion says, "Utnap, son of Ki, grandson of Antu, you must not leave the side of your mother to join the other young men. You must not search out a bride to lay with. You must stay with your own family. If you do go join the young men, I will track you down and I will eat you. And my brothers will track down all the other young men in your troop and eat them. And your bones will be picked over first by the hyenas, and then by

170

the vultures, and then by the ants, and then they will bleach white in the sun."

Utnap falls to his knees in front of the lion and starts crying. "Why? Why lion? Why would you eat me and why would your brothers eat my brothers? Why would you have my bones picked over first by the hyenas, and then by the vultures, and then by the ants, and then to be bleached white by the sun?"

"Because," says the lion, "you are a great hunter. You kill more antelope than the other men. You kill and eat the antelope that I and my brothers eat. If you would travel with the other young men, you would teach them to be great hunters as you are, and we lions would no longer have any antelope to eat. So you must stay with your mother, so we may continue to eat the antelope."

The view goes back to the fire with Utnap and his mother.

"I pleaded with the lion—I pleaded and pleaded and cried, but he would not listen," Utnap says, tears streaming from his eyes, and his mother goes to him and holds him and rocks him and says that everything will be all right.

"I will go speak to lion," Ki says. "I will talk to him and tell him to let you join with the other young men."

"No!" Utnap says with fear in his eyes. "The lion will eat you."

"The lion did not eat you," Ki replies calmly. "Also, I would like to hear a lion talk. I've never even imagined such a thing."

The scene changes to Utnap's mother walking the same path that Utnap had traveled when he saw the lion. There is no lion in sight. She yells out "Lion! Lion! Speak to me! I am Ki, daughter of Antu, granddaughter of Ninlil! We need to speak!"

Still no sign of the lion. Ki wanders on, travelling beneath the canopy of tall trees, through a rocky stream, through prickly underbrush, until she comes to the rim of a valley and sees a pride of lions in the distance. She brushes off her loincloth and strides bravely down to meet them. The alpha male, lying in the sun, raises his great maned head at her, disturbed by the strident walk of this human toward him. He gets up and braces his feet threateningly. Ki continues forward. "Lion!" she shouts. "Speak to me! We need to talk about Utnap! Lion! Speak to me!"

The lion rushes toward Ki. It isn't until he leaps up at her, claws extended, that she throws her arms in front of herself and screams.

Utnap stands in the middle of a large circle of people on the bank of the lake. All the people of the Gathering have come to hear his story. In his hands he holds the bloody shell necklace that had belonged to his mother. He raises it for everyone to see.

"So my mother went to talk to the lion to allow me to join the other young men. But the lion ate her. That is why I can't leave my family. I can't hunt antelope with the other young men. I will do as the lion says and live with my father and my sisters and their husbands and my gay brother and his husband. I will not travel and seek out a bride."

The crowd murmurs in shock and surprise at this announcement. After a few moments a young woman enters the circle with Utnap. She is not a beautiful woman; her nose is large and crooked and one ear is noticeably larger than the other. But she says with a strong voice, "My name is Shamhat, daughter of Inanna, granddaughter of Nin. I am not a beautiful woman, and no man has ever contested for my hand. But no man should live without a wife to lay with him and bear his children. So even though you are not in a troop, and you have not contested for my hand, I will allow you to be my husband, and I will join with your family." This is followed

172

by more shocked murmurs. Utnap walks to the woman and places his mother's necklace around her neck and the crowd bursts into cheers.

Up on a ridge overlooking the people, Spokesdog turns away from them and looks at you. "Utnap doesn't leave his family—in fact, he becomes its leader—one of the first male leaders of a family band. He and Shamhat have many children, and he teaches his sons to hunt, and they become great hunters. And they, like their father, stay with the family they are born to. Many people from other bands come to ask him for advice and guidance—some of them even stay with his band, which grows in size beyond the size of any other band, until it becomes a tribe, the first tribe. And his children, they can talk to lions, and to other animals too, and eventually to trees and to mountains and to the sun and the moon. And so, out of the insanity of hyper-anthropomorphization, religion is born. Religion becomes a force that is stronger than family bonds and allows for tribes to grow to hundreds of people—people who listen to Utnap's children, because who wants to get eaten by a lion? It was a useful insanity, back when people didn't know any better. So the children of Utnap, stricken with this tendency to imagine that animals think and talk like humans, are more successful than people who don't. Their huge tribe dominates all others, and eventually replaces them, so that in the end we are all descended from Utnap. We are all children of his insanity. Sure, it was a useful insanity then, but aren't you glad we've outgrown that kind of thinking?" He winks and says, "This edutainment has been brought to you by BioBetter—making a better you through neuroaugmentation. And don't forget, lunch is on me. Woof."

173

Chapter 31

"Uzziah is on the surface?" Tray asked after Astria told the subway car where to go.

"I don't know where he is," Astria said, taking a seat. "But I do know where someone is who can get word to him, and that person is on the surface, at one of the militia bases."

"The VDF has probably taken control of everything on the surface by now," Tray said.

"You don't know the CCM—they're not really big on surrendering. And each militia base has its own internal point-to-point network that will allow for coordinated RC action. The VDF might have a toehold in the civilian areas, but they won't try to crack the militia bases until they have to. Isn't that right, Raythen?"

Raythen nodded. It sounded like a good assessment.

"I still don't get why the UP is doing this," Edargo said. "They're risking a hell-of-a-lot with these A-Cons running around. Why not let the religious crazies have their stratoses?"

"Exponential growth," Tray said. "There are thirty-seven stratoses on Venus, producing half of the technical goods used in Sol System. Two of these stratoses are predominately MetaChristian. But MetaChristians breed at a rate that's four times that of the average secular Venusian, not to mention conversions and immigration. There's a big push by

174

MetaChristians on Terra to move to Venus. It's estimated in ten years there could be six MetaChristian stratoses here. In another ten years, twenty. In fifty years the majority population on Venus could be MetaChristian. That would mean that the industrial powerhouse of Sol System would be under the control of people who are throwbacks to a primitive, bloodthirsty superstition that technically makes them insane."

"If you're trying to get on my good side, you're doing it wrong," Astria said.

"I'm just being honest with you, Astria. The origin of the religious impulse is well understood to science. Spokesdog has an excellent edutainment on the subject."

"I love Spokesdog," Edargo said.

"Spokescamel is much better," Astria said. "He's funky, and his face looks like a penis."

Raythen stayed quiet about his partiality to Spokesgibbon—this wasn't the time for the perennial who's-the-best-spokes-creature debate.

"Real MetaChristianity doesn't argue against science," said Astria. "Most of us admit that humans evolved, and that the religious impulse evolved. God wants us to be made through the random processes of this universe. He wants followers that weren't designed directly by him."

"Like I said before, I'm not against religion per se, and I agree with your right to believe the universe is a computer program, but I do have something against any religion that advocates violence. The CCM has used their religion to justify having illegal weapons. I mean, you're a religious person and you aren't the poster child for rational pacifism."

"Pacifism isn't rational," Astria said.

"What? That makes no sense—it's obvious that pacifism is part of being more advanced."

"What makes it obvious? I don't see any logical connection between *advanced* and *pacifism*. If there's any relationship it's the inverse. The more advanced an organism or society, the easier it is for it to kill its enemies."

"Technically advanced, sure," Tray said. "But not morally advanced."

"How can you talk about morals?" Astria said. "Your morals aren't based on anything, they can be whatever you want them to be, which makes them nothing. You live in a crystal palace filled with hollow men. Is that what it means to be advanced to you? To have a meaningless life?"

"Morals are subjective, yes, but that doesn't make them meaningless. I base my moral system on something real—empathy. Genuine care for the well being of others. It's a real emotion—tangible, measurable. You can't call empathy nothing."

Edargo gave a sidelong glance to Raythen. Raythen shrugged.

"Why the hell not?" Astria said, visibly agitated. "You say morals are subjective, so it's logically valid for me to disagree with whatever ethical proclamation you make, even if I'm doing it just to be an asshole. You can be as fucking empathetic as you want and make yourself Saint Empathac of the Empathoids. It only matters to *me* if you can enforce your morality. Like the UP trying to enforce their morality on us with VDF troops. Ultimately, all ethics are decided by the power to enforce them, and God's ethics are right because he made this fucking universe."

"I believe in empathy as the foundation of morals," Tray said calmly and firmly. "It's my ethical system and the ethical system for lots of other people. My belief in it doesn't depend on convincing you that it's correct, its purpose is to help me guide my own life. Whatever power it needs to have is the power to move me. But even a cursory reading of the New

Testament shows that Jesus was a pacifist. Don't you feel any obligation to turn the other cheek?"

"I look at the New Testament as a cautionary tale. God sacrificed his only son to teach us that if you're a pacifist hippy who looks after everyone else and forsakes all worldly possessions, you end up flailed, stabbed, and nailed to a cross until you die."

"But . . . don't you believe in the resurrection?"

"The resurrection? Really? I may be a Christian, but I'm not a moron."

"Are you serious?" Tray asked.

Astria glared back at her with all seriousness.

"I think we're here," Raythen said quickly as the car slowed down. The door opened to an underground station platform. He poked his head out cautiously, looked both ways, and stepped out. The station was empty.

They walked down the hall and passed the open doors to a security shelter, like the one at the hotel. This one was completely empty.

"Odd," Tray said, "where is everybody?"

"Maybe the UP took them," said Edargo.

"Shit, I was afraid of this," said Astria. "One of Uzziah's plans was to have everyone gather at Cathedral Square and demonstrate against the attack. He must have put it into play before shutting down the network."

"We should go there then," said Tray. "Won't Uzziah be there, leading the demonstration? Or Theophilus? Plus, I'd like to get some shots of the mob." She looked at Raythen and Edargo.

"Theophilus isn't stupid enough to be out in the open," said Astria. "Anyway, she was against the whole demonstration idea. And Uzziah would be too busy coordinating the militia defense. I'm sticking to the original plan; you guys can do whatever you want to. I'm in a hurry." She jogged toward the stairs.

"Okay, we should split up," Tray said. "Edargo, Raythen, you go to Cathedral Square. Raythen, find a high spot over the crowd and pan around. Edargo, you get interviews. I want at least one from an average citizen, preferably a hot chick—"

"Can do," said Edargo.

"—then find whoever is leading the demonstration and talk to them. I'm going to stay with Astria—follow the A-Con module. I need to keep continuity with that story."

"I'm not taking the high ground," Raythen said. "I'm not hanging out in the open with the Torvalds around."

"Oh yeah, good point," Tray said. "Whatever, Edargo can handle the mob scenes alone. You lay low. I need to catch up to Astria." She was already out of sight up the stairs.

They went upstairs and entered into the lobby of an apartment complex. They caught a glimps of Astria as she was leaving through a side door. They followed her into a garage for two-wheeled vehicles—it held close to one hundred of them, lined up in neat rows. Astria was eying an electric racing cycle. She sat on it experimentally, started it up, and drove it to the closed garage door. If the network had been working, the cycle would have notified its owner that it was being ridden, giving the owner the opportunity to shut it down remotely. With the network down it was free to use.

Astria reached up to the side of the garage door and pressed a button. The door slid down into the ground with a gentle swoosh.

It was still night-time. From outside they heard a rolling crackling sound that seemed to come from all directions; little pops and hisses, like the sky was a frying pan filled with hot bacon.

"What the hell is that?" Edargo said.

"Dragonflies," Raythen said. "The VDF is swarming the sky with small reconnaissance drones—"

"And we're shooting them down with laser pulses," Astria finished.

"Yeah," said Raythen. "They have an average lifespan of three point five seconds, but given the millions that are sent out the VDF can get a good real-time view of what's going on. The must have plenty of drone dispensers attached to the dome." He shook his head. "I'm not going out there. If any of the Torvalds are connected to the dragonflies' point-to-point network, they could see me. I'm not taking the chance."

"Good-bye ladies," Astria said and zipped away on her cycle.

Tray hopped on to the closest cycle. "Raythen, keep low and safe. Edargo, big bonus for the crowd shots. I'll try to get to the cathedral if I can after this. Good luck to both of you guys, and thanks." She rode after Astria.

With the departure of the women, a calm descended on the garage that comes with being in the company of a good friend. They looked out into the white glow of the night, now making out the falling of ashes—the remains of the destroyed reconnaissance drones, decending like snow.

"I'm done here," Raythen said. "I'm just going to lay low until this is over." He moved to the far corner of the garage and sat on the floor, his good hand holding his forehead.

"Why did Sweet GG send me here? Why did she send me the text and ticket?"

"Maybe Torvald hacked her account? He *is* some sort of engineering genius, right?"

"Hacked her imp? Hacked the VuDyne? That's impossible."

"I've heard stories," Edargo said consolingly.

"She was just using me for training," Raythen said. "She and her team were training for *this* when they were in *Exo Arena*. They had to become expert exo troopers so when they replicated their neural patterns their A-Cons would be expert exo troopers. She was just using me."

"Yeah, but she didn't have to fuck you to do that, unless, you know, she was also training for something else."

"I just want to sleep. I just want to make this go away."

A few moments passed. Edargo fidgeted. Finally, he said, "Why don't you go down to the shelter? Pick out a nice safety chair and take a nap? It's not like any Torvalds are going to be searching all the apartment complexes, I'm sure they're all busy with the local militia. I bet the only Torvalds were the ones they planted here beforehand. And, uh, I think I'll head down to the demonstration."

Raythen pulled his hand away from his forehead and looked up at Edargo.

"Yeah," Edargo continued. "It'd be good to get the bonus, and, you know, unless you want me to stick around. That'll be fine too."

Raythen shook his head. "No, you go. You're right. I'll be safe here."

"Okay. Hey, we'll hook up again when the network is live," Edargo said, turning around and picking out a cycle. As he drove to the entrance he said, "Is life crazy or what?"

Chapter 32

Edargo was not one to hide from his own emotions, even when they were not all that flattering. As Shakespeare had said through the character of Polonius, "To thine own self be true." Self-honesty and the objectivity that comes with it makes it easier to read others, but the price was that he couldn't hide from the fact that there was a little piece of himself that was enjoying Raythen's plight.

Edargo raced through the empty, lighted road. The apartment complex had been near the edge of the city—Cathedral Square was about a kilometer away. He saw where he had to go on the map on his HUD, which his imp had stored when he had first arrived and was using to determine his position from landmarks.

He felt guilty about enjoying the situation, but seriously, hadn't he been second fiddle to Raythen for the past two years? In order to be popular you had to fit into pre-defined roles that people can quickly recognize with their hummingbird attention spans. And the role that he had fallen into was comedic side-kick. But that was when they were a couple of NPCs. This was reality. This was where it really counted. When they were in a truly dangerous situation in an honest to goodness shooting war, Raythen was curled up in a garage while he was the brave journalist going out to record the struggle of thousands of crazy people. He was going to push his way through to the leadership and get the emotional reactions of the loons, and maybe watch as the VDF (hopefully humans, not Torvalds) comes in and rounds them up. He was the star of the show, he was going to get the scoop, and with any luck he would end up with the girl. That Tray Wind was one cute elf. Those eyes! While he wasn't happy that his satisfaction was coming at the expense of his friend, he considered it completely understandable and human, in light of the circumstances.

Edargo, preoccupied as he was, didn't look in his rear-view mirror. If he had he wouldn't have been as surprised as he was when a hand grabbed the back of his neck and lifted him out of his seat. The cycle slowly drifted ahead as he saw the exo trooper running next to him, holding him above the road. He grabbed at the trooper's arm with both hands. The trooper turned off the road and ran into an apartment building. It didn't stop in the lobby but instead ran up the stairs and kicked in the first door it came too. The standard-looking apartment was empty of people. As the trooper quickly checked all the rooms to confirm this, Edargo realized how uncomfortable it was to be suspended by a firm robotic hand with a vice grip on the back of one's neck, and seriously wondered about the strength of his vertebrae supporting the weight of his body. The trooper tossed him onto the couch as a second trooper came through the door.

"Apologies," the trooper said with a metallic, anonymous, authoritarian voice. "We belong to the Venus Defense Force. You are a civilian in the middle of a dangerous police action. There is currently a no-travel restriction in the city. We have been tasked with ensuring that non-residents are brought to safe locations during the length of this police action. It would be best if you stayed indoors for now. Are you aware of any other non-residents in the area?"

Edargo, mouth half open, shifted his eyes between the blank helmets of the two troopers standing before him. He whispered, "Torvald?"

"Pardon?" the other trooper said. "Did you say Torvald? Who is he?"

"Not Torvald?" Edargo said hopefully.

"We don't have much time," the first trooper said. "We need to ensure the safety of non-residents. Our records indicate that you are friends with Dominic Rex, aka Raythen. Do you know where he is?"

Edargo got a very bad feeling about this. He collected himself and sat up. "No, I don't know where he is right now. We got separated at our hotel. I've been hired by a news organization to record the demonstrations at Cathedral Square. So . . . I appreciate you bringing me here but I've got to get going."

The two troopers didn't move. The second one said, deadpan, "Where is Raythen."

Edargo scrambled over the cushions to his left and was pushing off the arm-rest when a hand once again grabbed the back of his neck. He was thrown down flat on his back on the coffee table and a heavy knee leaned down on his chest.

"Hello Edargo," the trooper said. "Good to see you again. We really are pressed for time. I take it you ran into others of us during this operation. I also take it that Raythen is still alive. So where is he?"

"I don't know," Edargo gasped, having trouble breathing with the weight pressing on his sternum.

"We only have a small window of opportunity here. We don't want to hurt you—just Raythen. But we'll do what we have to do. *Your* window of opportunity is closing fast."

"You'll kill me anyway," Edargo said, his face turning red.

"We can get away with one murder, maybe, but two? Probably not. We don't want to push things."

Edargo didn't believe them, but he did believe that they definitely would kill him if he said nothing. Giving up nigh immortality is a hard thing. His only chance at life was to tell them *something*. He hated the thought of ratting out Raythen, but this was his *life*.

Then, in a flash, he thought of a convincing lie.

"Raythen and I split up. He went to the militia base, the one up toward starboard. He figured he'd be safe there."

The pressure on his chest let up a little. He gasped for a breath. The Torvalds were quiet for a moment.

"Was he alone?" Torvald asked.

The dragonflies, Edargo thought. *How long have they been watching me? Did they see me leave that apartment complex?*

"He kept under the trees, worried about the dragonflies. The rest of us took cycles."

"And who were the rest of you?"

"Reporters. Raythen and I were hired by reporters. They sent me to film the demonstrations while they went to the base."

"And why that particular base?"

"I don't know! I'm just here to get visuals! They wanted to interview the militia!"

"Edargo, you've always been a bullshitter, but you're also a selfish fuck. We need to crack a base anyway, so it might as well be that one. And you get to come along to watch."

Chapter 33

Sounds in a stratos carry; they don't dissipate into an endless sky like on Terra. Cacophonies ricochet off the dome, and depending on your position an event that happens a half-kilometer away can seem like it's happening right next to you.

The sound of the battle exploded into Raythen's consciousness. He went flat onto the garage floor and glanced desperately at the scene around him—he was still alone, but the ground vibrated, making the looser components of the cycles in the garage take on a life of their own.

Rail guns. Dozens of them. Striking a hardened target.

The weight of the raw power being expended shattered the night—and it went on and on, a continuous roar signifying the destruction of its object. Raythen remained on the floor, debating what to do. He was frozen by the thought of an unrestrained attack on a manned installation. They were not holding back. Then, after twenty minutes, the sound began to loosen, individual impacts could be discerned, and Raythen thought he could hear human screams amid the explosions.

They're attacking the base, he thought. *The military base Tray and Astria went to.*

This was over the top. He couldn't image the VDF, *his* VDF, using this kind of overwhelming deadly force in a police action. The battle had finally subsided to the point where there were actual moments of silence between the gunfire. He could make out the distinctive sound of exo armor being hit, and this time he was sure of the human shouts and screams. Some were cut off much too quickly.

Eventually the sounds of battle became sporadic. They were cleaning up. "Oh God! Oh God!" a woman shouted, high pitched and frantic. Then it was quiet for several minutes. Raythen took in a deep, ragged breath.

Scan, plan, react, he thought. *Scan, plan, react.* He couldn't do much scanning from the floor of the garage. Everything in his training told him to move. *But where? Where? Back to the subway? Find a room and lay low?* The VDF had just completely fragged the militia base. *What was their strategy? Concentrated power—easier to coordinate when communication was point-to-point, aided with dragonflies. Staying out of the tunnels.*

It's best for me to go underground.

Except, they would get underground eventually. They would send A-Cons underground first, to clear the way. What if those A-Cons were Torvalds? His best chance for survival was to be found by human VDF. If there were any human VDF they would be at the entry points, at the surface of the dome. Torvald wouldn't dare kill him in front of any human VDF, would he? He thought about the sounds of the assault on the base. There was something very wrong about that. That was the base he had reconed for Mr. Hang. It was close to the dome, there had to be an entry point to the VDF cruiser near it, cut into the dome. If he could reach it, maybe he could surrender to them.

He looked at the cycles and realized one was a Grand Faissa—and better yet—it had a helmet. *No one else took the Grand Faissa 526, what the hell were they thinking?* The helmet would give him some protection against recognition by the dragonflies. He got up and went to it, putting his good hand on the handle bar appreciatively. He put on the helmet and experimented hooking the hard cast thumb of his left hand to the rubber handle, successfully finding a position that allowed him to put his weight there.

He zoomed into the night, staying off the roads, driving in the shadows of the buildings and staying under the trees. The low light was not an issue; standard physical augmentation gave humans night sight that was better than cats. He followed the path displayed on his HUD, weaving between palmettos and flying through alleys. The most direct route to the dome would take him within a hundred meters of the attacked militia base.

What if Tray and Astria are hurt? What if they need help? As he approached the tree-line on the edge of the base compound, he heard a sudden explosion of sound that indicated a new assault—they were attacking another base. Better for him, they were preoccupied somewhere else. Not so good for the people in the other base.

Staying within the trees he glanced to his left at the ruins of the base as it came into view—across the clearing beyond the destroyed chain-link fence was a hectare of black smoldering rubble. He looked back and forth between it and the direction he was driving. He took a snapshot of the base and had his imp scan it for any humanoid forms. There were six fallen exos on the field, motionless. He glanced back at it and got another snapshot. There was someone in the rubble. He zoomed in. A person was lying prone on a flat slanted piece of fallen wall. The wall was facing roughly the direction he was travelling in, so as he continued to move he got a clearer view. He glanced back again. The person was unarmored, lying on his back, arms and legs splayed out. There was wet splatter behind his head. His imp made a positive ID.

Raythen turned hard into the field toward the base and went full throttle. There was no thought of dragonflies or Torvalds as he bounced over the uneven ground and went through a hole in the chain-linked fence. When he reached the rubble he clenched the front brake, almost flipping over the handle bars. He jumped off the cycle, landing at a run as he went to Edargo. Clambering up the fallen slab of wall he looked at Edargo's face, sightless eyes to the sky, brains and blood haloing his head.

"You were supposed to be at the crowd." Raythen cried. "You were supposed to be at the crowd!"

This wasn't the VDF. This was something else. This was something monstrous. Edargo had been murdered.

"Get the fuck in here!" a whispered voice hissed from somewhere in the rubble. Raythen jumped back away, almost tumbling down the wall.

"Come here," the voice insisted. It was Astria. He half crawled, half fell off the slab. His imp isolated her location in the shadow of two slabs that had fallen together to make a triangle of darkness. In a crouch, he ran to it. A hand reached out and pulled him in, bringing him deeper under cover. It took a moment for his eyes to adjust and see he was moving down something that had once been a corridor. Astria stopped and pushed him against the wall and said, "Are you trying to get yourself killed too?"

"This isn't right," Raythen said.

"What, like that means anything," Astria said. On her face was a pair of smart glasses, around her waist was a weapons belt with a pistol, slung over one shoulder was a satchel, on the other an MR-23 assault rifle. "We need to get to Theophilus. We have to stay underground. I think they're all up top now, zerging the bases one by one."

"This isn't right! They smashed his brain!"

"The Torvalds want you dead. Your only chance is to help me find Theophilus and get her to safety. Safety for her means safety for you. Got it?"

"But this is wrong! We've got to get to the VDF Command and have them stop this!"

"Listen to me Raythen because we have no time and you have to understand what the fuck is happening here." She jabbed her index finger in his chest. "So make like I'm Spokescamel and listen up." Jab. "There is no VDF Command anymore. The fucking douche bag plutocratic oligarchy that runs this fucking solar system has finally decided to stop jumping through hoops." Jab. "They've decided it's easier and more fun to take out anyone who defies them." Jab. "For the last few centuries the elite shit-slimes who lord over us have had to deal with democracy and rule of law and all that bullshit to get what they want. Sure, they ran things, but it stuck in their craws that they had to smile and suck up to us little people to keep the system working. And do you know what was the only thing that stopped them from the wholesale murder of the people who defied them?" Jab. "The one thing that kept them from openly declaring their homicidal hatred for the people who didn't bow down and follow their every whim without question?" Jab. "The military. The armed forces. As long as the military was made up of little people, they couldn't just order them to shoot at the other little people. As long as the military was made up of people who believed in the rule of law and freedom, the fuck-head douche-bag elites had to jump through frustrating legal hoops to get their way." Jab. "Now the shit-lickers are nigh immortal, and they're sick and tired of jumping through hoops. They don't want to spend eternity smiling and sucking up to the masses they despise. Now they don't need the human military." Jab. "Now they have their own army." Jab. "Now they have an army of sociopathic robot Torvalds who clearly don't give a fuck about the rule of law." Jab. "And it just so happens that this blood-crazed homicidal army of robo-fucks has a raging hard-on for your girlfriend. Which really sucks for . . ." she slowly traced a bull's-eye over his heart, and as she put in the center dot said ". . . you."

Raythen stared at her. It all made its own kind of insane sense. But if what she said was true then there was nothing he could do. There was nowhere he could turn. He was a dead man.

As dead as Edargo.

"Follow me," Astria said, turning around and walking down the hallway.

"Where are we going?"

"I have a mission. You're going to help me. Either die standing there or follow me and maybe live. Your choice."

He followed her.

Chapter 34

The hallway was illuminated by red emergency lights. The thick carbon composite walls were gouged with rail gun impact craters. They passed a bloodied corpse in a CCM uniform. Astria opened a door to the stairwell.

"What happened to Tray Wind?" Raythen asked. "Is she all right?"

"We saw the Torvalds approaching the militia base before we got here. The elf decided to record the attack from the safety of a nearby apartment building. That's the last I saw her. I stayed hidden nearby, to get access to the CCM tunnel systems when they were done. Then I found Edargo."

"What makes you think all the VDF exos are Torvalds?" Raythen asked.

"It makes sense. You have a bunch of A-Cons going into a battlefield with spotty communications. How do you get them to work together? Give them all the same brain. They showed remarkable coordination during the attack."

"I hope you're wrong."

"I'm probably not. Anyway, the CCM has its own underground network of passages. We need to use them to get to Cathedral Square."

"Why there?"

"I need to get Theophilus out of Corpus Christi. If she escapes their victory won't be complete."

"How do you know she's at Cathedral Square?"

"An educated guess. She's going to want to minimize casualties. Now that it's obvious the VDF is using deadly force she'll want to tell the people to get back to the shelters, and then she'll give herself up, hoping to end this. We can't let that happen."

"How are we going to get her off the stratos?"

"Leave that to me. Right now we just get to her and prevent her from doing anything stupid."

They reached the bottom of the stairs and went through double doors into a long, wide hallway with doors on either side spaced several meters apart. Some of the doors had been blasted open. A wrecked exo with legs missing was in one of the doorways. It was empty.

"Scratch one Torvald," Astria said. She crouched down and examined the armor. "The A-Con module is missing. Probably retrieved by one of his buddies. The Torvalds look after their own. Come on, the goodies are in here."

Following behind her he recognized the room as an armory. There had been a pitched battle here. Rows of cabinets, formerly containing armor and weapons, had been shot up and smashed, scattering their contents on the ground. Among them were four dead militia half-exos, torn to pieces, and one dead militia full exo trooper against the far wall.

Raythen went to a spilled cabinet with half-exo armor pieces scattered on the ground around it.

"No point going for that shit. Just get smart glasses and a belt. Light and fast." Something in an open tool chest caught her attention. "Well, hello there." She reached in and pulled out a crowbar. She spun it once deftly in the air with her index finger at the curled end and slid it smoothly into her belt.

Raythen found a pair of smart glasses and put them over his eyes.

ESTABLISHING POINT-TO-POINT CONTACT . . . CONTACT ESTABLISHED

<Raythen: tell @Astria> "Testing, Alpha bravo charlie."

<Astria: tell @Raythen> "I copy that."

It felt good to be on a network again, even if it was only with one person.

He found a utility belt and tried to put it on, swinging it behind his back and catching it on top of his cast left hand. As he was trying to move his bad hand to his good one Astria came over and grabbed both ends, pulling him forward and cinching them together. As the belt tightened onto him she kept her hands on it, looking up at him, her face just centimeters away. She gave an impish half-smile and pushed him back.

She seemed flirty. If anything seemed inappropriate to Raythen at that moment it was flirty.

Edargo was dead. He had been worried about the possibility of being spotted by Torvald, but why hadn't he thought about Edargo being spotted? That was stupid. He had been so preoccupied with the danger to his own life he hadn't thought that Edargo was in danger too. He should have realized that. He should have stopped Edargo from going into the open.

"Don't be a pussy," Astria said. She must have seen something in his face. "I'll get you a gun. It won't do shit against the Torvalds, but having a gun always makes me feel better. I imagine the same for you."

There were several MR-23s on the floor, but they couldn't be fired one-handed. Astria went to the wall and a small panel slid open, popping out a Glock 93 pistol. She handed it to him.

"I can't use this," he said. "I don't have the codes."

"Downloading," Astria said. Sure enough, a text box appeared next to the gun showing its status as active with thirty live rounds. He pointed it to the wall and saw the green cross-hairs where he aimed.

"How'd you get access?" Raythen asked. "You're not in the CCM."

"I have connections."

Raythen had a thought. "Wait! If you have security access you can get me into some exo armor."

"Yeah, I could if the Torvalds hadn't destroyed the fitting booths."

Of course they had. The two things that they would want to destroy in each base was the command and control center and the exo armor fitting booths. The base would be harmless after that.

They left the room and she led the way down the hall. At the end was a heavy blast door. He phanded it, trying to establish communications. The word DENIED appeared. Astria looked at the door and it opened.

Chapter 35

Captain Parvati Meyers reclined in her small quarters on the Pax Cythera. She was wearing blue flight-suit overalls—no naked reclining while on a mission. Her current race was East Asian; her blond hair was cut short and boyish. A flight helmet rested on the OmniServ, next to a glass of iced tea.

<Wilton: post> "Any word on the Achaeans?"

<Gen. Wong: post> "None. They may still be in the process of carrying out their mission—although I anticipated contact with them by now."

<Wilton: post> "Could there have been a malfunction? Or what if they were discovered beforehand? Would we know that?"

<Capt. Meyers: post> "A malfunction isn't possible, not for four separate units. And they would have sent out an emergency signal if they were discovered before the scramblers knocked out the network."

<Wilton: post> "Have we reconned the Hubein Regency yet? What if they met with superior forces?"

<Gen. Wong: post> "Our intel showed the hotel was clear of anything but cloth security at zero hour. Four exos should have easily secured Theophilus, but their return path might have been blocked. They might be traveling underground—or pinned down."

<Wilton: post> "Send a team to the Hubein Regency. We need to find Theophilus. I thought I made myself clear about the priority of her capture."

<Capt. Meyers: post> "I'm sure the Achaeans have secured Theophilus. Even if their escape is blocked, the local militia isn't going to risk shooting her. The Achaeans will ensure her safety until the city is under our control."

<Wilton: post> "Theophilus is our insurance policy. As majority shareholder in this stratos it will look much better to the public if we parade her into the courts after this is over and hold her legally responsible for whatever nastiness happens. And then it will be all done. If she escapes, the narrative becomes much more complex, she'll start to look heroic even to the non-Metas."

<Gen. Wong: post> "Rumor is among the Metas that we want to send her over to BioBetter and cure her of hyper-anthropomorphization disorder. If she believes that it would increase her motivation to resist."

<Wilton: post> "There's nothing I would love better than to send the whole lot of them to BioBetter. It's just not going to happen. Even just sending her would extend the media time-curve beyond what's acceptable. We have to secure her so we can have a nice boring trial that breaks her financially."

<Gen. Wong: post> "I'll send Oscar Team to the Hubein Regency, but we lost at least eight AUs taking Luke Base and we've already lost three at Mathew. By the time we get to John they will have a defense strategy in place or they will have bugged-out underground. Either way we are going to need all the AUs we have."

<Wilton: post> "As long as we have Theophilus all the Metas can rot underground till they grow mushrooms out of their ears. Find out where the Achaeans are and get Theophilus here."

<Gen. Wong: post> "Yes sir. I'm sending the command out now. Sir, there is another development."

<Wilton: post> "What's that?"

<Gen. Wong: post> "We have a group of civilians gathering on Cathedral Square. At least sixteen hundred, a significant portion of them children."

<Wilton: post> "Fucking savages. Why aren't they in their shelters?"

<Gen. Wong: post> "They may decide to make a stand at Cathedral Square and concentrate their troops there. We should disperse the crowd using nonlethal force before they bring in any exos."

<Wilton: post> "We have crowd control units—Gorgons—at the ready. Send them in."

<Gen. Wong: post> "With the surface unsecured we can't send manned Gorgons in, and the point-to-point isn't ready for tele-op. But I have an idea, with permission from Capt. Meyers. We can take the AUs salvaged from the fallen exos and use them to operate the Gorgons."

<Capt. Meyers: post> "I don't know. Torvald was never trained to run a Gorgon."

<Wilton: post> "From my understanding, which I got from *your* presentation, Torvald is smarter than the average human, and at least as versatile. He should be able to handle it."

<Capt. Meyers: post> "Rafe, crowd control is a very tricky operation. Without proper training things can easily get out of hand."

<Wilton: post> "When it comes to the AUs you have final say Parvati, but this sounds like a smart idea."

<Gen. Wong: post> "We're dealing with religious fanatics. There are children in that square. What if their exos decide to take the battle into the crowd? What if they lead our AUs to Cathedral Square and fire from crowds of children?"

<Capt. Meyers: post> "Torvald wouldn't fire back."

<Gen. Wong: post> "Of course not. And that would give them a huge tactical advantage. We need to eliminate that possibility."

<Capt. Meyers: post> "I'll discuss this with Torvald Prime. We have six retrieved ACUs. If he agrees we can have them in the Gorgons in minutes."

Capt. Meyers took a sip of her iced tea. Her hand shook slightly. She was worried about the Torvalds sent to capture Theophilus. They *should* have been back by now.

<Capt. Meyers: tell @Torvald> "Have you been listening? Are you up for driving a Gorgon?"

<Torvald: tell @Capt. Meyers> "I'm test driving a sim right now. It's fairly intuitive. I can handle it."

<Capt. Meyers: tell @Torvald> "Moving it from point A to point B is not what I'm worried about. Do you know what to do when you reach the crowd?"

<Torvald: tell @Capt. Meyers> "I'm looking through the tutorial. I'm sure once we get into view they'll disperse just at the sight of us."

As she spoke with Torvald, aerial views of Luke Base from the dragonflies flashed in front of her. *What a mess,* she thought. One image caught her attention and she froze it. *Shit, that's a civilian.* It must have been taken right before that dragonfly was fried, the image was blurred. But the person was definitely in civilian clothes. She got the coordinates and searched for a clearer image. The one she got was just a few meters above what was certainly a corpse.

Her mind went into a spin when she saw it. *Frak frak frak frak frak.*

<Gen. Wong: post> "Status on Gorgon plan, Parvati?"

Parvati stood quickly and caught her breath. She phanded a menu in the air before her, selecting *Torvald, Summon.* His life-sized avatar stood before her wearing a VDF flight suit.

"What's wrong?" Torvald asked.

She looked past him, searching the civilian registry. She found Edargo's last recorded location—Corpus Christi.

"What's the matter?" Torvald said with concern. Parvati grabbed the virtual picture of Edargo's corpse with her phand and shoved it in front of Torvald.

"Edargo is dead," she hissed. "What do you know about it?"

Torvald looked shocked. "I . . . I don't know. This is the first I've seen of this."

"I know communications are bad but everything we're getting point-to-point is going to you. Your brothers know about this. We're supposed to be taking extreme measures to avoid civilian deaths." She looked at him searchingly. "Are you lying to me?"

"You know I can't lie to you," Torvald said, his head and shoulders sagging. He looked at the ground, unable to face her. "I'm as shocked about this as you are." His voice was barely audible. "I need for you to believe me. I'll find out what happened. I'm sure there's an explanation."

<Gen. Wong: tell @Capt. Meyers> "ETA for the Gorgon decision please."

She took a step toward Torvald's image. Looking up at his face she said, "I can take your brain apart bit by bit. I can find out if you are lying to

199

me. I swear, if your brothers are killing civilians I will discontinue your entire line. I have everything invested in this—invested in you."

Torvald sniffed, a tear rolled down his cheek.

"You know that I love you," she said, her face and voice softening. "I need you as much as you need me. We need to make each other proud here. If you tell me this was an accident I will believe you."

"I don't know but it must have been an accident," he said, choking on his words.

"Then I'm sure it must have been. But you realize I will have to keep a closer watch over you all."

<Gen. Wong: tell @Capt. Meyers> "Gorgon status please."

"If I give you this mission with the Gorgons are you sure that you will be careful with the civilians?" Parvati said.

"We will be very careful."

"I'll be watching everything you do. If you get out of line I will be very, very angry."

"Yes Parvati."

"Okay. You've made me very proud up to this point." Yet she felt a little queasy thinking about the image of Edargo splayed out in the open, as if he had been exposed there for everyone to see on purpose. She had known when she first made Torvald that he would have to be put into situations where he might have to kill humans. She had designed characteristics in him that might be considered . . . psychopathic. She knew that when the decision had to be made to kill on the battlefield it had to be done without hesitation, without second thoughts. And one thing that she wanted to spare Torvald afterward was guilt—the torment of regret for anything she and the UP made him do. Perhaps she had gone a little too far with those psychopathic characteristics.

It was now too late for her to have second thoughts. She needed to have faith in her creation.

"You need to make me proud," she told him.

"Yes Parvati, I will."

<Capt. Meyers: post> "I'm giving the green light with the Gorgons."

Chapter 36

Raythen and Astria approached a metal door at the end of a corridor. The door slid open and they left behind the dull red of the emergency lights and entered into a room that had the elegant décor of a parlor from the nineteenth century. There were ornate wooden tables and chairs and the lighting came from silver chandeliers suspended from a high ceiling. Religious themed paintings from the renaissance hung on the walls. A delicate looking wooden spiral staircase was in the center of the room, leading both up and down.

<Lt. Rios: tell @Astria, @Raythen> "You are in possession of official militia equipment. Who authorized that? What are you doing here?"

Raythen looked around. There was no one else in the room. Rios must have been using the local point-to-point network of the cathedral.

<Astria: tell @Lt. Rios, @Raythen> "We have urgent information for Uzziah that can turn this battle to our favor. Are you in contact with him?"

<Lt. Rios: tell @Astria, @Raythen> "Raythen is supposed to be in custody, why is he armed?"

<Astria: tell @Lt. Rios, @Raythen> "The VDF does not have access to our hardwire network. We need to activate our network to coordinate our defenses. And the VDF is using A-Cons for their exos."

Several moments passed. Raythen said, "What if he doesn't believe us?"

"Stay here," Astria said. "I don't want you spotted by any Torvalds." She went up the spiral staircase. After she was out of sight for a few seconds a video image appeared on his HUD. It was from the interior of the cathedral above him.

<Astria: tell @Raythen> "You getting the feed?"

<Raythen: tell @Astria> "Copy."

<Astria: tell @Raythen> "I'll keep contact as long as they let us use their local network."

The interior of the cathedral, with its soaring gothic stone ribs, looked like the hollowed-out insides of some beached leviathan. Raythen watched the image bounce as Astria ran through the nave.

<Lt. Rios: tell @Astria, @Raythen> "Where are you going? I haven't given you permission to leave the parlor."

<Astria: tell @Lt. Rios, @Raythen> "Sorry lieutenant, this information is too important. We need to act now. The VDF have probably destroyed Mathew base already. Can you or can't you contact Uzziah?"

Astria passed through the atrium and headed for the ten-meter-tall open doors of the cathedral. Spotlights from outside gave the portal a glaring white glow. Silhouettes moved about on the broad stone platform that was at the top of the front steps. A male voice echoed in from the outside.

". . . together with our faith we shall show the unbelievers that we shall not be moved by their threats! We have the strength of God burning inside us! Jesus is here with his host of angels! There is one of the Lord's own angels standing next to each and every one of you!"

Astria stepped outside. There were about twenty people on the landing, several holding hands as they looked out on the crowd in the square below that now numbered over two-thousand. Astria could see the back of the man—well dressed and well coifed—standing at the lectern and speaking to the crowd. Lt. Rios, wearing a half-exo suit, ran over to her, lifted the visor of his helmet, and said, "You aren't authorized to be using militia equipment. Relinquish your weapons." He reached out his hand.

"Where are Uzziah and Theophilus? I need to talk to them."

"Relinquish your weapons or I'll take them."

"Your priorities are fucked up."

Lt. Rios thrust his hand forward for emphasis.

"Fine. We're wasting time." She unslung her MR-23 and handed it to him. He slung it over his own shoulder and held out his hand again. She pulled out her Glock pistol and gave it to him. "Okay, so can I talk to Uzziah or not?"

"I don't know where he is. We were all assigned to our positions and told to defend them. That was his last order. My position is here to keep the peace at this demonstration. Tell Raythen to get up here and relinquish his weapon now."

"I wouldn't bring Raythen out in the open unless you want a few dozen exoskeleton battle troopers up your ass."

"What? What does that mean?"

"Nothing." Astria said. "What about Theophilus? What was her last known location?"

"I don't know what happened to her after she left the shelter."

"Shit. Do you have any means of communicating with your commanding officer at all? You must have been given some instructions. Even carrier pigeons or smoke signals would be better than nothing for fuck's sake."

"I don't have time to deal with you right now. Get Raythen up here." Lt. Rios turned and walked to the edge to scan out over the crowd.

Astria saw Tray Wind's big ears at the other edge of the landing. She was also scanning over the crowd, getting some good shots for her news presentation. Astria walked over and stood in front of her, blocking her view.

"You made it out!" Tray said before shifting to the side to keep her eyes on the square. "I was worried." She didn't look worried; she seemed to be concentrating on something else very hard.

Astria moved to block her view again. "In case you're wondering, Edargo is dead."

"What? Dead?" Tray's full attention was now on Astria. "How?"

"Head cracked open. Seems the Torvalds are completely off the rails. Your finely honed journalistic sense wouldn't have a lead on Theophilus's location, would it?"

"Uh, no, I don't know where she is. Are you sure he's dead?"

"Oh yeah, I'm sure."

They both turned quickly to the square as screams came from the edge of the crowd, to the left of the cathedral. Bulky black shapes moved in the darkness beyond the lighted edge. The people closest to them started to move inward toward the middle, jostling the people who were already there.

"They're making their move!" Lt. Rios shouted to the other half-exos on the landing.

The six Gorgons, lined in a row, stepped in unison into the light. Five meters tall, the Gorgons were designed to control masses of people with the appearance of invulnerability. At the ends of arms the size of tree trunks were rectangular shields three meters tall and two wide. On the tops of their knobby heads were four black shiny tentacles, each as thick as a man's arm. The idea behind the tentacles was that when there was a mass demonstration, you could usually spot the most dangerous instigators by their body language and by the reactions of the people around them. The tentacles could extend up to twenty meters and pluck the instigators out of the crowd, dropping them into the paddy-wagons that usually trailed behind the Gorgons. There were no paddy-wagons here.

"Stay where you are!" the preacher cried from the lectern. "We are being tested by the Lord! Let your iron resolve match the iron demons that the VDF has sent against us!"

"Jesus fucking Christ," Astria whispered and walked purposefully to the preacher. Without warning she gave him a side-kick to the ribs that send him flying away from the lectern with a loud grunt. She took his place and said with a calm, authoritative voice, "Everyone must evacuate the square right now in a smooth, orderly manner. Please go to the nearest shelter and strap yourselves into one of the provided safety seats. We thank you ahead of time for your prompt cooperation."

As she spoke one of the militia half-exos rushed toward her, his arm extending to grab her. An instant before he reached her she turned around—pulling the crowbar out from her belt. The half-exo found himself grabbing the crowbar, his mechanical gloves locking onto it. Astria rapidly spun the crowbar clockwise while sweeping her leg underneath him. His mechanical arm, originally commanded by him to grab her and hold her still, was now a solid axel connected to a rigid shoulder which she used to spin his entire body, sending his head rapidly into the ground. She pulled the crowbar out of his now too late relaxed grip and looked around. Lt. Rios ran at her with arms extended to grapple her. She pivoted to the side and swung the crowbar at the back of his helmet, which flew off his head as he spilled into the lectern. She started to run for the cathedral door but something caught her ankle and she fell to the ground. She rolled onto her back and saw the first half-exo had lunged forward and grabbed her. She sat up and brought the crowbar down on the unarmored section at the wrist. He cried out and let go. As she scrambled to her feet she felt two vice grips on her shoulders that immobilized her.

"What are you doing?" she heard Lt. Rios say from behind her.

The half-exo in front of her stood and pulled out his MR-23 from its back-sling, holding it up with both hands to swing the butt into Astria's face.

"Harper! Stand down! I got her!" Lt. Rios yelled.

Harper ignored him and swung anyway. As the butt was coming down someone ran out of the cathedral door—falling into a roll and hitting Harper at the knees. Harper did an involuntary cart wheel and his helmeted head once again slammed into the ground. Raythen bounced to his feet and pointed his pistol at Lt. Rios's face.

"Let her go," he said.

"Who are you people?" Lt. Rios demanded with some measure of bewilderment. "Do you work for the VDF?"

Most of the people had cleared off the landing. Just a few stood around gaping, while the preacher was still on the ground, moaning and holding his side.

"Fuck no," Astria said. "I was just trying to save some people's lives."

Raythen was focused on Lt. Rios's face, on his forehead where his HUD placed the florescent green cross-hairs from his pistol. Lt. Rios starred at the barrel. If Rios made any fast moves, would he fire? Could he really do it?

<Astria: tell @Raythen> "You have to run into the cathedral now."

<Raythen: tell @Astria> "Once he frees you I'll run."

<Astria: tell @Raythen> "Run to the cathedral now. The Gorgons are coming, and they seem psycho."

Raythen glanced down into the square and saw the Gorgons rushing toward the stairs, tentacles waving.

Chapter 37

Half the people in the square were running away from the Gorgons—
the rest were defiantly holding their ground. The Gorgons, who had at first
marched slowly in an orderly line into the crowd, were now making a mad
dash toward the cathedral. A Gorgon at full gait could run at about forty
kilometers per hour. From the sudden swell of screams and screeches it
was obvious that the defiant ones weren't expecting this. All people in the
way were knocked aside by the riot shields with sickeningly fleshy
sounding thuds. Raythen saw one woman flung high into the air, spinning
wildly, her Bible fluttering out of her hands.

Everyone on the landing was now watching the Gorgons, even Lt.
Rios.

"Let go of me!" Astria ordered. Lt. Rios did and turned to face
carnage in the square—Raythen and Astria were no longer a priority.

Astria ran for the cathedral door, followed closely by Raythen and
Tray Wind. They were halfway through the nave when he heard the sounds
of crashing and wood splintering. He glanced back and saw the lead
Gorgon plowing its way through the benches, extending its tentacles
toward him. Looking forward again he saw some figures running out from
behind the altar. One of the figures was a full exo battle trooper, which
Raythen's HUD immediately identified as one of the Corpus Christi
Militia. Next to him was Erin Theophilus. The exo leaped over them and

started firing at the Gorgon. The pellets from the rail gun tore through the riot shields and impacted its body, exploding the armor with their ferocious kinetic energy. Two more Gorgons appeared from behind the damaged one, using their riot shields to send the church benches flying toward the exo trooper. Theophilus had stopped in her tracks.

"Get back to the stairs!" Astria yelled at her. "Turn around! Run!" Theophilus continued to stand and watch as the militia exo fired at the other Gorgons.

He should be moving, Raythen thought, looking at the exo. *He's just standing there, firing.*

Tentacles from the Gorgons extended toward the exo. He waved his rail gun as he fired, trying to hit the tentacles before they reached him. Normally, a single exo could easily take on multiple Gorgons, if the exo knew what he was doing. Raythen didn't think this exo knew what he was doing.

Astria grabbed hold of Theophilus's shoulder and turned her around. "Move!" she said. Raythen ran into the both of them and shoved them forward. They rounded behind the altar and went through the antique wooden doorway to the back room. Raythen slammed it shut. It was far too small for a Gorgon to fit through, giving him a sudden and welcome sense of safety. In the middle of the room Theophilus stood at the head of the spiral stairway and held up her hands to make them stop. "What happened out there?" she demanded.

"Get downstairs!" Astria yelled. "We're not safe here!"

To make her point a tentacle broke through the door, flailing widely back and forth, stopping, apparently at its full length, just a few meters away from them.

Another tentacle came through the door.

"Down!" Astria said. They didn't need any more prompting. They all raced down the spiral staircase, continuing down past the parlor that Raythen and Astria had first entered into. They ran down five more flights until the stairway ended at a subway terminal. They stopped at the glass wall in front of the track.

"Okay, what happened out there? What happened to the people in the square?" Theophilus asked Astria, her face looking red and possessed in the cavernous glow of the subway emergency lights.

"I think most of them got out of there safely," Astria said. "But more than a few got trampled."

"This has all gotten so out of control," Theophilus was hollowed out and exhausted. "I never thought the UP would use deadly force."

"Erin, you see the world in black and white, when it's really multiple shades of shit. Come on, let's get moving this way."

She led them up a short set of stairs to a pedestrian walk-way that ran along the subway line, protected by a hand-rail. It was wide enough for two people to walk abreast. The four of them went quickly down the walk-way, Astria and Theophilus in front with Raythen and Tray behind them.

"Where are we going?" Tray asked.

"We have to get to the next station fast," Astria said. "We should run."

They all ran at a brisk pace for several minutes until they came to the next station.

"Ray, you and Tray stay here for a minute," Astria said sternly. "I need a few private words with Erin."

"What about?" Theophilus asked.

"Come with me," Astria said, the glass door sliding open. She led Theophilus inside and the door slid closed behind them. She took

Theophilus around a corner so they were no longer in sight of the others and whispered, "Erin, I have a way for you to get out of here."

"What? How?"

"There's only room for one person. The CCM is almost finished. You have to escape. I can get you safely to the outer system. We can keep you hidden."

"I can't leave! How would it look if I ran off to safety! What would the people left behind think of me?"

"Erin, once the UP gets their hands on you they are going to *cure* you of religion. They are going to remove your ability to see God's hand in the world, to see God's hand in your heart. They are going to keep you buried until you yourself are going to condemn religion as silly, stupid and dangerous. And you are going to believe it."

Theophilus closed her eyes and shook her head. "No, no. That would never happen. I would never lose faith. Even if they . . . if they took away the feeling of God that I have, my faith would remain strong. I would not fail such a test."

"Erin, don't be selfish," Astria hissed. "This is not about you or your faith. This is not about passing any stupid test. This is about everyone else. This is about the faith of every believer in the solar system. If you walk out of that hospital condemning religion and God, the Godless fuckheads will have won. The only way for us to win is for you to escape."

"No, I can't run. I can't run from my people. We need to stand up strong together. We need to show the people of Sol System that we will stand for what we believe in. They will see the courage that faith has given to us."

"I'm sorry Erin," Astria said, taking hold of her upper arm. "I have to get you out of here."

Theophilus tried to jerk herself away, but Astria's grip was too strong. "Let go of me!" Theophilus yelled frantically. "Let go of me now!"

Astria let go suddenly like she had just touched a hot stove.

"Get me to John base now," Theophilus said, backing away. "Get me to John Base and then you can abandon the stratos if you want!"

"Erin—"

"Astria, I'm not discussing this any further. Get me to John Base."

Chapter 38

They were approaching John Base from a wide, underground passage when they saw an exo trooper and two half-exos running down the hall toward them—CCM soldiers. The exo trooper ran to Theophilus and said with a woman's voice, "I'm Colonel Kim Eun. Are you hurt at all? Are you under duress? Are you being followed?"

"I'm fine" Theophilus said. "I don't think we are being followed."

"Good. Come with us please."

They were led through several corridors until they came to a sliding metal door. It opened into a room about ten-by-ten meters. The room was bare except for several cots up against the walls. Sitting on the far cot was a man and two dark haired girls, one about ten years old, the other about six. The youngest was sitting on the man's lap. Colonel Kim's helmet vanished, showing her holographic head. She went to the man and the girls, putting her large robotic hand on the youngest girl's cheek.

"You being brave for daddy?" she asked. The little girl nodded. "Look who's going to be staying with you!" She turned to the door as Theophilus walked in.

"Ms. Theophilus!" the girl cried out and jumped off her father's lap. She was about to run but then stopped herself and looked at her mother. Her mother nodded. She ran to Theophilus and hugged her knees. "Theophilus Theophilus Theophilus! You have a funny name!"

Colonel Kim looked at her husband. He gave a wan smile. "How are you holding up?" she asked him.

"We pray," he said. "And then we pray more."

She looked at her oldest daughter whose eyes were staring down at her own feet. "Hey, Hana," she said. Her daughter didn't respond.

"I'll be back," Colonel Kim said to all of them. She turned to Theophilus. "These are privates Roland and Domingo." She motioned to the two half-exos. "They will be right outside your door. If you want anything, ask them. Whatever happens, you must remain with at least one of them at all times. I'll be back when the situation allows." She put a hand on her youngest daughter's head. "Look after Ms. Theophilus now." She hurried out of the room.

Pvt. Domingo said, "If you need to use the bathroom there's one down the corridor on the left." They went into the hallway and the door slid closed.

Theophilus picked up the little girl and asked, "What's your name?"

"I'm Hy!"

"Well I'm glad to meet you Hy." She went over to Colonel Kim's husband and sat down next to him.

Raythen sat down on the cot closest to the door. Astria was pacing back and forth across the room.

Tray Wind sat next to Raythen. "I heard about Edargo. I'm sorry. You two seemed tight."

Raythen rested his elbows on his knees and covered his forehead with his right hand. Thinking of Edargo, his eyes welled up with tears. Tray's hand gently rubbed his shoulder. He felt his shoulders shake.

"Jesus Raythen, man up," Astria said. "We're not in a good situation here. Not at all. No time to go all pussy on us. We need to plan our next move."

Astria was right. Raythen pulled off his smart glasses and rubbed away any tears from his eyes, straightening his shoulders. He then realized that he had to go to the bathroom.

"Always relieve yourself when you think it's safe," he heard Sarge's voice say. "You never know how long before the next bio break."

He sighed loudly and said, "I'll be right back," getting up and going to the door. It didn't open when he stood in front of it. He knocked a couple of times. It opened.

"Excuse me," he said to the privates, and went down the hall to the left.

Sitting on the cushioned toilet, the air was sprayed with fresh lilac scents and tinkly background music played. He took several deep breaths.

He heard someone else enter the room and go into the stall next to his. A second later there was a knock on the wall.

"It's me, Astria. We need to talk. I don't want to use the point-to-point; the militia might be listening. We have to get out of here."

"I need to get an exo suit. I can help them up there. We need to get to the exo booth."

"Not an option. Militias have a reputation for paranoia. I don't think they would much like giving an exo suit to a stranger, no matter what their situation. Hey, at the cathedral steps, was that your first Mexican standoff?"

"In real life, yeah."

"Gratz, achievement unlocked. Listen, we need to get deep down into the base, hide out until they rein in the Torvalds. Hopefully we will get found by some humans during the mop up."

"So, are you thinking that the two of us leave?" Raythen asked.

"We have to bring Erin with us."

"I don't think that's going to happen."

"We need to make it happen."

"How?"

"You've got a gun. We've also been given some conveniently cute hostages we can use to convince Erin to come with us. All you need to do is grab the little girl and put a gun to her head. I'll do all the talking."

Just when he was starting to believe that Astria couldn't surprise him anymore, she had to go and prove him wrong.

"Um . . . no."

"Come on! You can do it. From what I've seen you've got at least one testicle in there."

"I think enough people want to kill me already," Raythen said.

"If no one wants to kill you then you haven't really lived," Astria said, like it was her life motto.

"You're not going to convince me to take a little girl hostage."

The toilet decided that Raythen was done. It sprayed water on his bottom and then wiped him clean. He stood, pulled up his pants, and got out of the stall. Astria banged open her stall and glared at him. He looked down at her skin-tight white HAZMAT suit that was still sealed over her body. He found himself wondering if she had to relieve herself. She seemed to read his thoughts.

"I can go for days without pissing or pooping. I'm like a camel."

"Yeah?" Raythen said, momentarily distracted by the turn of conversation.

"Really. I've been modified. I can literally not go for days."

They stood there for an uncomfortable few moments. Then Raythen said, "I'm going to head back to the room."

"Me too. And if I do anything that seems insane or evil, just keep out of my way. It would be best for both of us."

Raythen believed her.

Chapter 39

In the far end of the room the father was telling his youngest daughter the story of the three bears while she sat on his lap in rapt attention. His oldest daughter was still staring down at her own feet. In the corner near the door Tray and Theophilus sat on the opposite ends of a cot—Tray had apparently gotten Theophilus to give an interview. Astria went back to pacing. Raythen sat across the room from Tray and Theophilus. He was looking at his encased left hand, a seemly solid dead mass. Astria walked past him, her feet flapping impatiently on the floor. He looked up to watch her, her thighs at the level of his eyes, their tensed muscles moving underneath the white, tight HAZMAT suit, her crowbar swinging against one thigh.

"Were there any indications during the negotiations that the UP would resort to violence?" Tray asked Theophilus. "Any sort of threats, however veiled?"

"There was no indication at all. There were no threats. They said they wanted us to cease construction of New Sinai until we could arrange a conference. That's all they were pushing for. I was perfectly willing to pause construction for a few days and was discussing it with the other share-holders in the stratos."

"But what about their demand to send in inspectors to your militia bases to see if you had illegal weapons? Didn't they threaten some sort of action if you didn't let them in?"

"We hadn't formally discussed that issue, not since the arrival of the Pax Cythera. We insisted that we had to discuss the status of the children first. We wanted a promise they wouldn't take any legal action about the custody of the children, they are our prime concern."

"As your prime concern, I take it that you don't agree with the Psychiatric Association's determination that teaching religion to children is . . . subjecting them to the psychiatric disease of hyper-anthropomorphization disorder."

Theophilus gave a bitter chuckle. "Actually, I agree with them on that one. Looking at it completely objectively, the way they have defined hyper-anthropomorphization disorder, it is the same as believing in God. And that's exactly what we are teaching them to do. I can't argue with that. What I can argue about is their determination that it is a mental disorder. Humans have been worshiping a personified metaphysical power for thousands of years. I can't see how they could call the normal behavior of humanity for most of history a mental disorder."

"Really? During that long history there were other behaviors that were considered normal. Racial prejudice, misogyny, child abuse, genocide. Many of these things done in the name of religion. So arguing that something was normal for most of history is not a valid argument that it is sane."

"People so easily forget the good that has been done in the name of religion." Theophilus retorted. "The abolition of slavery in the United States was spearheaded primarily by religious leaders. When indigenous people were being exploited around the world it was often the missionaries who were the only ones looking out for their well-being. During the Middle Ages the only hospitals that existed were those provided by the Church. But all that people remember today are crusades, jihads, and inquisitions. The seculars themselves say that religion *evolved* in human society because it allowed for the formation of larger tribes of people. It allowed for hundreds, thousands, millions of people to work together to build this civilization we live in today."

"Okay, for now, let's leave the arguments about history to the academics. Today, as we speak, people are fighting and dying just meters above us. Do you feel any personal responsibility for the deaths that have happened here today?"

Astria, just reaching the opposite end of the room, stopped and turned her head toward Tray Wind. She glared. A hand moved to rest on her crowbar.

Theophilus hesitated and brushed her hand over her smooth brown forehead. Her eyes seemed to lose focus for a second before she sat up straight and said "That is a fair question. That is a valid question. Of course, I've been asking that to myself all day." She took a deep breath. "We never know what our actions will bring to us and to those around us. We never know the full repercussions that come from standing up for our convictions. If I can't be free to live my life the only way I can understand life to be lived, and to do so peacefully . . . if that leads to *others* committing acts of brutal violence against us. . . then yes, I will take full responsibility for the deaths that occur today."

"Hmmm," said Tray, thinking about that. "Hmmm, that's very brave." She looked up, obviously reading some notes on her HUD. "Your born name is Erin O'Toole. Before you went public with your religious mission you changed it to Theophilus because it means 'one who loves God'. You

221

also changed your appearance to African. Is it true you became African because that old *Magical Negro* trope still has legs and you thought it would help you get converts?"

"Hold on there, spunky girl reporter!" Astria said walking quickly toward them. "You're going to experience some good old fashioned religious oppression first hand if you keep up that shit."

"Are you serious?" Tray said, getting up off the cot.

"That's okay," Theophilus said, holding a hand up toward Astria. "These are things that people are wondering about. It's best that I answer them." She turned back to Tray. "I took on this appearance because it looks like Nefertiti, one of the first monotheists in recorded history. She and her husband Akhenaten tried to replace the polytheism of Egypt with the worship of a single god of love and peace. She is a woman I admire. Also, someone at the time said that I had the poise and grace to pull off this look. What do *you* think?"

"Thank you for your candid replies," Tray said curtly.

"It's all bullshit," Hana said from her seat across the room. "I'm sick of all this religious bullshit."

"Hana!" her father said. "Don't talk like that!"

"I'm sick of this place! I never wanted to move here! I don't want to be a Meta! It's a stupid religion! Mommy is going to die because of this stupid religion!"

Hana's face was scrunched up with rage. Her hands were on her lap grabbing frantically at each other's fingers. They were the only parts of her moving. "Stupid," she whispered. Everyone watched her silently. Then she jumped up and ran toward the door. Theophilus stepped in front of her and grabbed her before she reached it. Hana thrashed in her arms, punching at Theophilus's shoulders and back as she lifted her up.

"Let me down! Let me down! I want to get out of here! Let me down!"

There was a series of loud explosions above them that shook the room. The door slid open and Pvt. Roland poked his head in and said, "Time to go people."

Chapter 40

The elevator opened to a large circular glass room. Beyond the glass was the factory level of the city, thirty meters below. Against the glass walls were consoles with chairs spaced every few meters. All the chairs were empty.

<Raythen: tell @Astria> "We got Theophilus down here just like you wanted and you didn't have to do anything crazy."

<Astria: tell @Raythen> "Hrumph."

They exited the elevator and spread out into the room. Pvt. Roland leaned over a console and viewed out over the factory floor. It was a spacious expanse, shiny black pillars ten meters in diameter reaching from the floor to the ceiling, the rows of them stretching into the distance like some postmodern reproduction of a prayer hall in an ancient Spanish cathedral. Rail tracks made a grid that connected all of the pillars to each other and to trails that weaved in between. Raythen could feel the hum of power that coursed through the air.

Theophilus was carrying Hy, who was looking around with wonder. Her father was whispering something to Hana, who went straight to a chair and swiveled it to face the glass wall with her arms folded. Tray walked to the center of the room and spun around slowly to record their surroundings. Pvt. Domingo positioned himself at the side of the elevator. Astria stood next to Raythen.

<Astria: tell @Raythen> "I lied to you. My plan isn't to hide out here till we get caught. My plan is to get Theophilus off this stratos."

Raythen tried to keep his face expressionless as he communicated silently with Astria.

<Raythen: tell @Astria> "How are you going to do that?"

<Astria: tell @Raythen> "That's a need to know. You don't need to know yet."

<Raythen: tell @Astria> "When will I need to know?"

<Astria: tell @Raythen> "Pretty soon. The plan is very time sensitive."

Text flashed in front of Raythen:

CORPUS CHRISTI CITY WIDE NETWORK ONLINE.
IMPORTANT BROADCAST INCOMING.

"Thank God," Pvt. Domingo said.

"What?" Tray said, unable to receive the message since she was without point-to-point smart glasses. "Thank God what?"

"The local network is back," Astria said, "although it's probably too late to do any good."

<Uzziah: post #Emergency> "Despite all of our most valiant efforts, our last militia base has fallen, and the unbelievers have vanquished our brave soldiers. But all is not lost. They may have won on the battlefield, but we can show the seculars that we will not submit to their hideous experiments on our souls. I and a few others have made it to the aerosail that is pulling the stratos. We have altered the direction so we are descending by a few degrees, hopefully not enough to get the attention of the VDF, but bringing us slowly to an unsafe altitude. In about a half an

hour I will put the aerosail into a steep dive and bring the city low enough that the air pressure will compromise the protective dome, which has already taken some damage from the fighting. We have overridden the safety systems that would have automatically deployed the helium balloons. This way, we will show the secular population of the solar system that there is something more important than this hedonistic life that they cling to like a pearl of great value, when the greatest value is God's love. So take these last minutes and pray together, for we are martyrs, pure in spirit, and will all be celebrating together with our Lord this day."

"Oh my God!" Pvt. Domingo said and fell to his knees. Pvt. Roland didn't move or say anything, but the blood had drained from his face.

"What?" Tray said. "What? 'Oh my God' what? What's wrong?"

Astria turned to Raythen and gave him a firm stare.

<Astria: tell @Raythen, @Roland, @Domingo> "Everyone be quiet and do exactly what I say. We don't have much time to save Theophilus's life. Raythen, grab the little girl from Theophilus and put her on the floor. Roland, grab hold of Theophilus and bring her to the elevator. Domingo, stay here and make sure the civilians stay put. Okay, on go—three, two, one, go!"

Astria has a way of getting out of this stratos, Raythen thought. If he did what she said she could perhaps also get him off. He went to Theophilus and grabbed Hy away from her, placing her at her father's feet. Roland was still standing by the elevator.

"Pvt. Roland go!" Astria ordered. He quickly moved over to Theophilus and grabbed her in a bear hug from behind, lifting her off her feet. Astria opened the elevator door and motioned him to get her in. He complied.

"What are you doing?" Theophilus cried. "Put me down!"

Astria went into the elevator with Raythen close behind. As the door started to close Pvt. Domingo ran up and held it open. "I have to get to my family!"

Tray slid in. "What the hell is going on? What's happening?"

"Hurry up then!" Astria said, stepping forward and pulling Domingo and Tray in, allowing the elevator to slide closed. They felt the elevator descend.

"What are you doing?" Theophilus repeated. "Astria, what are you doing?"

"Saving your life."

"How can you save her life?" Pvt. Domingo asked. "How can you do that? How many people can you save?"

"Only one," Astria said. "I think it's obvious who it should be."

"What the hell are you people talking about?" Tray asked, visibly shaken. "Raythen! Do you know what's going on? Where are we going?"

"We're going down." The words came out as a hoarse whisper from Raythen's dry mouth.

"Down? Down? Down the elevator? What do you mean down?"

"I mean all the way down."

The elevator door opened.

Chapter 41

<Wilton: post> "Is everybody watching the Cathedral Square footage? What the fuck was that?"

<Gen. Wong: post> "We're still analyzing the situation. Capt. Meyers?"

<Capt. Meyers: post> "Yes. We are analyzing the situation."

Capt. Meyers was staring at video from the cathedral steps, rewinding and playing the same eleven seconds over and over. *That's Raythen. What is Raythen doing there?*

<Wilton: post> "Why the fuck would they storm the cathedral? Did you see those civilians? Did you see the air some of those people caught? If any vids of that gets out to the public it's going to be top-viewed. This is not good."

<Capt. Meyers: post> "Unfortunately none of the AUs in the Gorgons made it back so we can't know for sure what happened."

<Wilton: post> "Of course none came back! They boxed themselves in the cathedral! They were sitting ducks!"

<Gen. Wong: post> "It seems to have something to do with that fight on the cathedral steps. Some half-exos were fighting some civilians. Perhaps the AUs were trying to protect the civilians."

<Wilton: post> "By storming through a crowd of women and children? I have to question the stability of your AUs, Parvati. We are

getting much larger than expected reports of civilian deaths. They *are* doing great against the CCM, better than expected, but fuck, they really flipped out at the cathedral. We need to make sure they behave themselves now that the fighting is settling down. And we need to find Theophilus. What's the latest word on that?"

<Gen. Wong: post> "Still no word about her or the Achaeans."

<Wilton: post> "We are about ready to send in some human troops, right? We have an engineering team ready to go in and find their jammers, don't we?"

<Gen. Wong: post> "Yes, we have some engineering teams ready to go in."

<Wilton: post> "Parvati, I want you to go in with the first team. I want you in as close contact with your AUs as possible to keep a leash on them."

<Gen. Wong: post> "Sir, with all due respect, that is a military decision. We should be able to reestablish the network soon—in my estimation it is not necessary to risk Capt. Meyers on the battlefield."

<Wilton: post> "This is a political decision. We are taking a huge political risk using AUs in the first place and I don't even know how to spin the cathedral mess. I put everything on the line trusting both of your opinions on them. We need to make sure we round them up as soon as possible and get this situation under control."

<Capt. Meyers: post> "I'm fine with going out there. I'm rated for a battle exo."

<Wilton: post> "See General, she's fine with it."

<Gen. Wong: post> "Very well. Captain, get ready to join Major Chin's team."

Capt. Meyers stared at the image of Raythen pointing a gun at the militia half-exo. *What the frak are you doing here?*

Chapter 42

Nigh immortality, the common condition of humanity that was once reserved only for the mythological, had been accepted by the general population with remarkable ease. Part of this could be explained by the slow increase in lifespan over the years—where people were first expected to live into their seventies, then eighties, then to the low one-hundreds. It wasn't any one breakthrough that made people nigh immortal, but many brilliant discoveries and refinements of technique that were introduced over time. This gradual introduction somewhat, but not completely, explained why people accepted this technological miracle so easily and without fanfare. Perhaps the most significant factor as to why it was so easily accepted into public consciousness was that most people, deep inside, had a part of them that didn't really accept in a concrete sense that death would ever happen to them. Once science confirmed this little wishful belief, once doctors started telling people matter-of-factly, short of any injury that destroyed the brain, that whatever was wrong was just a matter of a bit of biological engineering, it was as easy for people to accept their right to nigh immortality as it was for them to accept their right to be continuously entertained.

Tray Wind, for the first time in her life, faced her mortality.

They were all standing outside of the elevator door on the factory floor. Pvt. Domingo still held onto Theophilus. Pvt. Roland had run off.

"He can't destroy the stratos!" Tray screeched, her hands, made into claws, grasping the empty air. Her voice echoed through the ebon expanse. "I can't die! I'm going to get a Pulitzer! I'm going to be famous! Uzziah can't be that crazy! It's a lie! It's a bluff!"

"It would only be a bluff if he told the VDF." Astria said. "He hasn't."

"No! This is crazy! You're a bunch of crazy religious fanatic fucks!"

"Be quiet," Astria said, looking into the distance. "I'm trying to concentrate."

"Concentrate? On what?" Tray said angrily. "On your plan to get Theophilus out of here? What about the rest of us? Get the rest of us out of here!"

"I'm not leaving here," Theophilus said firmly. "Domingo, let go of me. We need to stop Uzziah."

"Even if we could get to the aerosail in time he'll have it defended," Astria said.

"What about the emergency balloons?" Tray said. "They're supposed to deploy when we go below a certain altitude, right? They're fucking fail-safes! That's what they tell everyone! I wouldn't have come to Venus if there weren't fail-safes! 'Go in the shelter, the balloons will deploy!' There are fail-safes!"

"Uzziah planned for that," Astria said. "He disconnected the fail-safes."

"What the fuck! They're fail-safes! Fail-safes!" she said, bending forward like she had to pee. "How do you disconnect fail-safes?"

In a quick motion that surprised even Raythen, Astria's right fist flew into Tray Wind's mouth. Tray took two stumbling steps backwards, swayed uncertainly, and then sunk down to sit on the floor.

Astria shook her right hand, grimaced, and muttered to herself, "Not in the mouth." She looked at Tray and said, "Dying is the last important thing you'll do in life. Try to do it well." She then went back to her concentrating as Tray rocked back and forth on the ground.

Raythen's mind was racing. He didn't want to die either. Strategies formed and competed in his mind. The obvious one was to use whatever plan Astria had for Theophilus for himself. There were impediments, the biggest being Astria. But he was armed—and she wasn't. Once he found out the plan . . . he could kill them. Kill them and live.

In *Gryphon's Claw*, Raythen was a rogue, a cad, a villain. A rakish villain, but definitely a villain. Would *he* think twice about killing some people in order to live? Raythen was supposed to live forever. And these people are going to die anyway. The person they were going to save didn't even want to be saved. It would be risky. He went through the steps, almost involuntarily. A shot from behind between the helmet and the neck in the seam at point blank wouldn't penetrate Pvt. Domingo's suit, but the impact might fracture his spinal cord. He could use Domingo's body as a shield as he shot Astria. He would have to act fast; they were now hooked into the network and she was probably watching them all from an overhead camera. And she seemed fairly competent with that crowbar.

Even as he planned this—there was something inside him—some unnamed hardened nugget of self—that was disgusted by the images that formed from the plan. Some *thing* that was wordlessly telling him that such a plan could not be on the table.

Forever is a long time. The hardened nugget stared at him facelessly, and Raythen knew that if he lived, that disgusted nugget of self would be there forever, reminding him of *how* it was possible for him to still be alive.

There had to be another plan.

"I need an exo battle suit," Raythen said to Astria.

She didn't move, didn't look at him, but after a second she said, "You can't get one; the militia bases are gone."

"There's got to be a repair shop in here somewhere. When I was in the military there were always one or two suits in the shop. If I had security access I could get a suit and run to the aerosail and stop Uzziah."

Astria's head shifted slightly toward him. "That's actually a good idea," she said. A schematic appeared in front of him of the floor they were on. A red line went from their current position to a rectangle marked "Repair Depot" about two-thirds of a kilometer toward the starboard side.

"Before you go, give me your weapon," she said.

Raythen pulled his pistol but hesitated, "I might need this."

"It won't do any good against a Torvald, and you can't use it in a suit."

He nodded and handed her the pistol.

"Now go," she said. "You have full security clearance."

He started running.

Chapter 43

Raythen displayed a countdown timer in the corner of his HUD that he set from the time when Uzziah said he was *taking the stratos down in half an hour*. It was at 24:43. It would take him a little over a minute to get to the repair depot. If there was a suit and if it was in working condition, he could get it on in about two minutes. That would give him twenty minutes to get to the aerosail.

As he ran he felt his injured leg buckle a little with each stride. He decided to have his imp stop blocking the pain. There was now a sharp sting from the muscle with each buckle, but the added feedback allowed him to compensate for it more effectively.

He ran between the towering black molecular assemblers, constantly looking back and forth for any movement. The Torvalds knew that both he and Theophilus were down here and they might come searching. But he was now connected to the Corpus Christi defense network and had clearance. He requested imagery intelligence for the factory floor. On his map he saw two orange dots in his vicinity—orange being the color for surveillance drones. *Dragonflies!* One was right on his six and trailing him.

<Raythen: tell @Corpus Christi Defense> "Request imint on this floor—battle exos."

Nothing appeared on the map.

In the distance up ahead he saw the repair depot. It was a large white building with several garage doors big enough for the passage of industrial vehicles. He phanded over it and clicked. A window showing its status appeared—there were no people inside. In the building menu, *Inventory* was a choice. He clicked it and he got a long list of items that scrolled off the page. "Exo battle suit," he said between breaths. The list slid down several hundred items and highlighted three exo battle suits. *Yes!* He clicked the first and it blew up to a 3D schematic. He saw immediately that both legs were inoperable. He clicked the second. It was fully operational. Breathing harder than what just could be explained by the run he requested that it be made ready in the fitting booth. The depot obliged.

<Corpus Christi Defense: tell @Raythen> "Possible targets acquired."

His map zoomed out and showed two red dots about a kilometer to the stern. Their estimated speed was 110 kph. After a moment their trajectories were projected—they were heading straight for him. The Torvalds had found him.

Raythen swiped away the depot menu from his view and focused on the door ahead of him. He didn't slow down as it slid open and he ran inside, yelling "Emergency lock-down! No one enters!" He ran through the expansive, hanger-like building weaving between heavy industrial equipment and mechanized freight movers. The building was without armaments, the lock-down would slow the Torvalds by about half a second. He followed a florescent trail overlay to the exo fitting booth, pulling off his shirt as he turned a corner around a house-sized jet engine nacelle. The booth was half-surrounded by an electronics repair station— benches strewn with tools and parts. The booth itself was a metallic cylinder three meters wide and twice as tall. The door slid open and Raythen kicked off his shoes, unbuckling his pants and pulling them off before stepping inside, turning around to get a look at the direction he had come before the door slid closed.

He put his arms out straight to the sides and stood still. The Torvalds were slowing down outside the depot. Security gave him visuals of their blurred outlines—their active camouflage partially compensated for by the stratos security. Carbon polymer rods slipped into his hip sockets and he felt the reassuring click as they locked in. The floor fell away and he dangled over the hole. The jellpack suit came on with four different parts, pulled on by robotic hands. From below him the jellpack stockings were pulled up to his waist—from above a jellpack poncho fell on him and became a vest as it stitched itself together. The sleeves were pulled on and all four pieces stitched into one full body suit. There were two simultaneous explosions at the depot wall. Wallinators. Every battle exoskeleton was equipped with a handgun that could shoot globs of plastic explosives, their main purpose being to destroy walls. The Torvalds were inside. Plastimuscle was weaved onto the jellpack suit, providing both protection and augmenting his strength. When it was finished wrapping over him, the outer armor was placed on in sections. First the chest and back pieces coming together and bolting on, then the lower torso and codpiece. The surveillance video was trying to keep track of the Torvalds, but would lose them on occasion as they zigzagged through the building. The Torvalds were keeping within visual range of each other to maintain point-to-point communication. The time it was taking for the suit to be fitted was maddening. The arms were bolted on—with a battle exoskeleton, the trooper's biological hands were kept in the wrist, and robotic hands were connected to the ends of the arms. As they were added Raythen took control of them and was relieved to have two good hands again.

It was then that he realized that he didn't have a rail gun. All of the ordinance was maintained in the military bases.

If he panicked he would die. Somehow, knowing that panic would kill him kept him calm. He needed a weapon. He scanned around the immediate vicinity with the surveillance cameras. He could just try to run, but they were almost on him—there was a welding machine there—*No, that wouldn't do.* He could throw that car engine block—*no, no, no.*

Then he saw his weapons.

The Torvalds were coming in from the same direction that he had arrived, from behind the large engine nacelle. The one on the right had a wider trajectory—he would see the booth first. The armored boots were being sealed onto his feet as the floor below him was returned. He put the surveillance angle as close to his view from the booth as possible—the camera was on the ceiling a little to the left and behind. He couldn't tell if the Torvalds could see his booth yet. A familiar band of text appeared before him:

ARMOR INTEGRATION COMPLETE—BEGINNING DIAGNOSTICS.

"Emergency! Cancel diags and open the booth now!"

The booth door slid open. Raythen leaped out and rolled onto the floor. The booth behind him exploded into shattered fragments that flew in all directions. He ran to a construction mech that was squatting a few meters away from the booth, one of its arms had been removed for repairs. Leaning against it were two sledge hammers—sledge hammers that were made to be lifted by a construction mech. Two-meter-long carbon polymer handles ended with lead-filled titanium heads that weighed fifty kilograms.

He grabbed one in each hand and swung them above his head. He turned and ran toward the nacelle.

Both Torvalds, still out of direct sight, were firing, sending a rain of pellets on either side of the nacelle. From the firing trajectories Raythen had a positive fix on their positions as they closed in. The work benches and construction mech were blown back from impacts. Raythen ran to the left side of the nacelle, swinging his sledge hammer as the Torvald came running in at sixty kilometers per hour. The hammer head connected solidly on the Torvald's chest—Raythen felt the impact shake his arm as the Torvald was flung backwards a dozen meters into the air. Raythen spun his body along with the momentum of the hammer head, landing on his feet and leaping up on top of the nacelle. He had hoped that the other Torvald would have run around it, but he had leaped up on top of the nacelle as well and was now pointing his rail gun at him. Raythen spun to the left as he came toward the Torvald. A rail gun pellet grazed his right hip, activating the reactive armor with an explosive pop. He swung his hammer low. Torvald jumped to avoid it. Raythen spun hard with the hammer and watched the Torvald arching through the air. Raythen's other arm swung its hammer down as the exo reached the apex. The titanium head hit him with an audible crunch and his trajectory was instantly altered toward the ground below—the curve of the rail gun's motion revealed by the destruction of a cross section of the nacelle underneath Raythen. He jumped away and dropped down next to the Torvald, sledge hammers raised. He brought them down in quick secession, one hammer striking and shattering the rail gun. The exo was trying to crawl away. Raythen rained down blows upon him—screaming as he did so, although he himself didn't realize he was screaming. Fragments of armor flew away, revealing twitching plastimuscle. The Torvald stopped making any meaningful movements.

The nacelle exploded and flew toward Raythen. He rolled away from it and scanned for the other Torvald on the surveillance cameras. He was running toward him from behind the remnants of the nacelle, firing his rail gun, swinging it left and right. Raythen got to his feet and ran to the left, getting an exact fix. As the Torvald came into view Raythen threw one of the hammers at him. It spun through the air as the exo caught view of Raythen and brought his gun to bear on him. The hammer struck the Torvald at the lower hip—he fell forward, flipping and tumbling to the ground. Raythen ran at him, holding his remaining hammer with both hands and swinging it down. The Torvald rolled out of its path as it cracked the floor. The rail gun pointed toward Raythen who made a desperate kick as it fired—pellets whizzing past his head. He raised the hammer as the exo sprang to his feet. He made a sweeping swing and the Torvald ducked below it. Raythen released the hammer and lunged forward, grabbing at the gun barrel with both hands, pushing it down as it fired. The floor exploded underneath them, creating a hole, and they both tumbled down into darkness in a free-fall.

Chapter 44

The shipping container slid noiselessly on the tracks toward Astria. It was a black, smooth, shiny cube—five meters tall and wide. It slowed to a stop in front of her. From the side closest to her a section slid out at about the height of her waist. Inside was a stasis chamber.

"Here's the plan," Astria said. "We are still in range of the sky hook. An automated freighter was supposed to take a shipment to it from here earlier today, but was canceled by the hostilities. I've reactivated its launch. Pvt. Domingo, put Theophilus in the stasis chamber."

"No, don't do it," Theophilus said, ineffectively struggling in Domingo's grip. "You can't make me stand still for this. I won't go in."

"Erin, I'm saving your life. Please, let me save your life," Astria said impatiently. "We don't have time for this."

Pvt. Domingo brought her close to the stasis chamber. Theophilus lifted her feet and tried to kick away from the rim.

"Wait a minute," Tray said, standing back up, tears and blood streaking her face. "Your plan doesn't make sense. The sky hook is sending the freight to the Sun-Venus L4 transfer station millions of kilometers away in space. It will take weeks to get there. Don't you think they will want to investigate the last shipment made *minutes* before this stratos's destruction? Don't you think they will suspect maybe someone was smuggled in with the freight?"

"We've already planned for that. There's nothing to worry about," Astria said firmly.

"Planned for that?" Tray said. "How could you have planned for that? The UP will send one of their interplanetary ships to investigate. Even if they didn't get to it before it reached the transfer station you could be sure they will have *that* place locked down. There's no way your people can get to her before the UP does."

Standing next to Astria, Pvt. Domingo had stopped pushing Theophilus forward. Even Theophilus had stopped struggling.

"We have plans for everything. Erin, we're going to get you to safety," Astria said.

"Of course you are," Tray said, pointing an accusing finger at her. "Because you work for the UP! They want her alive so they can cure her of hyper-anthropomorphization! They don't want her to be martyred! You're a fucking spy! You work for the UP!"

Astria let out a tired, impatient sigh. With a lightning fast move she pulled out her pistol and, without looking, placed it on the seam at the back of the neck of Pvt. Domingo's armor—where Raythen had contemplated firing minutes before. Astria did more than contemplate. As the pistol fired she pulled it back away—Pvt. Domingo's suit released Theophilus. The suit, sensing a neck injury, inflated small air-bags around his neck to immobilize it and dropped him to his knees before guiding him to a prone position flat on his back.

Astria pointed the gun at Tray. Without hesitating she fired two shots. Tray's head jerked violently back—two holes in her forehead. She fell onto the floor.

Theophilus stood at the edge of the stasis chamber. She turned numbly and whispered, "Astria?"

"No time."

She kicked Theophilus in the stomach—as she doubled over the butt of the piston came down on the back of her head.

A few moments later the stasis door closed with Theophilus inside, being prepped to be frozen for her interplanetary flight. Astria watched the shipping container slide away. In her own mind she didn't use the name "Astria" for herself. She had a different handle.

She thought of herself as Crowbar.

As Crowbar watched the shipping container recede into the distance, she thought, *As far as missions go, this one is about as fubar as they get.*

She smiled inwardly at the thought that the Universe might actually manage to kill her this time.

Chapter 45

Raythen locked his grip on the barrel of the rail gun as he plunged down into the darkness with Torvald. His imp told him he was ten meters from the floor, now nine. Torvald was thrashing and kicking. They tumbled in freefall. Raythen grabbed Torvald's upper arm with his free hand and jerked his body almost instinctively—they struck the floor, Raythen on top of Torvald.

They were in the service floor underneath the factory—no lights—the suit's light-amplifying vision making the most of what was coming in from the hole above, revealing a labyrinth of pipes and cables. Torvald attempted to pull away the rail gun while simultaneously trying to stand up. This pulled Raythen forward, he hooked his foot on a pipe on the ground and yanked back, swinging Torvald forward. As Torvald lost his footing he fired, sending pellets spraying behind Raythen. With all his might Raythen pushed the barrel down toward Torvald's knee. Torvald stopped firing, but too late. Torvald's leg was blown off below the knee. Raythen planted his foot on Torvald's chest and pulled at the barrel. The rail gun came free of Torvald's grasp. Of course, Raythen couldn't fire it, it was a secured VDF weapon, but he could use it as a club. He swung the gun down on Torvald as exo tried to maneuver out of the way. He kept swinging, keeping him down. As he pounded on Torvald he remembered that he had to be elsewhere—fast. Torvald was trying to fend the blows with his arms—it was a very human-looking action. Raythen wanted to penetrate the armor, to tear it open and grab hold of that cemi field unit that contained Torvald's mind. He wanted to strike it against the ground till it shattered into tiny pieces—but he did't have the time to do that. He stepped back. *Got to go and stop Uzziah from killing everybody.* He raised the now broken gun up in the air and shook it in a gesture that came off as one of both threat and frustration.

<Raythen: tell @Corpus Christi Defense> "Requesting fastest route to aerosail tether."

A blue florescent trail appeared on the floor. Torvald hadn't moved since Raythen had stopped beating him. His arms were still up in a defensive position. So disconcertingly human. At least he wouldn't be able to follow him with that missing leg.

Raythen ran after the trail.

Chapter 46

There was the problem of the head. Crowbar pulled out the standard issue military knife from her belt and by habit tested its sharpness by lightly brushing over the edge with her thumb. Of course it was razor sharp; all knives were always razor sharp these days. She squatted over Tray Wind's body and grabbed her blue hair in her fist, stretching the neck. *Start with the trachea and work back. Blood blood blood.* Good thing she was wearing the HAZMAT suit, the blood just rolled right off. It was always easy until you hit the cervical spine. She felt around with the blade for the space between the vertebrae. *Got it. Need a little more force.* Tray Wind's mouth opened and closed, as if trying to say something while Crowbar sawed rhythmically through the spine, those huge green eyes staring off into nowhere. Finally, she was done. As she lifted the head up she heard the elevator door open. Crowbar spun around, splattering blood on the floor in a spiral from Tray's neck.

In the elevator was that little girl, whatsherface. Crowbar's imp displayed the name *Hy* over her, with a helpful little arrow. Hy stared silently wide-eyed at Crowbar and the head.

What's the kid doing down here alone? Crowbar had to get moving, the mission wasn't over yet, but she felt bad that this poor little kid had to see a decapitated head. It was the sort of thing that could really fuck someone up. On the off chance that they survived this, Crowbar thought she should do something to mitigate any trauma. She knew that kids often responded to a situation depending on the reactions of surrounding adults. She could make this all seem like a prank. Putting on what she hoped was a silly grin she thrust the head forward and yelled, "Happy Halloween!"

Hy screamed and pressed a button, closing the elevator door.

There, done my good deed for the day.

Head still in hand, she started running for the repair depot. She wondered how Raythen was doing. She got his location from the security cameras. She frowned when she saw he was in the floor underneath her, only a quarter-kilometer away.

<Astria: tell @Raythen> "You're taking your time."

<Raythen: tell @Astria> "Ran into a couple Torvalds."

She requested video of notable events in the depot. As she watched a replay of the battle she thought, *Jesus fuck, that is so hot.*

<Astria: tell @Raythen> "Still, you need to hustle. I'm going to do a personality analysis of the remaining militia; there might be some who don't want to go all Masada with Uzziah."

<Raythen: tell @Astria> "Good idea. I still don't have a rail gun. I can't get any imint from the aerosail. I don't know what kind of defenses Uzziah has in place."

Crowbar felt a little self-conscious running with a decapitated head. What if Raythen requested a visual of her? There would be some serious 'splaining to do, and there wasn't any time for 'splaining. She hoped that getting a visual of her wasn't one of his priorities, at least not at the moment.

She got a list of the remaining militia battle exoskeleton troopers. Only four. Ah, but Colonel Kim was one of them. She had a family; she had incentive to stop Uzziah. *Excellent.*

<Astria: tell @Kim> "Colonel, we have to stop Uzziah. You can get to the aerosail in time to prevent his mass killing."

No response.

Where are they?

She requested their positions and saw they were in battle formation moving toward the entry point of the Pax Cythera.

<Astria: tell @Kim> "You need to break from formation and assault the aerosail. I know you want to. I know you want to save your husband and daughters. Policies can change. People can change. If we live we can work toward being accepted. If we're dead we can't do anything."

She reached the depot. Running through one of the holes blasted by the Torvalds, her destination wasn't far inside—an industrial incinerator—a massive metal box with a thick hatch and a small circular window. She opened the hatch and threw the head onto the grate where it clanged about before coming to a rest. Closing the hatch she said, "Medical emergency. Disposal of contaminated biological waste."

"Unable to comply," the incinerator said. "The item has been identified as human remains. Until this unit can establish communications with the proper authorities the item shall not be incinerated."

"Fuck." Crowbar opened the hatch and took the head back out. She dropped it on the floor and pulled out her pistol, firing a couple more rounds into the skull. She holstered the pistol and took out her crowbar. She swung it down on the head a few times and then kneeled on the ground, placing the head firmly between her knees. Using the knife she cut through the scalp and pried open a section of skull. She reached her fingers into the brain tissue, swirling them around. When she felt the filaments of the imp tighten on her fingers she pulled them out. Following her fingers were thin strands, visible by the blood and tiny bits of brain that were on

248

them. Every fiber filament of the implant was connected with every other one, so she was sure she had the whole thing. *If you took all the filaments of an implant and stretched them in a single line they would go from Terra to Luna and back, or some such bullshit.* Here they just looked like a clump of bloody wet hair. Crowbar went back to the incinerator and threw in the imp.

"Medical emergency. Disposal of contaminated biological waste."

This time the incinerator complied.

Chapter 47

Mark was the closest militia base on the way to the aerosail. Raythen had asked the network if there were any working rail guns there. The network obliged with a blip on his map. He made it there through the underground tunnels without incident. Most of the Torvalds were still scouring the industrial levels.

He stood in the dusty rubble of one of the chambers in Mark Base. The dead exo trooper at his feet had both of his legs blown off. He couldn't help stepping through the blood to get to the rail gun that was lying just beyond the dead trooper's outstretched arms. He gripped the handle and requested an ammo count. About half full. He turned to go but then remembered something. Bending down he took the wallinator from the trooper's belt.

9 minutes and 43 seconds.

The tether to the aerosail was attached at the tip of the nose cone of the stratos. The surface level of the stratos was about a quarter kilometer below it—the ground sloping steeply up a rocky facade that was supposed to simulate a mountainside on Terra. A winding trail led up for hikers and sightseers. There was also an underground passage with an elevator. The elevator might be safer, but would be too slow.

Raythen sprinted out of Mark Base toward the front of the stratos. The air was empty of dragonflies, he supposed the VDF had either run out or decided they didn't need them anymore. The sloping peak of the mountainside was silhouetted by a line of golden glow on the horizon beyond that heralded the start of sunrise. Raythen ran past picnic tables as he reached the base of the rocky facade. He leaped, aiming for an outcropping a dozen meters above. He landed on it and ran forward, spotting his next target. He leaped again.

He was an easy target if any Torvalds spotted him on the surface. The network didn't see any, but the network was less reliable on the surface. There were plenty of places to hide among the trees, and private buildings weren't connected to the emergency land-line network. He noticed that he was connected to the network by only two point-to-point nodes, and one of those was iffy.

8 minutes and 21 seconds.

<Raythen: tell @Astria> "Any luck getting the others to join us?"

<Astria: tell @Raythen> "Negative. They are engaging some troops at the Pax Cythera entry point. Trying to take out as many as they can, I guess. It's not pretty. I'm shadowing an engineering team. They are almost to our jammers. If they take those out and the Torvalds' network goes up we would be in serious trouble."

Raythen laughed bitterly.

<Raythen: tell @Astria> "Like we're not in serious trouble already."

He reached a metal platform that ended at a door with a sign saying *Authorized Personnel Only*. He opened it and went inside. He was relieved to make it to cover, no longer exposed. He followed a virtual trail through gray metallic passageways inside the stratos bulkhead, the ceiling high above in the darkness. He hurried to the closed airlock that led to the tunnel inside the tether that connected the stratos to the aerosail.

<Astria: tell @Raythen> "Don't go that way."

<Raythen: tell @Astria> "What? Where should I go?"

<Astria: tell @Raythen> "We're blind to what's in the tether and the aerosail. You'd be a sitting duck in there. Go up that ladder to the maintenance airlock above the tether. Then run on top of it."

<Raythen: tell @Astria> "Run on top of the tether!?"

<Astria: tell @Raythen> "Tick-tock."

It was insane, but she was probably right about Uzziah monitoring the tunnel.

Just do it. It's a plan. Go!

He climbed the ladder until he reached the maintenance airlock in the ceiling. Opening it manually, he pulled himself inside, head first. He could barely fit through it in his armor, it was primarily used for maintenance bots to monitor and repair the tether. He crawled to the outer door—trying not to think about what he was about to do. He opened the door and poked his head outside—not the outside of the city surface, the outside he had known most of his life—but the real outside of Venus. The tether, a twelve-meter diameter hollow tube, was stretched out directly below him, a gray tendril that seemed to become insubstantial as it joined the aerosail in the distance. The tether and aerosail melded into the golden line of the horizon with the diffused sunlight that was just starting to split the surrounding clouded darkness. It was like he was in the throat of an enormous dragon that was opening its mouth, and he was preparing to run out on top of its tongue. He could hear the wind whip by him and felt its force try to push him back. His suit had its own oxygen supply that would last about an hour. He slid out on the tether and crouched. The bottom of his feet stuck its surface—they were equipped with gecko-grip setae that could stick to just about any surface by command.

7 minutes, 45 seconds.

He ran. He couldn't go full speed under these conditions—he had to make sure one foot was descending to the surface as the other was leaving it. Eight kilometers to go. He was running at forty kilometers per hour. Not fast enough. A strong cross wind could blow him off if both feet were in the air. But he had to risk it. Fifty kilometers per hour. Still not fast enough. The dragon's mouth opened wider. The shadow of the aerosail stretched across the tether and touched him. He had to go faster. Sixty kilometers per hour. As the foot behind him left the tether he felt suspended in nothing, a little eternity before the leading foot landed. He should make it. If he didn't get blown off the side he should make it.

The aerosail grew in front and its features became clearer as he reached the half-way point of the tether. At the end was a large spherical knob, the command and control center. Four spokes radiated from the knob, each a hundred meters long, connecting to the interior of the cone section. The cone, wider in the back that faced Raythen, tapered forward to a hole that was fifty meters in diameter. From the outer surface of the cone were four massive wings, two horizontal stretching left and right, and two vertical going up and down.

Raythen started planning his attack. He would enter the top of the control center using the wallinator. Drop in and kill everyone. That's it.

A cross wind hit him at mid stride.

Vertigo shook him as his forward motion was shifted suddenly to the right. He immediately bent forward and brought his arms across his chest, extending his feet down. His left foot hit the surface first and gripped. His body fell forward and he commanded his left foot to continue its grip as hard as it could. He sent his right foot forward to step on the tether. He felt the tug of the bolts in his hip sockets as his body continued forward into the interior jell-packs of his suit. It took him a moment to recover himself from the sudden stop.

"Whoa," he whispered as he recovered his stance.

5 minutes, 54 seconds.

He continued his run.

Chapter 48

<Lt. Aleksy: post #IMINT> "That's odd."

<Lt. Sogga: post #IMINT> "What's odd."

<Lt. Aleksy: post #IMINT> "There's a Meta exo running on the tether."

<Lt. Sogga: post #IMINT> "What tether?"

<Lt. Aleksy: post #IMINT> "Here's the feed."

<Lt. Sogga: post #IMINT> "Shit! *That* tether! Look at him go!"

<Lt. Aleksy: post #IMINT> "What the fuck he doing that for?"

<Lt. Sogga: post #IMINT> "He's probably running from the AUs. Those AUs are tearing the Metas to shreds."

<Lt. Aleksy: post #IMINT> "Bro, he must be scared shitless to be running like that. What's he planning to do? Hide in the aerosail? Those Metas are stupider than I thought."

<Lt. Sogga: post #IMINT> "Think we ought to tell the General? She wanted to know if we spotted anything out of the ordinary."

<Lt. Aleksy: post #IMINT> "She's kind of busy dealing with that suicide assault they're making on our entry point. It looks like those AUs really did the job in there."

<Lt. Sogga: post #IMINT> "Good for them. They can have the shitty jobs while we watch."

<Lt. Aleksy: post #IMINT> "Holy fucking shit! Did you see that?"

<Lt. Sogga: post #IMINT> "Fuck bro, he almost lost it."

<Lt. Aleksy: post #IMINT> "Oh man! He must have dumped his ass! I bet it doesn't smell so good in his suit now, hehe."

<Lt. Sogga: post #IMINT> "We should send a tell to the General. She should at least know there's a hostile moving to the aerosail."

<Lt. Aleksy: post #IMINT> "Yeah, I'll do that. Bro, it's times like this that I regret we can't post our on-duty vids. This would make a killing."

<Lt. Sogga: post #IMINT> "Especially if he falls."

<Lt. Aleksy: post #IMINT> "Fuck yeah! That would suck for him though. He would survive for a while in his suit—and cook like a lobster. You think he would live up to impact?"

<Lt. Sogga: post #IMINT> "I don't know. I don't think the suits are rated for that kind of pressure."

<Lt. Aleksy: post #IMINT> "He wouldn't be under the pressure for very long."

<Lt. Sogga: post #IMINT> "The impact would definitely kill him."

<Lt. Aleksy: post #IMINT> "Holy FUCKING shit nipples! HOLY FUCKING SHIT NIPPLES!"

<Lt. Sogga: tell @Gen. Wong> "Emergency! Emergency! The aerosail is going down!"

Chapter 49

Raythen was about three hundred meters away from the aerosail when he saw the massive horizontal wing flaps point downward, pitching the rear upward and the nose down.

2 minutes and 54 seconds.

He's early!

The tether was lifted up with the tail of the aerosail. The increased incline on the flexible tether moved toward him like the wave of a rubber garden hose that is jerked with a quick flick of the wrist. He watched in horror as the wave rushed toward him. Beyond, the aerosail seemed to have become frozen in the air from its stall. He stopped running, making his feet stick to the tether. He pulled out his wallinator and pointed it at the tether skin. The surface of the tether was made of thickly corded carbon fiber—he wasn't sure if the explosive could penetrate it. He needed to get inside the tether passageway. The aerosail seemed to come back to life— like a sperm whale diving into the ocean—and plunged sharply downward. The wave of the tether, twenty meters higher than him, was only seconds away. He fired the wallinator at a point three meters in front of him. As he was about to command it to explode he realized that such a hole would probably not be good for the structural integrity of the tether. What if it tore completely away, severing the stratos from the aerosail? In this case that might not be a bad thing since this aerosail was trying to pull the stratos down. But a stratos without an aerosail would be at the complete mercy of the Venusian winds, and be flipped around like a leaf in a storm.

As all this was going through his mind the wave hit him. He was surprised by the speed that he was sickeningly shot up—and a question came to him too late—at what force would the gecko grips holding his feet to the tether fail?

After he crested the top of the wave the bottoms of his boots made a loud pop as they released their grips. He was flung straight up in the air.

Focus.

The tether shrank away below him with disturbing speed.

His legs peddled behind as the tailwind caught his body, pushing him forward.

He had experienced free-fall before—in simulations. The first rule is to relax. He stretched his arms forward and up as he stopped pedaling and stretched his legs behind him, his body falling into the arch position with his stomach parallel to the ground. Below was the aerosail. That had been his destination. It was still his destination. He had his imp calculate his trajectory and display it as a florescent blue line. It fell short of the projected trajectory of the aerosail, far to the right of the tether. He put his arms behind his back and adjusted his body to steer to the left. He watched the imp's projection. Now he was going too far to the left. He lost sight of the aerosail as it plunged into the clouds. *That's okay* he thought as his imp continued to track its calculated movements.

He was flying.

The tactile sensors of the suit allowed him to feel the wind rushing past him. He could hear its roar as it buffeted his body. The roar changed pitch as he tensed and then relaxed his limbs. With fine adjustments to his body he managed a shaky intercept course with the aerosail. His imp calculated his speed relative to it—about forty-five kilometers per hour. That was survivable. He was still accelerating slowly.

He was just five-hundred meters to impact when he made a horrifying realization—the falling wave of the tether was going to hit the stratos, making the tether go taught and stop the forward motion of the aerosail—it might already done so. He thrust his arms in front of him to slow his forward motion. Before he could get a rear view to see status of the tether behind him the aerosail broke through the clouds below with the back edge of the cone less than a hundred meters away. If he hit the top of the cone he would tumble away into oblivion. The aerosail was inclined down at about a forty-five-degree angle. He was rushing toward it at over eighty kilometers per hour.

He pointed his head straight down, tucking his arms against his sides. He felt the change of air pressure as he rushed past the edge of the cone.

The large spherical knob at the end of the tether, the control center, surged to meet him. When he was thirty meters away he extended his right hand forward and fired the wallinator. As the wall exploded he fell inside.

Chapter 50

Raythen fell through a room that was angled forty-five degrees downward. He struck something that was sticking up from the floor, a control console of some sort, and bounced off, sending a jolt through his hip sockets that caused his entire skeleton to shudder. He ricocheted off the ceiling and fell to the floor, sliding down a long corridor on his back, feet first. About thirty meters ahead at the end of the corridor was a large room, beyond he could see a wall-sized window that looked out at the clouds that he had just narrowly escaped. The blast door to the room suddenly slid closed, blocking his descent. He switched the wallinator to his left hand and fired at the door as he grabbed the rail gun off his back with his right hand. The charge detonated and the blast door fragments fell down into the room below. His heel caught against the lip of the sliding door track and his momentum was transferred to the top half of his body. As his head and torso fell forward he brought himself into a crouch and jumped toward the roof, simultaneously spinning his body.

There were three rows of control consoles with chairs, all facing the window, exposed to the glow of the morning sun. To the left of the entrance was a trooper in battle exoskeleton armor, facing Raythen with his rail gun, firing. He was standing on the slanted floor, his legs spread wide for stability. Two other men in half-exo armor were strapped into their seats to the right of the entrance. They were also firing with their assault rifles. Raythen didn't have to think about them—they couldn't hurt him. The spin of his body was distributing the impacts from the trooper. As Raythen spun he saw the trooper bend his legs, getting ready to leap. True to exo strategy, always keep moving.

Normally, a wallinator is useless as a weapon in an exo battle. Exoskeleton troopers were too fast and the reactive armor didn't allow for the goop to stick. However, Raythen saw the direction where the trooper was ready to go—as Raythen spun he sent a glob of explosive at the plexiglass window. The trooper was in mid jump over the window when it exploded. Violent wind rushed up into the room—the full blast hitting the trooper and throwing him up into the back above the destroyed blast door. Raythen had been pushed to the right by the rail gun impacts and landed in the far corner of the room. He paused just long enough to position himself and get a fix on the trooper and then started running up toward the back, scrambling over consoles and firing. The trooper fired randomly as he fell down into the consoles. Raythen, now at point blank range, stopped, aimed for the trooper's rail gun and fired. The rail gun shattered, the pieces of it flying out of his hands. The trooper propped himself up against a console. Raythen stopped firing. The two militia stopped firing and watched as Raythen pointed the rail gun at the trooper's chest. The roar of the wind filled the room. Raythen clicked on the trooper with his phand. It was Uzziah.

<Raythen: tell @Uzziah> "Move the aerosail back up."

Uzziah projected his face onto his helmet, a face twisted with rage. Artificially amplifying his voice so that it could heard over the wind, he yelled, "You can't stop the will of God!"

Raythen projected his own face onto his helmet and yelled. "Pull the aerosail up or I will kill you!"

"If God didn't want me to martyr ten thousand people he would come down and show himself to me! This will get his attention. Do you think he would let me martyr them if it was against his will?"

There was no reasoning with him. Raythen replied, "Just call me God," and shot him square in the chest. Uzziah flew backwards and bounced off the wall. As he ricocheted into the middle of the room his body was caught in the vortex of wind, a black cloud of reactive armor dust whipping around him like a malevolent spirit. He quickly rose once again, arms and legs spread wide, and then was buffeted by the turbulence, send down in a spiral and sucked out through the hole in the plexiglass, down toward the surface of Venus.

Raythen turned to the two half-exos. Maybe he could talk to *them,* without the influence of Uzziah perhaps he could get them to help him get the aerosail back up. As he was about to speak one of them pointed his rifle at the console where Uzziah had been and fired. Raythen jerked his weapon desperately in his direction and pulled the trigger. The half-exo's armor ruptured, the kinetic energy tearing his body in half.

Raythen then fired at the remaining half-exo.

He was now alone in the control room, alone with the deafening roar of the wind. He went over to the console that Uzziah had been at and sat down in front of it. It had a dizzying array of physical controls. He tried to phand over them to get instructions but there was no response.

"Computer! Computer!" he yelled. There was still no response.

In front of him was joystick—its purpose seemed intuitive enough. Two bullet holes darkened the metal surface several centimeters from it. Grabbing the joystick he put his thumb on the biggest red button and pulled it back. Above the joystick was something that his imp told him was the attitude control. It was a circular window that normally displayed an artificial horizon—if they happened to be facing the horizon. It currently displayed all brown. There were hash marks on it that showed the number of degrees from the actual horizon. It was currently near 44. He held his breath, holding the joystick as far back as he could.

The attitude control started to move.

Chapter 51

Raythen was breathing heavily. The attitude control read zero degrees. He slowly released his grip from the joystick.

<Astria: tell @Raythen> "I see you made it to the aerosail."

Raythen was startled by Astria's tell. He phanded around to see if any of the local controls would now respond to him. Nothing did.

<Astria: tell @Raythen> "I've managed to open communications with the aerosail, but that's about it. Hey, I've got good news and bad news."

Raythen waited two seconds in silence.

<Astria: tell @Raythen> "Which do you want first?"

<Raythen: tell @Astria> "I'll take the good news. I can use it."

<Astria: tell @Raythen> "The good news is that the Pax Cythera broke away from us in a panic when they thought we were going down. Bunch of fucking pussies."

<Raythen: tell @Raythen> "And the bad news?"

<Astria: tell @Raythen> "The bad news is they left over a dozen Torvalds, two of which just entered the tether passage to where you are."

<Raythen: tell @Astria> "What! You should have told me that first!"

<Astria: tell @Raythen> "You said you wanted the good news first."

Raythen quickly got up out of his chair. He turned around and looked down the corridor.

<Astria: tell @Raythen> "You're going to have to return the way you came."

She was talking about going over the top of the tether again. Considering his experience out there the first time he actually contemplated facing the two Torvalds. Yeah, he probably couldn't take on two of them in a confined area, especially if one used the other for a shield.

<Raythen: tell @Astria> "Yes, I suppose so."

<Astria: tell @Raythen> "I can't talk much longer, we're about to take out an engineering team they left behind. Get back as quickly as you can. We need the firepower."

<Raythen: tell @Astria> "Copy."

Raythen grunted with annoyance at Astria and ran down the corridor. He couldn't believe she could be so flippant about the two Torvalds coming toward him. After all, *he had just saved all their lives.* A simple *thank you* would have been nice.

Chapter 52

The engineering crew had almost made it to the jammers.

Thank fucking God the jammers were so deep in the bowels of the stratos. And thank God Colonel Kim has some skills.

The VDF exo trooper with the engineers had taken out the other two remaining militia troopers, even though the Metas had gotten the drop on them.

What really surprised Crowbar was that the VDF trooper, who was lying against the thick cabling of the dimly lit chamber wall, was actually bleeding from the stumps of the knees, and from the empty shoulder socket where the right arm used to be. The bleeding was only a slight trickle, the suit had applied tourniquets, but it was obvious to her that this was no Torvald.

Colonel Kim, standing next to Crowbar, was pointing her rail gun at the VDF trooper's head.

"Remove your helmet trooper!" Crowbar yelled harshly, pointing her own assault rifle. "Remove your fucking helmet now or my friend here will remove it along with your fucking Godless head! Remove it now!"

Crowbar heard the clicks as the seals of the neck came undone. The VDF trooper reached with her remaining hand and pulled off the helmet. The woman's short blond hair was plastered to her skull with sweat. She was gritting her teeth.

She looked familiar. Crowbar's imp provided an identity.

"Hey," Crowbar said, lowering her weapon, "you're sort of famous."

There was no response from the woman, except for the defiance in her eyes.

"I'll go check the perimeter, make sure we got them all," said Colonel Kim.

"Good idea," said Crowbar, not taking her eyes off the VDF trooper. Colonel Kim silently slipped away.

A grin overspread Crowbar's face. "It's a pleasure to meet you. Golly gee! I am surprised to find the likes of you here, Professor Meyers. Imagine, meeting an expert in the creation of A-Cons, of all things."

"If I was you," Professor Meyers said evenly, "I would strongly consider giving myself up. You can't hold the VDF off forever."

"If I was you, I would consider shitting my pants now, because I know that you are the mad scientist who's responsible for much of the carnage that has happened here today."

"I am not a mad scientist," Professor Meyers said with real annoyance.

Crowbar saw that she had struck a raw spot. When someone doesn't seem perturbed by losing a few limbs, but gets upset at being called a 'mad scientist', you know that's *some* raw spot.

"Not a mad scientist? You created an army of killer robots. I think that's automatic honorary membership into the Mad Scientist Club."

"They are not robots. They are people."

"Sure, people. People who live in little metal tubes. Hey, just changing the subject, have you ever gone by the name Sweet GG?"

Meyers was clearly startled by the question. "Who told you about her?"

267

"Duh, her boyfriend—or is it *your* boyfriend?"

"No, no . . . he's not my boyfriend. Sweet GG is an assistant of mine. That's all. She helps me with . . . training."

"What was she training the Torvalds? Cunnilingus? Because they really want to kill Raythen. I hate to tell you this, but your robots are crazy. I mean batshit crazy. But you know what? It's kind of sweet that they can feel so jealous over a human, really. I bet they're kind of fond of you too, aren't they? Do you think they would put down their weapons if they knew you were in danger? If they saw that you were down a few limbs and had a gun to your head? Do you think they would surrender and play nice?"

For the first time, Crowbar saw worry in Meyers' eyes. "I am not at liberty to discuss this operation with unauthorized personnel," she said.

"Of course not," Crowbar said. "That's okay, I don't need you to say anything."

Colonel Kim returned. "We're all clear."

"Excellent," Crowbar said. "Colonel, do you think you'll be able to carry her?"

"No problem."

"Good. I'd like to talk over a plan with you. To make it work we need a motorcycle and some explosives. Lots of explosives."

Chapter 53

Raythen entered back into Corpus Christi, sliding through the airlock, breathing a deep sigh of relief. He dropped to the floor, went into a crouch, and took some moments to assess his situation. There were still plenty of Torvalds left—he had to be ready to fight. He probably couldn't win against all of them, and there weren't enough CC militia left to put up an effective offensive. The Pax Cythera had backed off, so there was no hope of human VDF troopers taking over from the Torvalds, at least not for several hours.

Taking another deep breath he stood and retraced the path back to the door overlooking the interior of the stratos. He opened the door and ventured a peak down upon the city from his high vantage point, now illuminated by the difuse Venusian sun. Smoke rose from the ruins of the four militia bases, reaching up to the dome and collecting at the apex. There was no visible activity.

If I survive this, what's going to happen to me when the rule of law is restored?

What was his legal position? He had to surrender himself to the authorities eventually. He had killed people. He had actually killed people. Uzziah and the two half-exos. He had torn them up pretty bad. He had killed so many people in simulations—yet he never thought he would ever kill anyone in real life. He had been forced to do it, he had saved himself and thousands more. The UP would understand once they downloaded his imp. And, he hadn't killed any human VDF.

But, he had to accept the fact that he killed human beings. Beyond the legal aspects, it was something he would have to live with.

The stupid religious fanatics! That second half-exo—he hadn't even raised his weapon. What if he wasn't going to fight? What if I didn't have to kill him?

The reality of that thought was an immense red wave poised to rush in and overwhelm him. He quickly turned away from it and cleared his mind. He had to survive. Survival was first. He had to decide what to do. He had to hide until law and order was restored.

CORPUS CHRISTI NEWORK CONNECTION ESTABLISHED

The jammers are down!

What had Astria said before, that there was an engineering crew searching for the jammers? Had they found them and disabled them?

EMERGENCY BROADCAST MESSAGE TO ALL PASSENGERS OF CORPUS CHRISTI

A video image appeared on Raythen's HUD. It took him a moment to register what he was seeing. The room in the video was lit by red emergency lights. A woman in a battle exoskeleton was on the floor with her back against a wall. Two legs and an arm were missing. Her face had been badly beaten—her nose broken with blood pouring down onto a swollen, half-open mouth. It looked like several teeth were missing. Her half-open eyes showed semi-consciousness. Astria was crouching over her, holding her head up by gripping a fistful of the woman's short blond hair. Astria leered at the camera gleefully. She put down the crowbar that was in her other hand and pulled the long military knife from her belt. She gave the woman's head a shake and said, "Hey Torvalds! Who's your mommy?"

Then she slit the woman's throat.

The woman's eyes flipped wide open, showing mostly whites. Her mouth opened and gurgled. As the blood started to cascade down her neck, the image vanished.

NETWORK CONNECT LOST

"What the fuck," Raythen whispered.

That woman's face! It was badly beaten, similar, not exact, but so similar. He brought the image back up and focused on it. He had his imp do a comparison with Sweet GG's avatar. There was some room for error due to the injuries—but the imp came back with the results.

91% match.

Chapter 54

Raythen raced across the surface of Corpus Christi. When Astria had broadcast over the live network, her position had been revealed—she was on the far side of that stratos that was under construction—New Sinai. He tried to message her but there was no response—the point-to-point network wasn't operational on New Sinai. He did a search for any of the remaining militia and saw that Colonel Kim was available.

<Raythen: tell @Colonel Kim> "What the hell is Astria doing?"

There was a few seconds delay before she responded.

<Colonel Kim: tell @Raythen> "I didn't know all that she was planning, but I think I understand it now."

<Raythen: tell @Colonel Kim> "That homicidal insanity she broadcast is part of a plan?"

<Colonel Kim: tell @Raythen> "I know, I was shocked by it too. She told me she was going to get all the VDF over onto New Sinai. I thought she was just going to threaten the woman. Once the VDF are over there we're going to blow up the tether connecting it to us."

<Raythen: tell @Colonel Kim> "Who was that woman with Astria?"

<Colonel Kim: tell @Raythen> "She's a scientist, she created the A-Con troopers. That's why they're rushing to her. Hey, if I were you I would stay put, hide someplace. Hopefully this will be over soon."

<Raythen: tell @Colonel Kim> "How is Astria planning to get off New Sinai before you blow the connection?"

<Colonel Kim: tell @Raythen> "She has a motorcycle—although I don't think she has a chance getting out, not with all those VDF intent on killing her."

Raythen saw that Colonel Kim's position was just outside the hull, by the tether connecting Corpus Christi to New Sinai. She was still in the process of placing the explosives. He could also see several Torvalds entering the tether on the security feeds. They were passing just meters away from her on the other side of the hull and didn't know it.

What if Astria had just slit Sweet GGs throat? The image came back to him involuntarily in his meat memory. It drove him crazy. This woman who he had shared so much with, who he really cared about; he had to face it—he *loved* Sweet GG, as crazy as that sounded. He couldn't let her just bleed out like that. If he got her to a stasis chamber she could still be saved—but what about the Torvalds? They were trying to save her.

Should I help the Torvalds save her?

But why had she asked him to come here in the first place if she knew that it was going to be attacked? He had to reach her and talk to her. He had to find out.

<Raythen: tell @Colonel Kim> "Do you know what path Astria took to get to her current position on New Sinai?"

<Colonel Kim: tell @Raythen> "I went with her; I carried the scientist over there."

<Raythen: tell @Colonel Kim> "Send me the path you took."

A map of New Sinai appeared on Raythen's HUD. A blue dotted line showed the path. They had gone on an arching trajectory halfway between the middle of the city and the outer edge along the port side. Raythen knew that was the way Astria would be trying to return—she had traveled that way to get a lay of the land.

So far eleven Torvalds had passed through the tether to New Sinai. No more had gone through in the past twenty seconds. Maybe that was all of them—except for the two on the aerosail.

<Colonel Kim: tell @Raythen> "What are you planning, trooper?"

<Raythen: tell @Colonel Kim> "I have to go in there."

<Colonel Kim: tell @Raythen> "That's suicide."

Raythen didn't respond. He was running up the slope in the stern, up to the airlock that led to New Sinai.

<Colonel Kim: tell @Raythen> "I have to warn you, I've just finished placing the charges. I'm going to get to a safe location now. Astria told me that if I saw any Torvalds trying to leave New Sinai I was to blow the connection, whether she was back or not."

<Raythen: tell @Colonel Kim> "Sounds like a smart plan. I would stick to it."

Raythen leaped up toward the airlock.

Chapter 55

Best fucking mission in years.

Crowbar raced her silent electric motorcycle through the half
constructed molecular manufacturing units of the factory floor. There was
no roof above her; the ground level of New Sinai hadn't been built yet.
Nothing between her and the golden clouds of Venus except for the
plexiglass dome far above. The ride was bumpy—there were the tracks on
the floor as well as exposed sections with heavy cabling. She had the
motorcycle at full speed—two-hundred kilometers per hour.

There was still a high probability of death. It would be a good death—
Theophilus was safe—mission accomplished; and she always thought the
ideal way to die would be with her fingers clenched on the throat of her
killer—taking him down with her. While this upcoming way of going out
would lack the visceral tactile satisfaction of the *ideal* death; it was, in a
way, its grander metaphorical twin. *Dying while trapping my enemies in a
stratos that plunges into the furnace of the Venusian surface—that is pretty
epic.*

But she wasn't dead yet.

What was that!

She only had the barest glimpse of a movement to her right, but that
was enough to get her to perform evasive maneuvers. She started to slalom
the motorcycle, going low at each turn so that her knees would almost

touch the ground. Suddenly, there was an eruption a few meters to her right causing dust and fragments of debris to fly toward her. A second and then third eruption followed immediately afterwards, moving along her same trajectory. She saw a manufacturing unit ahead of her; she maneuvered so that it was between her and her attacker and turned sharply to the left to keep it that way. She heard explosions as supersonic pellets struck the unit.

She was now moving toward the port side of the stratos. She would have to turn back toward the exit eventually. The Torvald was aware of that and would probably try to cut her off.

Aw fuck it, let's go for broke.

She turned a sharp right toward the exit and opened the cycle up, crouching low with her head between the handlebars.

<Raythen: tell @Astria> "What the fuck did you do to Sweet GG?"

The point-to-point connection placed him about where the Torvald had been, and there was now no longer any sign of the Torvald. Crowbar was really starting to like this kid.

<Astria: tell @Raythen> "That's the first time I've heard you swear. You must be really angry."

<Raythen: tell @Astria> "If she dies I'll tear your arms off!"

She bet he really meant it. He was attempting an intercept course with her. She was faster than he was and could easily get away with some maneuvering, as long as he didn't fire, but that would delay her arrival at the exit, and there were a bunch of killer robots coming after both of them.

<Astria: tell @Raythen> "And here I thought you came in to rescue me."

<Raythen: tell @Astria> "Turn around—we're going back to save her."

Now that's really crazy, Crowbar thought. *Time to stop playing.*

276

<Astria: tell @Raythen> "That wasn't your girlfriend. Your girlfriend is one of Dr. Meyers' assistants. Watch this."

She sent him a vid of her talk with Dr. Meyers. A few moments passed before Raythen responded. He was less than a hundred meters away.

<Raythen: tell @Astria> "But she looks so much like Sweet GG's avatar."

<Astria: tell @Raythen> "Probably just sucking up to the boss. Your girlfriend is safe Ray. Let's get the fuck out of here."

Chapter 56

They reached the slope that went up to the front cone of the stratos. Without any scenic façade it was just a black tapering incline that curved up into the distance. Astria popped a wheelie as she hit the edge.

<Astria: tell @Raythen> "Let's boogey. Watch your six."

Raythen pointed his gun behind him as his rear-view screen expanded on his HUD. The scene behind him was a labyrinth of towers and deep crevasses. The Torvalds would be racing back up here soon with their creator. He was exposed and they were homicidal. He wouldn't last long if they appeared.

Astria had pulled away from him. She was going straight for the exit, not bothering with any evasive maneuvers. Against his better judgment he leaped up toward the top. As he reached the apex of his jump he felt a jarring impact against his back that sent him rapidly forward toward the slope. Another impact hit his right shoulder, sending him spinning. He was upside down when he hit the ground, facing the interior of New Sinai. He immediately rolled to the left—he had to get off the X. The ground exploded where he had landed. His HUD showed two contacts firing on him. He scrambled on his hands and knees to point himself back to the exit and then tried to get to his feet. They were still at long range—if he kept moving they would have trouble concentrating their hits—his armor could still hold out.

There was another solid impact on his back. The reactive armor was almost gone. The exit was still about fifty meters away, and the Torvalds were moving forward fast as they fired.

A voice yelled out from above him—he could hear it clearly, amplified by the sound sensors of his suit. He looked up and saw Astria standing in the circular exit hatch pointing her assault rifle out at the stratos.

"Hey morons! I'm the one who slashed your evil brood-mother's throat! You fucking idiot toasters!"

She started firing, not that it would do any good against the battle exo's armor, but Raythen was no longer getting hit. Instead, trails of destruction moved up the slope from his position toward the exit. Raythen followed as fast as he could—running through dust and debris—making the best of the opportunity Astria afforded him.

Astria jerked back once, then twice, as pellets passed through her flesh. Then she was thrown backwards violently into the tunnel, making a loud throaty grunt. Raythen dived in after her. He found her lying on her back, moving her head side to side slowly, processing what had happened to her.

"The fuckers got a vertebra," she said, as if in disbelief. "Well, I guess that's better than my skull." She watched as Raythen crawled next to her. They were out of the angle of fire, safe for the moment. "You're going to have to carry me the rest of the way. I can't feel me legs. Heh."

Raythen went to holster his weapon but realized the damage to his shoulder prevented the full motion of his right arm. It just swayed back and forth with his hand at waist level. Instead he scooped up Astria with his left hand and hoisted her over his good shoulder, her face against his back. She exhaled raggedly with pain. He started running through the tunnel.

279

"Thanks for that," he said. "I was almost dead."

"Yeah, yeah, save it for later. We still have trouble. I'm going to detonate the charges at the entrance to New Sinai when the Torvalds get there, but check out the surveillance at the Corpus Christi side."

He did. There were two VDF exos waiting there, one on each side of the open airlock. He looked ahead down the tunnel. The connecting tether between Corpus Christi and New Sinai was flexible and not perfectly straight, curving slightly so he could not see the entire length to Corpus Christi. If it had been a straight view the Torvalds would be shooting them to pieces right now. But if they continue forward far enough they would be spotted, and they'd be dead meat.

"Brace yourself," Astria said. The roar of an explosion burst from behind them. The tether they were inside of—now suddenly freed from New Sinai—rocked violently to the left. Raythen stopped running and planted his feet to the ground using the gecko-grips.

"Good-bye New Sinai!" Astria yelled in the roar of the wind. "Good-bye Torvalds!"

The tether was now like a paper streamer behind a bicycle—at the mercy of the wind. Thirty meters behind them it opened up to the Venusian atmosphere. The tether suddenly changed its course up and to the right. Raythen could feel his body shifting against his hip suspension. He tightened his grip on Astria.

He was about to say something, but decided to use electronic communication instead, figuring Astria would have trouble hearing him. She might have even blown out her eardrums.

<Raythen: tell @Astria> "We have to figure out what we're going to do about the remaining two Torvalds. If you can hold out we should wait here until they leave, I don't think they know we're here. They're going to

want to get to a defensive position until the Pax Cythera returns. The air seems to be blowing outward."

<Astria: tell @Raythen> "The air seems to be blowing out, but I'll tell you, it's starting to smell really farty in here. We should kill them now—tell Kim to take them from behind while we rush them." She then coughed and spit blood onto Raythen's back.

<Astria: tell @Raythen> "Shit, I think I punctured a lung."

The tether made a sudden drop-Raythen's stomach rushed to his throat—then they bottomed out and rose slowly.

<Raythen: tell @Astria> "I don't think we can take them. I can barely raise my arm. Those guys look like they're still in pretty good shape."

On the security feed they saw the Torvalds back away from the hatch and move toward the door that led back into Corpus Christi. They moved cautiously with their weapons ready. They were retreating away from the airlock.

"Shit!" Astria yelled. "We need to take them out! They can still do damage."

<Astria: tell @Colonel Kim, @Raythen> "It's vital that we eliminate the remaining Torvalds. If they get word to the Pax Cythera about how weak we are the VDF will finish their assault. If we wiped out the entire attack force there's a better chance they'll give up."

<Astria: tell @Raythen> "Get a move on!"

Raythen obliged and started running forward.

Chapter 57

Raythen stepped out of the flexible tether onto the solid ground of Corpus Christi. He closed the airlock behind him.

<Colonel Kim: post> "The Torvalds have holed up in Mathew Base; the place is so toasted we have very little working surveillance. I think they originally wanted to get back to the aerosail but they realized they would be sitting ducks in transit. We managed to scrounge another exo suit and give it to Captain Jakovich. The two of us are keeping watch."

Raythen gently laid Crowbar on the floor, on her back. She grimaced in pain, her white teeth painted over with streaks of blood. The wounds that she had on her body weren't visible—the HAZMAT suit had done its job and repaired itself over them. Raythen saw that she was obviously in pain and said, "Have your imp anesthetize you."

"It can't."

"What?" he said, confused. "Is it damaged?"

"My imp can't anesthetize. Anesthesia is for pussies."

Raythen thought, *Of course,* and said, "I've got to get you to the hospital."

He moved his gun to his fully functional left arm and holstered it to his back. Then he picked her up, cradling her in both arms.

<Raythen: post> "I'll join you at Mathew after I drop Astria off at the hospital."

<Colonel Kim: post> "Copy."

As Raythen started running down the slope, he viewed New Sinai from a live-feed. There was a sizeable hole at the nose cone from the explosion. It was falling away fast, and listing to the side. He wondered if the hole was large enough for the stratos to lose its buoyancy—and if the Pax Cythera would attempt a rescue. It would be tricky, with the stratos out of control like that. If those were human troopers in there he was certain they would go after them. He requested the location of the Pax Cythera and saw that it was on a parallel course with the Corpus Christi, about five kilometers above.

He reached level ground and ran along a tree-lined road.

Another mission completed, Crowbar thought, looking at the blank mask that was Raythen's helmet. *Almost got killed saving this kid's life. I guess it's only fair; he somehow managed to save the stratos.*

The image of Tray Wind's decapitated head rose to her mind's eye. How would he react if he knew?

Hey kid! I killed your little elf friend! What do you think of that?

Would he get mad? Would he lose control and crush her to death in a flash of blind fury? She was intrigued by the thought. Feeling his massive mechanical hand gripping her shoulder, her legs without feeling, she knew she was absolutely helpless and at his mercy. It had been an exciting mission, lots of close calls—but she could use one more thrill for the road.

"Hey Ray, I need to tell you something important," she said.

<Raythen: tell @Astria> "What's that?"

"About Tray Wind. I guess you were kind of friends with her so it's only fair that I tell you this. I killed her."

283

Raythen didn't flinch from his run, but his helmet shifted to look down at her face. And his grip did tighten on her—oh yes, his hand did squeeze her shoulder—not enough to do real damage, but it hurt, and it probably bruised. She felt a little shivering jolt go up the remaining undamaged spine, her nipples hardened visibly under her slick white suit.

<Raythen: tell @Astria> "What? How?"

She let out a little gasp. "I was worried about Theophilus—about her escape. If the jammers had gone down and if Tray Wind had communicated what she knew, Theophilus would be intercepted for sure."

<Raythen: tell @Astria> "How did you kill her?"

"I shot her in the head," Crowbar said, feeling a smile tug at the edge of her mouth. She forced it down—no need to be completely reckless.

<Raythen: tell @Astria> "You murdered her to protect Theophilus from being *captured?*"

"It wasn't only that," she said hurriedly. "She also accused me of being a VDF spy. She was really fucking things up. The only way I could save Theophilus was to kill her. And you have to remember, I thought we were all going to die anyway. How was I to know that you were going to save the day?"

He didn't respond. His head faced forward once again. She debated trying to reestablish communications with him, and then decided to let him get her to the hospital in silence. After all, he was a fucking hero.

Chapter 58

Torvald 17, or Buck, as he had been nicknamed by his fellow Torvalds, watched Raythen carrying that evil bitch down the slope. She looked wounded—good—he hoped she was hurt bad. He could shoot at them now—it was so tempting, but that would give away his position. He switched his view to Mathew Base, which he could also see from his vantage point on top of a tree near the slope. He was pressed against the trunk with his active camouflage on. He had hopped his way there on one leg from the bowels of the city where Raythen had left him. It was easy for an exo to hop on one leg over long distances. It *does* present a serious disadvantage in combat, however, which is why they had decided to place him in the tree. It had tortured him to be stuck up there when the bitch slit Parvati's throat—how he had wanted to run in to try and save her! But now he was glad to be where he was. He was their ace in the hole, their element of surprise. And most importantly, he was in communication with the two other Torvalds. Some of the remaining VDF dragonflies had taken refuge at Mathew Base—one poking its antennae up out of a ventilation shaft. Through a series of several others he shared a point-to-point network with the base's interior.

<Buck: tell @Spoof, @Cruiser> "Big news, big news—look at who's in my sights."

He sent them a live-feed of Raythen and Astria.

<Spoof: tell @Buck, @Cruiser> "What's the downside of killing them now?"

<Buck: tell @Spoof, @Cruiser> "The two militia preparing to assault your hidey-hole would tag me. I might not even be able to finish the job with Raythen before they knocked me out of the tree."

<Cruiser: tell @Buck, @Spoof> "We should come out there. Do you have visuals of Alpha and Bravo?"

<Buck: tell @Spoof, @Cruiser> "They're keeping low; I haven't had a visual for over a minute. I have a thirty-meter probability zone for Alpha, fifty for Bravo. I'd be careful about Bravo, he knows how to move in a suit."

<Spoof: tell @Buck @Cruiser> "We should come out now and engage Alpha and Bravo while you kill Raythen and Astria."

Buck knew what Spoof and Cruiser were thinking—they were thinking exactly what he was thinking. With this whole mission becoming a disaster, they *had* to kill Raythen and Astria, had to justify all this sacrifice for revenge. But they also had a chance to salvage what little remained of their original mission, which was to eliminate all of the Corpus Christi Militia. Theophilus was still missing—they had failed to capture her. But they had been so close to destroying the militia—it had been so easy—it had seemed like no risk to divert some resources to kill Raythen. But then that bitch somehow captured Parvati—and slit her throat! Why had Parvati come out from the safety of the Pax Cythera? Why had she put herself in danger?

Deep down, at near-repression, Buck suspected why she had been sent out. It was to watch over him and his brothers, to make sure they were behaving themselves. Because they *weren't* behaving themselves—they were being bad—and the humans running the show had been worried. So they had sent out Parvati to make sure that the A-Cons behaved.

Buck understood why humans hid so much of their emotions from themselves.

<Buck: tell @Spoof, @Cruiser> "Raythen's trajectory is taking him to the hospital."

Buck, Spoof, and Cruiser all conceived of a plan within 800 milliseconds of each other. They were so confident in their ability to come up with identical plans that they didn't have to confer. They just all said "Copy."

Although it was painful to do so, Buck allowed Raythen to run to the hospital. The hospital building itself was partially visible at the edge of the hub of the city, the top few floors poking beyond an apartment complex. Alpha and Bravo were hunkered down, which meant they were waiting for reinforcements, which meant they were waiting for Raythen. What they didn't know was Raythen would never arrive.

Buck watched as Raythen turned a bend around the apartment complex, out of sight. Spoof and Cruiser could see everything he saw— they knew approximately when Raythen would reach the hospital. That was when they would strike—which would be right—about—now.

Spoof and Cruiser came out of the ruins of Mathew base on the side closest to Alpha, firing as they did so. Buck's main view was on the road to the hospital, but he had a sub-screen observing the action. No sign of Alpha for about three seconds—and then he pops up like a flea. It was stupid to jump up like that; he obviously didn't know what he was doing. Maybe they should have gone after Bravo first.

And there was Raythen! Running to the rescue! He was going along the road, by the fastest route, holding his weapon in his left hand.

I thought you were smarter than that Ray, Buck thought. *You really should be keeping to cover. Ah, but you're rushing to save your new friends. And you've forgotten about me.*

At six hundred meters away there was a small building on Buck's side of the road; he lost sight of Raythen as he ran behind it. Buck set his crosshairs on Raythen's projected movement and tracked him. When the crosshairs reached the end of the building Raythen reappeared. Buck fired, feeling a level of joy he had never experienced before. Raythen was flung from his trajectory and was blown back toward a tree. Buck grinned inwardly as he kept up a steady stream of fire. Raythen hit the tree and pushed off of it with one hand while swinging his gun around with the other. Buck aimed for the gun and gave himself a congratulating "Yes!" when he saw it shatter in Raythen's hand. Black reactive armor spray rose up around Raythen as he was trying to get his feet planted. The impacts from Buck's rail gun prevented him from doing so. Raythen sprawled backwards into the drain ditch on the other side of the road. He only lost sight of Raythen for an instant before he bounced back up into view. Buck continued firing. Now Raythen was rolling up the slope into some bushes—seemingly inert, without control, moving only from the pellet impacts.

It was beautiful.

Buck kept firing. Inside, he was both laughing and crying. He thought of Parvati, of his brothers floating to oblivion in the husk of New Sinai. He thought of Sweet GG—such beauty, intelligence, and yes, such complete sweetness. Such a perfect being as her was beyond the understanding of the worthless, useless meat-bag that was now twisting in the bushes under his relentless assault.

288

Then his weapon was empty. He grunted in anger when he realized he couldn't fire anymore. But it didn't matter. A cloud of reactive armor dust settled slowly on the dead husk that contained Raythen. And Raythen must be dead or dying within. With that much concentrated fire—he had to be gone.

Buck wanted to get word to Spoof and Cruiser, but the point-to-point network was spotty. They were in full combat now, moving fast. No matter—he had one mission left. It was going to be his privilege to kill that bitch Astria before she got away. Then he would go back and make sure Raythen was truly dead.

Chapter 59

Dr. Brown was having trouble with his patient. The hospital gurney she was laying on was not responding to the commands from his smart glasses, particularly the command to restrain her. It was odd that he couldn't control the gurney; he could control everything else in the emergency room. She was refusing to be sedated, and she kept batting away his hand that held an injector. He had half a mind to just slide the gurney into the stasis chamber in the wall behind her.

"Blast it, stay still ma'am; it's only a mild sedative."

"No sedative!" Crowbar hissed through clenched teeth. "I need to be fully awake while there are still hostilities. Just fix me up!"

"And I need to take off your glasses."

"Fuck no!"

"I can't fix you up until you calm down." Dr. Brown saw an opening and jabbed toward the side of her neck. The injector wouldn't work on the HAZMAT suit—he needed to hit exposed skin.

One of her hands came down hard and chopped at his wrist, making his hand numb for a second causing him to drop the injector. She was fast!

"I don't need a fucking sedative! Do what you need to do to fix me, but no sedative!"

"Alright," Dr. Brown said, backing away a step, holding up his hands. "Alright, you win."

There was a horrified scream from the hallway. Dr. Brown spun around in time to see a body fly by the glass doors of the emergency room. His imp calculated the speed of the body as sixty-six kilometers per hour. It also identified the scream as belonging to Dr. Lito.

"We need to get the fuck out of here now doc," Crowbar said.

A VDF exo hopped into view behind the glass doors. It did another hop to shift its position to face them. It looked comical as it did this, Dr. Brown would have laughed if he was watching this from somewhere else, preferably very far away. The building knew this was a security breech and the doors would only open for authorized personnel. However, the doors to the emergency room weren't made to hold back a battle exoskeleton. With a single push both doors shattered inward. Another hop brought the battle exo in front of Dr. Brown. The exo grabbed the top of his skull with a massive mechanical hand and squeezed. The skull crunched beneath the exo's grip, and the mechanical hand was suddenly filled with scalp, blood, and brains. Dr. Brown dropped to the floor.

Buck had always wanted to do that.

The gurney in front of Buck was empty. He flicked the gunk from his hand and slid the gurney aside to see that evil bitch Astria on the floor, her back to him, reaching up toward her satchel and gun belt that were both hanging from hooks on the wall. She pulled herself up, her motionless legs splayed on the floor behind her.

Heh, idiot. Like that pistol can protect her, Buck thought. It was fun to watch her desperate scramble, to witness her fear. After all, once she was dead, she wouldn't be able to feel pain—to suffer the way he was suffering now at the emptiness and crushing sorrow she had brought to his life.

291

One hand was in the satchel, she used it to pull herself up so the other hand could reach the gun belt. She pulled out her pistol and fell back down, simultaneously grabbing something from within the satchel. Using her elbows, she flipped herself to face him.

Buck had hoped to see fear and desperation on her face—that would have been satisfying. But instead he was shocked to see something else. She was grimacing from exertion—but underlying that grimace was a look that he was strangely interpreting as triumph. Yes, the crazy bitch was smiling as she pointed her gun at a cylinder in her hand—a cylinder that he recognized.

"Alright Gimpy—make one more hop and this Torvald dies," she said evenly.

Chapter 60

Raythen knew he was in trouble from the first impact. He was flung to the side—he knew he had run onto the X and he had to get to his feet and get off of it quickly. He felt himself hit against a tree and he rolled his body so his free hand was against it. As he pushed off he felt his gun arm blown back as his rail gun was shattered to pieces. *Bad.* He needed quick cover—where was the firing coming from? His imp traced the sound of the pellets and projected a red line to the top of a tree six hundred meters away. The building he had just passed was between him and the shooter. He planted his feet to leap for it but pellets struck him dead on the chest, throwing him into the air again. As he fell toward the drainage ditch— arching through the air, looking at the sky—time slowed and his mind stilled itself. This was bad—very bad. The black cloud of reactive armor dust obscured the view of the branches above him. He was falling toward the ground; his armor was quickly losing its integrity. His weapon was gone. Where had this Torvald come from? He should probably do something, like twist around and try to land in a crouching position so he could leap toward the building. It was stupid of Torvald to strike so close to cover. Even though, being completely honest with himself, he didn't think he would be able to make it to the building now.

As he hit the ground on his back he had an idea.

"Eject!" he yelled.

The exoskeleton armor suit split in two—the front half flung up in one piece into the air above him while the back half was thrust against the bottom of the drainage ditch. Pellets hammered at the armor above him, throwing it against the grassy slope. He remained flat on his back, not breathing, as the pellets made an invisible ceiling of death above him. The front half of his armor was being pulverized into a shapeless black heap. The firing seemed to go on forever—that was a good sign; it meant Torvald had bought his ruse. Then, all was silent and still.

Raythen started a timer from the end of the last shot. He had to decide how long to stay in the ditch. Assess the situation. Torvald had been stationary—in a tree! That would usually mean certain death in *Exo Arena*—there must be some reason why he wasn't on the move.

Then it came to him—it was the Torvald he had left on the factory floor, he only had one leg. He had limited mobility—since he was damaged he must have taken the role as look-out and point-to-point node. But now that he had exposed himself he would have to move. There were so few exos that even an impaired one could make a difference in a battle. He was probably going to aid the other Torvalds at Mathew.

30 seconds since the last shot. Raythen decided to make a try for the building. He rolled out of the bottom of his exo suit into the ditch. Still hidden from the Torvald's last position, wearing only his Jeef's and socks, he crawled until the building was between him and the tree. Then he got up and ran to the front door.

It was an apartment complex, much like the one he lived in back on Lu Shin. There was no virtual doorman to greet him—of course there wasn't—he was no longer connected to the network. And he no longer had his point-to-point smart glasses. He was blind and deaf and mute in that empty lobby. He had to know what was going on, how Colonel Kim was doing at Mathew Base. What he really needed to do was tell Colonel Kim about the one-legged Torvald—but he had no way to do so.

He needed to get back on the network, and the only way he knew to do that was to get a pair of smart glasses from Astria. He had to run back to the hospital.

Chapter 61

How much love do these Torvalds have for each other? Crowbar wondered. Her gambit had at least made Gimpy pause, balanced in front of her on one leg, both hands reaching halfway out toward her, surely wanting to crush the life from her.

"He would gladly die," Torvald said, "if he knew that it led to *your* death."

"You sure about that?"

Torvald barked out a laugh, and she guessed that he was sure. This was it. His knee bent. Here she was yet again, facing death, and yes, it was a good death, taking out one of these fucking toasters. She fired at the cylinder in her hand, the impact shooting it away, sending it across the room.

Torvald, however, did not jump at her. He instead hopped straight up and spun mid air so that when he landed he was facing the door. In the shattered doorway Crowbar saw Raythen standing in his Jeefs, looking in at the scene.

Where's his fucking armor? Why doesn't the idiot have his fucking armor on? she thought.

"But I killed you!" Torvald yelled and jumped at him.

There was a reason Dr. Brown couldn't get the gurney's restraints around Crowbar. She had overridden the controls through the point-to-point network. The gurney's many functions were under her complete control.

She now had it collapse down to its lowest height, about half a meter above the floor, and sent it rolling at full speed at Torvald.

When Raythen saw the exo coming at him he dodged to the side, rolling to the ground in the hallway. When Torvald landed at the doorway he awkwardly tried to shift his stance toward him. That's when the gurney struck, just below the knee. He fell back, landing on the gurney. Crowbar ordered the restraints to seize him—several black tentacles came out from underneath and wrapped themselves around Torvald's arms and torso. He let out a scream of rage. Against the wall to Crowbar's right the doors to the stasis chamber opened. The gurney rolled toward it as Torvald struggled. He rode into the coffin-sized chamber and the doors closed, abruptly blocking the sounds of his screams.

Raythen stepped uncertainly into the room, careful to avoid the glass on the floor. Crowbar was laughing—then coughing up blood—then laughing again.

"You think that will hold him?" Raythen asked.

Crowbar still convulsed with laughter. She wiped some blood off her chin with the back of her hand, looked at it, said "Eeww," and then laughed again.

"What are you laughing about," Raythen asked.

"He said . . . he said, 'But I killed you!' Heh. I love it when they say that. Whew. Heh." Her face became serious. "I think there are pieces of lung in my mouth." She felt around her mouth with her tongue and then chewed on something. "And I broke my hand when I shot the Torvald out of it." She looked at Dr. Brown and said "You better find a doctor that's still living; I think I'm ready to call it a day."

"Okay, sure—but, what about the remaining two Torvalds?"

"Colonel Kim has that under control. The other guy she went out there with is dead, but she'll be fine."

"What? What if she loses? They'll come after us."

"You ever hear of an Exo Arena player named Slipknot?"

"Of course."

"That's Colonel Kim."

Raythen raised his eyebrows. While he was still worried, he was much less so.

Chapter 62

Raythen was back in his hotel room, in the hot-tub. The local network was back up, but they were disconnected from the rest of the planet, and the solar system. He was watching news reports, the VDF was shadowing Corpus Christi with two cruisers now, but they were keeping their distance. A Red Crystal ship was docked with Corpus Christi, their personnel providing assistance for those who needed medical help and acting as neutral observers to the damage done to the stratos and its inhabitants.

He learned the fate of New Sinai; the hole had been too big for it to maintain buoyant air, it had been carried uncontrolled by the stormy winds until it entered the heat and pressure of the lower atmosphere—cracking its hull and plunging to the surface.

He had spoken with Colonel Kim (or Slipknot, as he now called her) in the hospital when he was being treated for his injuries. She had said that he was under the protection of the Corpus Christi Militia, and she vouched for it as its new commanding officer. But she also warned that all of their legal statuses were uncertain—this situation was unprecedented and no one knew how things were going to turn out.

They had removed his left hand. He had a temporary robotic hand strapped in its place—the doctors where currently growing him a permanent biological replacement.

He really didn't know how all of this was going to affect his life. The Red Crystal personnel were saying that word of the Torvalds was getting out to the rest of the solar system and that the VDF and UP were getting a lot of heat for it. People were talking about the illegality of using A-Cons in combat and that the MetaChristians could even bring a lawsuit against the UP.

Raythen didn't want to think about the future. He wanted to lay in his bubbly hot water and enjoy the fact that no one was trying to kill him now. He closed his eyes and eased into the water up to his chin. He was able to relax for about three minutes before he heard someone step into the room. He opened his eyes—his imp should have warned him someone was there, but it didn't.

The man was wearing a Red Crystal t-shirt—a red diamond on his chest with a smaller white diamond inside it. Raythen sat up, startled. "Who are you?"

The man didn't say anything—he just pointed a stun gun at Raythen and fired.

Chapter 63

Rafe Melon-Smith-Tagart-Sanchez-McRay-Wilton tramped through the snow to the front porch of the secluded white farmhouse. His breath misted around his head, but he wasn't cold, even though he was only wearing his pinstriped suit. Temperature was never a part of virtual environments. It was his first trip to the Farm, that's what Parvati had called it, the virtual environment where she had raised her A-Cons.

He stepped onto the porch and stood at the front door, lifting his hand to knock. He stopped himself—this was his house now—there was no need to knock. He opened the door and stepped into the small foyer, tracking snow and mud onto the dark hardwood floor.

The furnishings were tastefully rustic. To his left was a living room—to his right a dining room with a farmhouse table and wooden chairs. Ahead was a stairway. Very quaint and homey.

"Hello? Where are you?" Wilton called out impatiently. No reply. However, he did hear something from the direction of the dining room. He stepped inside and saw her in the adjacent kitchen, sitting at a small round table with her back to him. Her shoulders were shaking and he heard her sobs.

"Oh fuck," Wilton muttered as he entered the kitchen. "Sweet GG, shake it off. I have some questions for you."

Sweet GG spun slowly on the armless wooden chair so she was sitting on its side, her hands clasped on her lap. She was wearing a white sweater and blue jeans, appropriate clothes for her surroundings. Her eyes were puffy and red.

"Yes," she said, composing herself. "I read the report."

Wilton's political life was now over. He had taken the fall for the Corpus Christi fiasco and had been forced to resign. Worse yet, he had been kicked off the board of United Shendry, and all his stocks in that company spun off into the new company called Zelta Corp., which consisted entirely of United Shendry's former weaponized A-Con division. In other words, he was now the biggest target for any lawsuits and legal investigations into the Corpus Christi affair. And why had he agreed to all this without so much as an injunction? Why had he rolled over without calling together an army of lawyers to sniff around for anyone else who could possibly be blamed?

Because the powers-that-be had wanted him to take the fall and if he ever wanted to enjoy dinner at the adults' table again he would have to do what they said.

In the meantime, he would get all the information he could. The person he most wanted to place the blame on, Parvati Meyers, was dead. *She* had let those psychotic A-Cons out into the open when they were clearly not ready. The problem with relying on technical people is you don't know they are incompetent until they fuck up, and then it's too late. Still, if he could place blame on anyone else that was *not* at the adults' table, they were fair game.

Unfortunately, the woman in front of him didn't count.

"So you know what kind of clusterfuck you and Parvati made with those Torvalds."

"Parvati is dead because of you," Sweet GG said, her crying giving way to anger. "You sent her out into the stratos! You put her in harm's way!"

"Hold on there, you can't talk to me like that. I now own everything here. I own you. And it's because you decided to have a boyfriend outside of your little . . ." He tossed his hand into the air uncertainly, ". . . family, or whatever, that Torvald went ape-shit out there."

Sweet GG looked at the floor, stung by the truth.

"Why did you date that NPC anyway?" Wilton asked. "Was it the excitement of dating a real human? Did it turn you on that he thought *you* were human? That you were out there like one of *us*? After all, you're supposed to be some engineering marvel, one of the most sophisticated A-Cons Parvati ever made from scratch. What made you want to fuck some NPC?"

After a moment of silence, Sweet GG said softly "He was nice."

"*Nice? He was nice?* So what do you think of Torvald wanting to kill this nice person? We've talked to Torvald—Torvald Prime. We worked him over real good and he spilled most of his story, except one part. He refused to talk about you. Did you know that he used company money to finance Raythen's trip to Corpus Christi? That he used your account to send messages to him? Did you want Torvald to kill Raythen?"

"No!" Sweet GG yelled, standing up to face him. "I had no idea!"

"Then how did he get on your account?"

"Those were special military accounts that were set up for us! Obviously we don't have standard imps! He made a mirror account from mine!"

Wilton shook his head. "I can't believe she let you out to mingle with humans. It was irresponsible."

Sweet GG's face lit up with fury. "Parvati wanted us to be as free as possible! She cared about us! And you let her die out there! You put her in danger! You let her die!"

Wilton had been kicked around for the last few days by people he had once considered his friends, his equals—and to a certain extent he could understand their behavior. But this A-Con, this *thing*, there was no way he was going to put up with her talking to him like this.

He pulled his hand back and slapped her face as hard as he could. He felt the sting on his hand as her head snapped to the side and she made a shocked yelp. It felt good. It felt surprisingly good. She could feel it, feel the pain. And she wasn't a real human—there was nothing she could do about it. She was his *property* for goodness sake.

He grabbed her roughly by the upper arm to have her face him and he slapped her again. She looked up at him and he drank in the dawning helplessness that was revealed by her eyes.

Yes, he thought, *there might be some perks to this shitty situation after all.*

Chapter 64

Raythen knew he was in zero-g even before he was fully conscious. The disorientation and slight nausea was a dead give-away. When he did open his eyes he saw Astria sitting a few meters away, facing him. She was wearing a plain gray jumpsuit and was strapped into a chair that was affixed to an inward-curving metallic wall. He was strapped into a similar chair, wearing a similar jumpsuit. They were inside a tube-shaped chamber with several other chairs, empty, along the walls. There were hatches on each end of the tube.

"About fucking time you joined the party," Astria said. "Have a drink." She thrust a clear plastic container labeled *Russian Standard Vodka* at him, straw first.

He shook his head, "No thanks. I can use some water though." He noticed his prosthetic hand was gone, leaving only a stump.

Her eyes followed his to the stump. She said, "Don't worry about that. We're working on your new one. New hand."

Even though she wasn't slurring her words, he could tell she was quite drunk—the way her head swayed in the weightlessness and one eye was more closed than the other.

"What's going on?" he asked.

"Guess where you are," she said and grinned mischievously.

"Space?"

305

"You're on a fucking spaceship. I mean an interplanetary spaceship, not some fucking shuttle."

An interplanetary spaceship? he thought. *Do the MetaChristians actually own an interplanetary spaceship? No one is allowed to own interplanetary spaceships except for the UP.* Then he thought ominously, *Does she work for the UP?*

"Astria, am I under arrest?"

"Ha! No. And stop calling me Astria. That's just an alt. My main is Crowbar." She brought back the vodka and took a sip. The container was half empty.

Crowbar?

"So…Crowbar, what's going on?"

"Yeah, you're on a fucking interplanetary spaceship motherfucker. It's called the *Wanderer*, by the way. You really should have a drink. It's bad luck not to drink after a mission. And we kicked fucking ass. Complete success, better than the boss could have expected. Outstanding."

Raythen was suspending all emotion until he knew what his situation was. "Crowbar, who's in charge here?"

"Wouldn't I like to know. Jorn and I have pondered that question many times. Maybe you can figure it out. Although you're not really an intel guy. You're muscle. Have a drink. It's real vodka, from Russia."

"Where are we going?"

"I'm not going to answer any questions until you take a drink." She thrust the bottle forward again and made a zipping motion over her lips.

He hesitated a moment before giving a quick nod. She gave it a little push and it floated toward him. He reached out and plucked it from the air. He noticed by the way her legs floated freely that she was still paralyzed. He put the straw to his mouth and took a sip. More vodka went into his mouth than he expected. He immediately felt the burn. He swallowed and pulled the straw from his mouth. She motioned with her head and said, "Take another." He took another and sent it back to her.

Alcohol and zero-g didn't mix well for Raythen. He immediately felt a disconcerting sense of vertigo.

"Alright," said Crowbar. "Here's the rumpus. We belong to a super-secret organization called *Manos*. That's right, you heard right, *Manos*. I guess it's because we're the 'hands of fate' or something. I wanted to change our name to the Crazy 88, but then everyone was like 'but there aren't 88 of us', and I was like 'if there were 88 of us then we couldn't be called the Crazy 88.' Anyway, we get sent on secret missions throughout the solar system." She laughed. "God that sounds so corny. We work for a mysterious man who goes by the handle of *Dr. Happy*. We don't know who he is, but he sends us on missions and provides us with money and material and network resources. Jorn thinks he's someone high up in politics who uses us to do his doodoo. His dirty doodoo. I personally believe myself that he's an insane trillionaire who just likes to fuck stuff up. There doesn't seem to be any rhyme or reason to the missions he gives us. I mean, why the fuck did he want to save Theophilus? Are the stars just pinholes in the curtain of night? Who knows?"

"Who's Jorn?" Raythen asked.

"He's the captain of this bucket. You'll meet him eventually."

"Are you really a MetaChristian?"

"Fuck no! But, you know, I hate snotty atheists. That's why Dr. Happy knew I would rock this party. Hey, do you want to know my belief system? It's real simple. I just think about what I would do if I was all knowing and all powerful, and then I call that God. And that's God. And why the hell not? I'm sort of a...Nietzschean Ubermensch by proxy."

His imp started to explain to him what a Neitzschean Ubermensch was but he phanded away the text as it appeared.

"It was a successful mission. And we did succeed! I mean, it was a crazy shitty mess—we destroyed a fucking stratos! Ha! I never did that before. We kicked major league ass."

Now Raythen decided to ask the question that was really pressing him. "Why am I here?"

"What? You think I'm going to let a killer like you get away from us? You've been recruited kid! You are now among the select elite few to join our super-secret organization! Manos! Be proud!"

Raythen wasn't proud. He was horrified. "You can't be serious. I have a life! You can't just kidnap me like this!"

"You *had* a life. It's gone now. You killed people in that aerosail. That life is locked up by Venusian legal authorities in a little tiny metal box. There's no way you can go back to your happy little NPC existence with your minor celebrity status and your geek girlfriend."

"I *had* to kill those people in the aerosail. It was the only way I could save the stratos!"

"Really Raythen? Really? Did you really have to kill *all* of them?" She gave him a knowing wink, her half-closed eye not having to close very far.

"Listen!" he said, visibly panicked. "I am willing to defend my actions legally! It's the VDF's fault that they used psychotic Torvalds to invade!"

"Exactly," she said, pointing the straw at him. "It's their fault. And *you* know exactly why it's their fault. And *you* are proof as to what a huge cluster fuck that led to that . . . huge cluster fuck. So what do you think they're going to do with you? Huh? Have a big public trial? Fuck you. You'll be disappeared."

"No," Raythen said, shaking his head. "It's not like the twentieth century where the government can just disappear someone. There are too many records . . . too many witnesses. It's ridiculous."

"Poof! Disappeared."

"Just get me back. I don't want to go with you. Just turn around and I'll take my chances with the authorities. They're not going to disappear me."

"We can't turn around. We have to pick up Theophilus. Heh heh. She's gonna be soooo pissed."

"Well, after we get her."

"Well no. Listen kid—there are two kinds of people in the world— those who consume more than they produce—and those who consume more . . . no, those who produce more than they consume. Yeah. Before you came to Corpus Christi you were the former—no wait—yeah, you were the former. Now you're the other one. It's productive to kill someone who is destructive. I mean, sure you made money, but you weren't really *making* anything. You weren't adding anything—you weren't making any sort of difference that mattered at all. Rich people where just jacking off while they killed you. But now look at what you did—you saved the lives of ten thousand people!" Her face lit up. "Think of it—thousands of people who would be dead now, not the least of which—" she pointed a wobbly hand with deliberate care at her chest "—me. For the first time in your life you actually made a real difference in the universe. You're not just a dancing monkey."

"Second."

"What?"

"Second time in my life," Raythen said. "When I was in the VDF I was part of the rescue at the Falstaff collision."

"See? You're just a fucking natural hero. You couldn't go back to that other life anyway. You know it. You know it is meaningless squat."

"It wasn't that meaningless," Raythen said quietly.

"Really? Are you sure."

"Yes. She was there," he said at barely a whisper.

"What? Who? Oh yeah, your GG girl. Yeah, why *did* she send you into a death trap? I'd like to know that."

Raythen wanted to know that too. But he certainly didn't want to talk about it with a drunken sociopath. He kept quiet, and Crowbar took a long draw from the straw.

"Sometimes you just have to kill people. You know?" she said suddenly. "You don't kill the sheep, you know? The sheeple. You kill the people who are at least trying. That's the funny thing. You kill the people who are at least trying to be something more. Like Tray Wind. She was trying to matter. She even had her own little ethical system. I mean, it's the cutesy little squeak toy of ethical systems." She made her fingers into a hand puppet and had it say with a high-pitched voice, "Empathy! Empathy!" She let her hand hang in the zero g. "Heh. The people who are trying are the people who get in your way. And sometimes you have to kill them."

The hatch to Raythen's left opened. A tall, lanky man with a bushy blond beard floated in, assisted by Doc Ocks—two tentacles attached to a bundle that fit onto hip sockets. Each tentacle could extend up to ten meters and ended with a robotic hand.

"Here's our captain—Jorn Jornson," Crowbar said.

310

Jorn nodded briefly to Raythen, and then said to Crowbar, "I just got new orders. I'm going to have to put you two into suspended animation in a little over three hours. There's a shipping crate leaving L4 that's going to transport you to your next destination. I have a small window to insert you into it before I intercept Theophilus."

"Oh fuck," Crowbar said. "I hate getting frozen when I'm drunk. And I wanted to see Theophilus's face when she woke up." Crowbar made a pout that was surprisingly girlish.

"On the bright side," Jorn said, "vodka goes well on ice. Heh heh."

Raythen said, "I don't want to be frozen."

Jorn turned briefly to Raythen, his rosy cheeks plumped by a smile, and then turned back to Crowbar. "He needs to go to orientation."

"Yeah," said Crowbar, "I suppose that'll happen when we end up where-ever the fuck we end up."

"I want to find her," Raythen said. "Talk to her."

Crowbar knew who he was talking about. "Well, that depends on our boss now. But like I said, there are perks in this job, we don't just work for money. And they don't call him Dr. Happy for nothing!"